D0130821

The Law in Charity

The Law in Charity

CHELSEA QUINN YARBRO

A DOUBLE D WESTERN
Doubleday
NEW YORK LONDON TORONTO SYDNEY AUCKLAND

A Double D Western
Published by Doubleday, a division of
Bantam Doubleday Dell Publishing Group, Inc.
666 Fifth Avenue, New York, New York 10103

Double D Western, Doubleday,
and the portrayal of the letters DD
are trademarks of Doubleday, a division of
Bantam Doubleday Dell Publishing Group, Inc.

Library of Congress Cataloging-in-Publication data applied for.

0-385-23955-6
Printed in the United States of America
July 1989
First Edition

for
DAVID and TAMMY TANQUERAY
it's been a long time coming
but here it is
with love

The Law in Charity

1

Liam Cauliffe was waiting on the steps of the clapboard Presbyterian Church when Jason Russell finally rode into Charity on a grey afternoon in October. Since the church was located at the far end of the main street, situated diagonally across from the bank, Cauliffe had plenty of opportunity to see the response the new sheriff received; the dour Scottish preacher rarely laughed, but amusement flickered at the back of his narrowed eyes.

When Russell dismounted in front of the church he took the time to secure his three horses and pack mule to the hitching rail before going to shake Cauliffe's hand. "Liam."

"Jason." He patted the newcomer on the arm. "How was the journey?"

"Uneventful, once I reached Santa Fe." He put his hand to his unshaven chin. "I came on the Fort Smith–Santa Fe Trail," he went on, "because they said there might be trouble with Indians further to the north."

"There's been a little," said Cauliffe. He indicated the church. "Want to come in?"

"Actually," said Russell, his words clipped, "what I want is a bath, a shave, and then the opportunity to meet the men who've hired me. I'm not fit for presentation just now; would an hour be—"

"Hey!" yelled a boy in the muddy street.

Both Cauliffe and Russell turned, and Cauliffe spoke. "Sam Ramsey, if you—"

"What kind of a saddle is that?" the boy demanded, unimpressed by the critical attitude of the circuit preacher.

Russell regarded the boy thoughtfully and answered, "It's a hussar's saddle."

"It looks funny," said the boy with the overwhelming contempt of his eight years. Without waiting for any comment from the two men, he sauntered away.

"I suppose you don't see many saddles like that out here," Russell mused. "The hotel a block down—I assume it's the only one?"

"Yes," Cauliffe said. "The owner's expecting you. Don't let her catch your eye, Jason; she's a strapping German widow, and you're just the sort of man she'd like to capture." He pointed toward the building—one of three with a second story—"I'll meet you there in an hour."

"My horses?" He nodded toward the hitching post.

"There's a livery-and-smithy at the foot of the street. I'll take them down for you." Cauliffe clapped Russell on the arm again. "It's good you're here."

"Umm," Russell answered, clearly withholding his own opinion until he had taken the measure of the place. "Be careful with the chestnut; he's head-shy," he warned as he went to untie his horses, handing the lead of the mule and one of the horses to the preacher.

The two men walked down the wide, muddy street, taking care to keep out of the worst of the ruts. There was little traffic except on the wooden sidewalks this dreary afternoon, and the two men did not hurry.

"The general store and the bank are owned by Mister Fletcher; you'll meet him later today," Cauliffe explained as they walked, pointing out the general store. "There's a post office of sorts in there, and Hosea Olfrant will take shipments for you, one way or another."

"Good to know," said Russell, stepping around the end of a small wagon.

Cauliffe nodded to three middle-aged women who bustled along the sidewalk, two of them dressed for hard farm work instead of the chores of housewifery. "We're starting to get more families in here in the last year or so. I've been marrying as much as burying these last six months."

They reached the hotel and here the preacher took the leads of Russell's other two horses as Russell took the largest carpet bag from the saddle of the chestnut he had warned Cauliffe against. "Where will you be in an hour?"

"At the church, if you'll come there. And I'll tell Calvin that you'll be in later to give him your instructions."

"Thanks," Russell said, and looked up at the front of the hotel. He pulled his fur cap from his head, revealing iron-grey hair, then he went toward the double doors and entered the building, turning back to wave to Cauliffe as he continued down the street to the livery stable.

There was a young man behind the counter; he wore an ill-fitting dark jacket and was encouraging a straggling moustache on his lip. "Yes, sir?"

"I need a room and a bath, please," Russell told him as he looked around the lobby and drew off his gloves.

"For how long?" asked the young man, all eagerness.

"For a week at least, I should think," Russell said, coming up to the counter. "The bath I want immediately."

"Hot water'll cost you extra," warned the youth, clearly trying to gauge the ability of this new patron to pay for such a luxury.

Without speaking, Russell reached inside his coat and drew out a small pouch. He opened it and counted out three twenty-dollar gold pieces. "This should cover the whole."

The clerk swallowed hard. "Yes, sir. I think that should. If you'll wait, I'll get your bags and take them up to your room."

"Thanks; I'll manage. If you'll be good enough to give me the key and tell me where to find it?"

The clerk was still mesmerized by the three gleaming coins. "If that's what you want, fine." He recovered himself enough to open the register. "If you'll sign—or make your mark and tell me your name."

With a trace of a smile, Russell took the pen and inspected the nib before entering his name in a precise, sloping hand: Jason E. N. Russell. For his address he gave London, England. "Which room?"

"Number seven, it's at the corner." He pointed toward the ceiling, indicating the far end of the room. "The bath's at the end of the hall, and the tub will be ready in twenty minutes. Towels are extra."

"Fine," said Russell as he hefted his bag and accepted the key that the clerk held out to him.

The room was larger than Russell had expected, and the four windows gave an excellent view of the street as well as the long slope down the mountain. He opened his bag on the chair, unwilling to dirty the crewel-work quilt that covered the bed. He arranged his things neatly and took the time to strop his razor before going to bathe. The last thing he removed from the bag was his baton, the eagle removed from the top of it but otherwise just the same as when he had refused to surrender it, eighteen years ago.

An hour later, bathed, shaved, and dressed in clean clothes, his high boots glossy with polish, and his baton carried slung in a holster from his belt, Jason Russell made his way along the wooden sidewalks to the church.

"I have to be blunt," announced the florid George Fletcher with a calculated scowl. "You are not what we expected, Mister Russell."

"I didn't suppose I would be," Russell answered patiently. He had spent the last forty minutes listening to George Fletcher, Hosea Olfrant and Barton Purvis expound on the various problems that had beset the burgeoning new town of Charity, and he had expected that this observation or one very like it would be forthcoming.

"You are hardly the sort of man we had in mind," echoed Purvis, whose conversation so far had consisted of restating everything that Fletcher said.

"And what would that be?" cut in Liam Cauliffe, who was growing restive. "Were you looking for a bully with guns and a temper to ride roughshod over the town? There are plenty of other places where that has happened."

"Of course not," protested Fletcher, a little too quickly.

"Not in the least," Purvis agreed.

"Gentlemen," Russell said mildly, and gained the attention of the four men in the church, "let me simplify this for you; I am qualified for this work, though I grant I am not a gunman—which I gather you do not need —nor am I a military man as such."

"My point exactly," said Fletcher, nodding portentously. "I'm relieved that you—"

"On the other hand," Russell went on smoothly, apparently unaware that he had done the unthinkable in interrupting George Fletcher, "I have experience in enforcing the law. I began as a Bow Street Runner when I was just nineteen years old. When that force was disbanded—"

"And why was that, pray?" inquired Hosea Olfrant.

"The Runners were disbanded in '29 when the Metropolitan Police were established in London. Our . . . services were taken over by the Peelers."

"Peelers?" questioned Purvis, speaking for himself for once.

"The Metropolitan Police," explained Cauliffe. "Sir Robert Peel's blue boys."

"They wear blue uniforms," Russell said. "The Runners did not wear uniforms. At the time there was a tremendous debate about it." He nodded to Cauliffe. "I understand that you knew about this."

"Something of the sort was mentioned," Fletcher said with deliberate vagueness.

Russell nodded. "For the last eighteen years, I've worked for the East India Company, and for Office of the Governor General of Australia. I have letters of reference from these, and I will be happy to present them to you."

"If you have been so well employed, why do you want to work here?" demanded Olfrant.

"Because," said Russell slowly, "I am tired of being a company man. I want to establish something of my own. My family . . . well, there are difficulties, and I hope that some of them can be resolved if I make my way here, in this country." He glanced at Cauliffe before he went on. "Also, I truly believe I can do what you need done."

George Fletcher pursed his lips. "Why do you say that?"

"Because I was trained as a thief-taker and I have worked at that profession for over twenty years," Russell stated. "I am very good at what I do."

The three most influential men in Charity considered this. At last Hosea Olfrant said, "What might that mean to us?"

Russell gave a quick, tight smile. "For one thing, I will keep the peace. That, gentlemen, is a promise. If there are crimes, I will bring the criminals to justice, and I will do so without needlessly endangering innocent citizens. If there is an emergency here, such as a robbery or a killing or a fire, I will organize the men of the town to deal with the problem quickly and safely." He folded his arms and moved a little closer to the warmth of the wood-burning stove. "I will also do my utmost to make Charity the sort of village that criminals avoid."

"You're taking on a lot," Cauliffe said.

"That, so far as I can determine, is the work to be done," Russell said, and looked at the other three men in turn.

George Fletcher sighed and fingered his luxuriant moustache. "I believe that a term of . . . shall we call it a trial? is in order. Let us say six months." He held out his hand, but to his offended amazement, Russell did not take it.

"Let me propose that a year would be more reasonable." While the three men exchanged uneasy looks, Russell went on. "I have my reasons for the suggestion. For the first, winter is coming, and during that time, it is reasonable to assume that there will be less crime than there is during summer, in part because most of the people who live in this part of the Texas Territories will not travel very much or very far. The time of greatest risk is the summer, and that is the time when you will find out whether or not I am able to handle the job you want done."

"He has a point," conceded Olfrant, watching Fletcher for some suggestion of his wishes.

"Yes, you do have a point," said Fletcher. "Very well. I assume that you will inform us if you change your mind at any point along the way." He raised his massive chin and did his best to stare down Russell.

"Certainly," Russell said, apparently unaware of the challenge Fletcher was offering. "Am I to assume that my tenure begins at once?"

Fletcher, Olfrant, and Purvis exchanged signals, and it was Purvis who answered for them. "Yes. We will expect you to take up your responsibilities tomorrow morning."

"If you will come by the bank, I will give you a badge of office and establish the terms of your salary." Fletcher hooked his thumb in his belt and stared around the church. "I expect that you will give us regular reports of your activities and expenditures. As the Town Council, we have to be kept informed."

Russell nodded.

"We have a jail," Purvis added. "It's one block off Main Street, near the

Catholic church and school." He said this last with distaste and an apologetic air.

"There is a Catholic church here?" Russell asked in some surprise.

"Don Maximillian insisted that it be made part of the town," Fletcher admitted in angry reluctance.

"And who is Don Maximillian?" asked Russell.

When Fletcher did not speak, Purvis supplied the answer. "He is one of the Spaniards. He has a Spanish claim to some of the land around here. His family came here three generations back, and to hear him tell it—" He broke off at a sign from Fletcher.

"You will have to decide how you wish to deal with Don Maximillian," said Fletcher, washing his hands of the issue.

"If you are willing to abide by my decision, that's quite satisfactory," Russell said. "About this Catholic church—who services it? Is there a priest?"

"Yes," said Fletcher almost angrily. "And two nuns. They have established a school of sorts there, for Catholic children. The Good Lord alone knows what they are being taught—"

He was cut short by Liam Cauliffe. "Mister Fletcher, we all bow to the same God, and if I can accept the Catholics, it would behoove all the rest to do the same." He did not remind them of his vocation; they were in his church.

"All right; I will say that the Padre is a reasonable sort of man, for a Mexican." Fletcher glared at his two companions.

"Padre Antonio Mardronez," Cauliffe supplied. "He's an Augustinian; the Greater Canon, I believe is the designation." He regarded Russell with curiosity. "Have you any experience with Catholics?"

"Yes, and with Jews and Hindoos and Aboriginals, for that matter." He paid little attention to the reaction his statement created. "I will want to see this Padre Antonio . . . Mar . . ."

"Mardronez," said Cauliffe. "I'll arrange it, if you like."

"No, I think I'd rather do it myself." He paced down the central aisle of the little church. "I would like to know the names of all those who own businesses in the town, as well as those ranchers and farmers who come within the purview of Charity. I would like to know the companies who service the area, and how frequently the service is available. I would also like to know the names and methods of any criminals known or suspected to be operating in this area." He tapped his baton with the flat of his hand. "What about housing? Am I to arrange that for myself?"

"Well . . ." Purvis cleared his throat. "I can rent you a room in my house. The Missus don't like boarders, but you're not quite the same as a boarder, are you?"

Fletcher patted Purvis on the shoulder, just as he might pat an obedient hound. "They're good people, Mister Russell. Missus Purvis will look after you just as she ought."

Russell hesitated. "It's a very generous offer," he began with better manners than truth, "but since I cannot anticipate my comings and goings, I think my presence might be more disruptive than either Mister or Missus Purvis would like." He saw relief in Purvis' face as he went on. "At the moment I am at the hotel, but I think I ought to plan to establish myself in a house as soon as it is convenient."

"That could be a tall order. Houses don't come cheap around here."

"I'm not entirely without means," said Russell quietly. "My father's will provided some funds for me, and if things work out well, I plan to purchase land so that I can breed horses."

This announcement silenced the men in the church, and it was a little time before George Fletcher said, "Well, it's settled then."

"And Mister Fletcher," Russell went on in his calm way, "I know my worth. Pray don't think to offer me a lower salary in the belief that it would be a sensible economy. My value as a sheriff has nothing to do with my father's legacy."

"It never entered my mind," Fletcher protested, although his suddenly ruddy cheeks belied his words.

"Of course not," Russell said at once. "I'm too cautious, but a good sheriff ought to be." He stopped and regarded the men. "Tomorrow I take office. Unless you have reservations?"

Fletcher, as usual, spoke for all three. "We need a sheriff and—"

"And you will not find a better," Liam Cauliffe declared stoutly. "I've know Jason Russell these twenty years, and I tell you that no better man for this job walks the earth." The Scots preacher could be daunting, and now he dared anyone to contradict him, including Russell.

"We'll have a one year trial," Fletcher grumbled. "There is a badge, and you shall have it tomorrow."

"Thank you," Russell said. "If there is nothing else? I have been riding most of today and I still must speak with the liveryman about my horses before I dine."

"Horses." Hosea Olfrant said the word as if it were unfamiliar to him.

"I have three, and a mule," said Russell as if this were nothing unusual. "I'll send for the others when I am established."

"What others?" demanded Fletcher, intrigued in spite of himself.

"My father left me three horses from his stud annually; recently I have had to ask my . . . half-brother to continue to keep them for me. He will be relieved to be rid of them at last." Russell clearly did not want to discuss more of this.

"Your half-brother," said Olfrant. "He is still in England."

"Yes." Had the three men known Russell better they would have recognized the tone of his voice and would have changed the subject.

"Where he raises horses?" Purvis asked.

"Among other things." Most of the cordiality had left Russell now, and he was becoming brusque.

"You've suffered the fate of the younger son, it seems." Fletcher was satisfied, and the tension lessened. "Second marriages are often so disadvantageous for their children."

Olfrant nodded. "Lucky thing your half-brother abides by the terms of the will. There's many another who would not." He rose from the plank bench that served as a pew. "We'll see that you have the information you requested. That way we all get off to a good start." He picked up his hat and put it squarely on his head. "I have some maps at my store, if you want to look at them. And I know most of the farmers and ranchers around here. I can show you where they're located." He went to Russell and held out his hand. "It's a pleasure to meet you, sir. I, for one, am delighted that you accepted our offer of employment."

Fletcher, nonplussed at this disregard for his leadership, stared at Olfrant. "Yes," he agreed, doing his best to reassert his authority. "I believe that I did the right thing in speaking with Preacher Cauliffe."

"It was good of you to do it, Fletcher," said Purvis, returning to his role.

When Fletcher and Purvis had shaken his hand and left, letting Olfrant fend for himself, Russell turned to Cauliffe. "Laid it on with a trowel, Liam."

"It's the only way to get their attention," said Cauliffe. "Mind you remember that."

"I suspected it," Russell admitted. "How much longer do you remain here before you continue the circuit?"

"Another week," said Cauliffe. "Then I take the road toward Pueblo." He folded his large-knuckled hands and bowed his head. When he raised his eyes, he sighed. "Still an unbeliever, are you, Jason?"

"Anything else would disappoint you," said Russell. "Come to the hotel in half an hour and I will buy you a meal. If the kitchen is decent, we'll spend a pleasant evening."

"Thank you, and I will count it an honor." He paused and added, "The Widow Schmidt has a Chinese cook, so the food is tolerable; better than in most of these isolated towns."

Russell smiled briefly. "It's settled." He and Cauliffe shook hands on it.

2

Padre Antonio Mardronez had severe lines in his young face that were the tokens of a childhood spent in deepest poverty. He stood in the door of his small church and regarded Russell with curiosity tinged with suspicion. "You are the one they have hired as a sheriff?"

"Yes; Jason Russell." He waited for the priest to hold out his hand, and was not surprised when he did not. "May I come in?"

"This is God's house. Everyone is welcome," said Padre Antonio, stepping aside. "What do you want me to do for you?"

"Nothing, as such. I was hoping to meet the townspeople and find out what their circumstances are." He was deliberately affable.

"I am a priest," Padre Antonio said stiffly.

"And you have a church and a school here, and you have the assistance of two nuns. Is that correct?" Russell asked.

"Surely there is no law against that." It was an effort for him to be polite.

"Of course not. But those who teach children sometimes know of the activities of their—"

Padre Antonio cut him short. "The Confessional is sacred. Nothing revealed to me in Confession can be spoken of."

"I know that," Russell said, noting the distress the priest showed and wondering what he had heard that caused him such discomfort. "But sometimes there are other problems, problems that you might need the assistance of a sheriff, such as when townspeople treat your students with disrespect, or are impolite to your nuns."

"God sends us many tests," Padre Antonio said.

"God also provides laws and sheriffs to aid you in the tests," said Russell, moving back from the priest. "Remember that, if you will."

"Of course." He made an automatic blessing in Russell's direction before the sheriff left the church and went back across the muddy street to the three-room jail.

There was a small stove in one corner, and it produced barely enough heat to warm the small front office of the jail. Russell kept on his marten-lined jacket as he took his place at the desk and pulled a heavy journal toward him, adding his notes to three closely written pages that followed the heading *Charity*. He was finishing his observations when the door opened and a tall man in an engulfing coat strode in.

"Good afternoon," Russell said, closing the journal and looking at the newcomer. "What can I do for you?"

"You the new sheriff?" asked the man as if the question itself were amusing.

"Yes; Jason Russell. And you?"

"Jack Johnson," said the man, grasping Russell's hand in his own. "Called Smilin' Jack most places. I heard you wanted to know about any outlaws in the neighborhood, so I just came by to tell you that Coffin Mayhew's in the area."

Johnson was about to depart, but Russell stopped him. "Who is Coffin Mayhew and how do you know about him?"

"Mayhew's got a gang of about twenty men. They specialize in holding up travelers and destroying outlying farms and ranch houses. You know— come in, shoot the men, rape the women, steal the food, burn the buildings, take the livestock, if it suits 'em." Johnson had his hand on the door latch.

"Why do you know this? And how?" Russell was perplexed by the man, and his curiosity sharpened.

"I'm a driver for Helston Drayage, out of Denver. We cart and haul, and when there's travelers, I bring 'em up in an old Thompson coach. They keep us informed of men like Mayhew. You just got here, so I figured you hadn't heard about him yet." He almost stepped out the door, then stopped. "I hear you come from London."

"That's right," said Russell, wondering why Johnson had mentioned it.

"My Pa came over from Plymouth, on the south coast." He grinned. "Biggest liar this side of the Mississippi, but I always believed what he said about England because it never changed." He chuckled. "Figured I had to warn you, 'cause of Pa. You understand."

Russell was not entirely sure that he did, but he answered, "Certainly," as he tried to puzzle it out.

"Mayhew's dangerous. They don't call him Coffin for nothing. Word is he likes to see people die, and sometimes takes his time with 'em. A place like this, Charity'd be a good target for him. Better be on the lookout is all I can say."

"Thanks; I appreciate the warning." He studied the man with more attention than at first.

"Be careful of Mayhew, and don't underestimate him."

"I'll try not to," said Russell. "Is there anyone else you've heard about you'd like to mention?"

Johnson laughed. "Mighty smooth-spoken, aren't you?" He shook his head. "No, nothing comes to mind. But I'll keep my ears open for you, how's that?"

"Fine," said Russell, still puzzled by Johnson.

"Y'know," he added, "the Mayor here—"

"George Fletcher," Russell said.

"That's him. He's slippery as river ice. He might look like he'd be rock-solid, but from what I've heard, he'd turn tail if he thinks he might be accountable." He shook his head. "He's a banker."

"I know," said Russell, nodding in agreement. "I thank you for that warning, too."

"No trouble," said Johnson, then went out leaving Russell to enter a few more lines in his journal.

Of the eight men in the hotel bar, only two were doing anything more than drink; Frederick Fletcher and the young clerk Martin Corley, were engaged in a senseless and acrimonious argument that carried through most of the building.

"An' I say a man like m' father deserves more than that from the likes of you," bellowed young Frederick.

"Y'r father's nothing!" yelled Corley, his voice almost cracking.

The other six men at the bar did their stoic best to ignore the disruption. One of them hitched his shoulders a little higher as if to create a barrier between himself and the two belligerent young men.

"You'll answer for that!" Frederick grappled with his chair as he strove to reach out and throttle Corley.

"Don't you *touch* me!" yelped Corley, all but tipping his chair over in his effort to escape.

"Gentlemen," said a voice in the door, "perhaps both of you had best stop now." Russell strolled into the small, malt-scented bar, his baton held easily in his left hand. "Mister Corley, I think you ought to go to your rooms at once."

"Now see here . . ." Corley protested with alcoholic courage.

"At once," Russell said, his voice low but the words sharp. "Now." When Corley hesitated, Russell hooked one toe around the leg of Corley's chair, jerking sharply.

Corley and the chair lurched over backward.

"That's great!" crowed Frederick Fletcher. "I'm going to remember that."

Russell turned on him. "And you are coming with me, Mister Frederick."

As he struggled to disentangle himself from the overturned chair, Corley swore steadily and vehemently. When he got onto his knees, he rounded on Russell. "You're nothing but a lackey, that's all you are." He was not precisely sure what a lackey was, but he had heard the word used as an insult and he thought it sounded more dignified than some of the others he knew.

"Merely a sheriff," said Russell as he caught Frederick by the collar of his jacket. "Come along, Mister Frederick."

"Let go of me, Russell," Frederick said, his face darkening. "You can't do this to me."

Russell took Frederick by the arm, and in the next instant he had shoved his baton into the youth's armpit. "Get up, Mister Frederick."

Frederick was now as pale as he had been flushed. "Don't—don't do—"

"I won't," Russell assured him, indicating the door with a nod of his head. "If you'll come along."

Sun Fan-Li, the hotel cook and man-of-all-work, appeared in the inner door of the bar. "Trouble?"

"Mister Corley could use a bucket of water over his head," Russell suggested, keeping his hold on Frederick. "He's likely to be sick, as well."

"Trouble," said Sun fatalistically, coming to help Corley to his feet.

"I hope he chokes," Frederick declared with more bravado than truth.

"Mister Frederick," Russell said gently, "you're not using good sense, talking that way. Come along." He propelled the young man toward the door without apparent effort.

As he stumbled through the bar doors into the dusk, Frederick vented his anger on Russell. "You're going to answer for this, Russell. You're my father's employee, and he'll see you discharged for this. You're exceeding your authority, doing this to me, and you'll find out my father won't stand for it." He was so preoccupied with his wrath that he did not realize at first that he was being prodded down the hill instead of up it. "Where the devil are we going? The house is the other way."

"The jail is this way," Russell said as if reminding him of an unfinished chore. "You are disorderly in public, and for that you are going to jail."

"Are you mad?" Frederick started to fight, but the pressure of the baton grew more insistent and he quieted.

"I have sworn to keep the peace, and I will," said Russell as he kept Frederick walking down the wooden sidewalk. "It does not matter to me who breaks it, that person will answer for it." They had reached the corner and here Russell propelled Frederick to the left. "We've only locked rooms, not proper cells yet, but by spring the bars should be installed."

"You're not putting me in jail!" This time the protest was more of a whimper.

"Yes, I am. And if Corley is not confined at the hotel, I will put him in jail as well."

A few more steps took them to the building itself, and now Frederick looked scared. "There's ten dollars in my pocket. You can take it if you'll let me go."

"Is that a bribe? Bail hasn't been set." Although he sounded amused, there was a note in his voice that warned Frederick that he had gone too far.

"Bail. It's bail." He climbed the three steps to the narrow porch.

"I doubt if it will be as much as ten dollars." He opened the door and escorted his charge inside. "I will put you in the second cell. There are two windows so that I can keep an eye on you. I'll send word to your father." He did not relish what the senior Fletcher would say, but he had faced much worse than an indignant banker in the past.

"How long will you keep me here? You won't tell anyone?" Frederick now seemed much younger and more callow than he had a few minutes before. "Sheriff?"

"I must tell your family, naturally. As to how long you will be here, I can't say." He had taken a ring of keys from the top drawer of his desk and now he led Frederick toward the detention rooms.

Frederick took one last desperate chance; he swung wildly, his fists churning and hammering. He felt his knuckles bruise on bony flesh, and then there was a sharp hurt under his arm. He yelled and his knees almost buckled.

"That was very foolish," Russell told him as he tightened his grip on Frederick. "And it makes your situation worse, not better."

"I—"

"That's enough," Russell warned him as he opened the door and propelled the young man through it. "I will give you an hour to come to your senses, and then we'll send for your father." He stepped back and locked the door, paying no attention to the imprecations Frederick hurled at him.

While he waited for Frederick to calm down, Russell took one of the sheets of paper from a wooden box he kept in a lower drawer, selected and trimmed a nib for his pen, and then started to write.

Messrs. Dawlins, Faulett and Bragonier
Solicitors

He then added the full address of the London firm, and went on to his business.

*In regard to my inheritance, I am now requesting that the horses be-
queathed me in my father's will be sent to me with all due dispatch. If it is
acceptable to my half-brother, I would prefer that half the stock sent be
good coach-and-draft breeds instead of Thoroughbred, for draft animals are
much needed in this part of the Texas Territories. I will include full instructions for finding this village, as well as names of those to contact along the
way in order to make delivery less arduous.*

*The tack and harness as well as the firearms provided me will be very
welcome, and I would appreciate it if you would see to it that additional
bits and bridles are included in what is shipped to me. I authorize any
expenditure necessary from the funds left to me by my mother. You have
records of the account as well as the necessary documents to enable you to
arrange this, for which I thank you in advance.*

*I ask you to extend my greetings and good wishes to my half-brother and
his family, and assure him once again that I have no desire to seek legi-
timisation. When I swore to that upon reaching my majority I did so with
no regrets and I have none now. I am grateful to the Right Honourable the
Earl of Mindenhall for his dutiful and continuing discharge of our father's
instructions.*

Believe me in all things your most obt. svt., etc.
Jason Everard Nicholas Russell

"I cannot believe than a son of mine would forget himself so completely," blustered George Fletcher as he faced Russell across the front
parlor. "Drunk in the hotel bar!"

"There were others who saw it, sir," Russell said without emphasis.

"I don't doubt it. You wouldn't dare to say this if there weren't some
others who—" He stopped abruptly. "He is a very difficult boy. Nothing
like Horatio or Newton." He rocked back on his heels. "Missus Fletcher is
convinced that it was coming from St. Louis that altered him. She has said
that he ought to be sent back to her brother and allowed to live there at
least until he has a better sense of how—"

"How to get on in the world?" Russell suggested.

"Yes," said Fletcher. "That's it exactly. She has said that he is not
suited to so rough-and-tumble a life as we have here." He cleared his
throat. "She says that he takes after her in that way."

Russell remained expressionless but there was something in his eyes that
was close to sympathy. "What would you like me to do with him? I can
hold him overnight and release him to your custody in the morning, or
your can come with me and pay his bail."

"You are not going to charge bail on such an offence, are you?" Fletcher
demanded, once again asserting his position as Mayor of Charity.

"I would for anyone else who disturbed the peace," Russell said. "I think it would be a bad precedent to establish privilege for him, don't you?" This last gentle question had impact.

"Precedent."

"There are bound to be others who would believe themselves entitled to similar favor, and if they were given it, others would also want it. In no time at all there would be no real law or discipline possible in Charity." He watched while George Fletcher struggled with this unwelcome notion.

"So there are," Fletcher said at last. "You have an excellent point, Sheriff Russell."

"Then what is your decision about your son? Do I keep him overnight?"

Fletcher took a turn about the room. "No," he said. "I will be down within the hour to pay his bail. What bail have you established for disturbing the peace?"

"A dollar for disturbing the peace, a dollar for public disorder. You have all the fines, haven't you? You and the Town Council agreed on them." Russell stood still, letting Fletcher pace the room.

"That would be two dollars, then." He cleared his throat.

"Or he could be set to work cleaning the streets. That is the alternative to the bail," Russell pointed out. He thought that it might be best for Frederick if his father decided to let the young man clean streets for a week instead of paying for his release, but he kept this to himself.

"Missus Fletcher would never stand for that; never." He went the length of the room again, then came back and planted himself in front of Russell. "I will collect the boy in an hour or so. No word to my wife about this. She would be too distressed if she knew."

"In a town this size, she's bound to hear of it sooner or later," Russell reminded Fletcher.

"Better to hear of it later," sighed Fletcher. "She will be less upset if the whole thing is over and done with, don't you know."

Russell remained silent.

"Well," Fletcher said on a more cordial note, "I thank you for your discretion. It reflects well on you. And don't think I will not remember it. I can see you had to do your duty. That's plain."

"I'm glad you understand that," Russell said sincerely.

"A man in my position has to take the broader view. Nothing else makes sense," said Fletcher, dismissing Russell with a gesture. "I'll come in an hour or so."

Four hands from the Mattington ranch were the next men that Russell confined in his jail. They had arrived around noon, determined to get drunk and cause a general disturbance: they reckoned without Jason Russell.

The confrontation lasted less than three minutes, and at the end of that time, two of the hands had knots on their heads and the other two were nursing aching hands.

The next morning Hepsibah Mattington arrived in Charity, demanding to know what had become of her hands.

"I have them in jail, Madame," said Russell when he presented himself to her in the hotel lobby.

Hepsibah Mattington was close to fifty and had been born and raised on cattle ranches. She was a woman without any pretense; her greying hair was drawn back in a bun, she wore her skirts split up the middle so that she could ride, and there was a rifle slung across her back. "Why?" she demanded.

"They had been at Lorinda Dooley's house," Russell said, aware that everyone in Charity and for thirty miles in all directions knew Lorinda Dooley's house for what it was. "They were drunk. One of the men had taken a new girl upstairs and he wanted to use his belt on her. Miss Dooley does not permit that in her house. So she sent for me."

"I see," Hepsibah said. "What did you do to them?"

"I arrested them," Russell said blandly.

"You had Catty, McPhee, Tuck, and Hunter to deal with. None of those men are easily handled." She folded her arms. "You shoot them?"

"I don't carry pistols," Russell told her.

"Just that fancy club," she added for him, nodding to the baton.

"That's right." He indicated one of the three chairs in the lobby. "Would you care to sit down?"

"No, I would not care to sit down," she snapped. "I want to know how you brought those bullies under control. Or do I have to go ask Lorinda how you did it?"

Russell shook his head. "Missus Mattington, would you believe me if I told you that your hands are not as difficult to deal with as you might think? Catty and Tuck were the most belligerent; I had to knock them out. Hunter and McPhee . . . they each tried to draw on me. And now they each have broken hands. I was sorry to have to do that."

"You know, I think you mean it," she said measuringly.

"I do," he said.

"How bad's the damage?" Hepsibah asked.

"Two of them have a bad headache but I've had Doctor Clayton examine them and he says they're in no danger."

"Hah! Henry Clayton's a fool!"

Russell continued as if she had not spoken. "He's bandaged the hands for McPhee and Hunter. If they're sensible they should not have any lasting trouble."

"McPhee and Hunter are range hands. You can't expect men like them to be sensible. I don't know what I'm going to do with them until their hands heal. Why'd you have to break them?" Before he spoke, she went on. "They were going to draw on you, yes, I understand that. And I suppose a broken hand is better than a bullet in the shoulder any day, but Lord bless me, why'd it have to be my men who made such wumps out of themselves?"

By now Russell was smiling slightly. "Missus Mattington, I wish everyone—"

"Call me Bess," she interrupted. "Saves breath."

"Thank you," Russell said.

"They tell me your first name is Jason," she persisted. "Mind if I use it?"

"If you insist." He regarded her with respect. "How long have you lived on your ranch, Missus Matt . . . Bess?"

"Came here in '38; that makes it ten years now. Before then, we had land in Missouri." She indicated the entrance to the dining room of the restaurant. "Had your supper yet?"

"It's early," Jason said.

"No reason not to have some of Widow Schmidt's ham," Bess Mattington said roundly. "Come on. I want you to tell me everything that happened."

Russell cocked his head. "You'll be disappointed."

"In Dorabelle's ham? never!" She started toward the dining room entrance. "You coming?"

Russell shrugged and followed her.

3

"I suppose it's useless to ask you how you got that?" Henry Clayton said to Jason Russell as he examined the cut in the sheriff's arm.

"There was a disturbance," Russell said.

Clayton shook his head. "Those rowdies up from Pueblo, I suppose."

When Russell neither confirmed nor denied this, Clayton went on. "You need some help, Jason. You can't take on six armed men and expect to walk away from it unhurt."

"Does that mean you're advising me to carry pistols?" Russell asked, flinching against the bite of alcohol as Clayton cleaned the wound.

"I've advised you to do that since the day after you got that badge," the physician reminded him, concentrating on the cut. "At least the blade was clean. You were lucky. Some of those men never sharpen their blades, and they cut like saws."

It took Russell a minute or two before he could trust himself to speak evenly. "I have pistols and two rifles. I would rather not carry them."

"Why in the name of all that's holy not?" Clayton pleaded.

"Because if I carry a pistol, there's a much greater risk of getting shot. If all I have is my baton, I have a very good chance of getting nothing worse than an occasional cut." He reached to roll down his sleeve. "When I was in the Runners we were taught that it was part of our duty to keep the general population as safe as possible. That meant that we were ordered not to fire pistols unless we had already been fired upon. Even then, in a crowded area, we were expected to make every effort to deal with the situation without resorting to firearms."

"That's fine for London; this is Charity." Clayton stepped back. "One of these days, you're going to find yourself up against someone who doesn't play by your rules, and you're going to get your damned head blown off."

"I have met several men who don't play by my rules. I am still alive." Russell stood up slowly. "The others are not."

Henry Clayton regarded his patient with curiosity. "You killed them?"

Russell nodded, his face blank with distress. "I do not like killing people, Henry. I would rather not have to do it." He stood up, holding the back of the chair until the room stopped wobbling around him.

"I still have to bandage that," Clayton reminded him a bit distantly.

"Fine." Russell was grateful for a little more time before he would have to go back out into the cold, for he felt chilled bone-deep already. "Don't make it too tight," he advised.

"You don't want it coming loose, do you?" Clayton asked as he sorted through his linen gauze strips.

"No, but I don't want my hand going numb, either." He waited stoically while Clayton finished his work, and then he flexed his fingers experimentally; it was painful but not impossible to move them, which was reassuring. "Do you have anything I can take for this?"

"Morphia," Clayton muttered, not meeting Russell's eyes as he spoke.

"I'd rather not have anything that drastic," Russell said as he fastened his cuff. "Is there anything milder?"

"A couple shots of whiskey," said Clayton in a lighter tone. "Or go find William Red Pony. He'll give you whatever it is the Indians use."

"Does he know that?" Russell asked with real interest which surprised the doctor.

"He says he does," Clayton answered cautiously.

"Then I'll certainly talk to him," said Russell as he picked up his fur cap. "I wanted to speak to him about land around here in any case."

"Why to Red Pony about land?" Clayton inquired.

"Because he is likely to know more than others. He has lived here longer than anyone I've met. The only other person who would have better advice—if he would give it, which I doubt he would—is Don Maximillian. Since he and I have yet to meet . . ." He left the rest up in the air.

Henry Clayton nodded slowly. "You're a sensible man, Jason, except when it comes to your occupation."

Russell was able to laugh once. "I'm most sensible about my occupation, but you don't realize it yet. One day you'll discover that I'm not being as reckless as you think I am." He started toward the door, walking with care, not swinging his arm. Once he was on the street, he would have to force himself to move naturally, but for a few more minutes he could pamper himself.

"What about the Indian medicines—you aren't really going to—" Clayton was too distressed to go on.

"Of course I'm going to use them. If I hadn't used native medicines in India I would be long dead. The Company surgeon thought I was insane, but four other men died and I lived." He opened the door and breathed in sharply as the cold air struck him. "They tell me it will snow tomorrow."

"Or tonight, possibly." Clayton watched him. "Take care you don't get too cold. Have Frau Schmidt give you a good supper and make sure you have an extra blanket or two. Cuts like that one can cool the body too much."

"All right," said Russell. "After I speak with William Red Pony." He closed the door and steeled himself for the short walk to the jail.

William Red Pony was in the little room at the back of the livery stable; he often earned extra money looking after the horses for Daniel Calvin. As Russell came in the side door, William stepped out of one of the stalls.

"Good afternoon, William," Russell said.

"Sheriff."

"How are my horses doing?" He had learned the first time he met Red

Pony that one of the few things that drew out this taciturn man was horses.

"They're fine horses, Sheriff." He folded his arms. "What is it you want?"

"Two things, if you please." Russell stepped nearer the stove that ran the forge as well as warmed the stable. "I need your advice on land, for one."

"And the other?" Whatever Red Pony's reaction to Russell's request might be, he revealed nothing in his expression of face or voice.

"I was hoping . . . that is, I was told you have some knowledge of native medicines."

"Indian medicine is all useless; that is what all white men say." He spoke flatly but his head lifted enough to show his resentment.

"This white man says nothing of the sort," Russell said. "This white man would appreciate your help, if you're willing to give it. If you aren't, I will understand." His arm was aching and he hoped that whatever William Red Pony might tell him would work.

Red Pony picked up a brush and set to going over Russell's big brown gelding, starting at his neck and working back and down. "I might be able to find something. What is the matter?"

"I was cut in the fight." He knew he would not have to say more, since most of the town had seen it.

"Henry Clayton will tend to you."

"He already has. Unfortunately he is limited. He can offer nothing to stop pain that does not also muddle thoughts." He did not press further.

"And land. Why should you speak to me of land."

"Because you raise horses and you are familiar with this place, more than anyone else," Russell said patiently. "My half-brother will be sending me horses that were left to me by our father, and when they get here, I hope that I will have a good place for them." He saw Red Pony's face brighten. "I trust your suggestions."

Red Pony cleared his throat. "The horses from your brother—they will be like these?"

"Some of them. Others will be work horses—larger and stronger, for farm work and hauling. But they will be fine animals of their sort." He knew he had said enough. "I will be at the hotel, if you want to speak to me."

"Perhaps in an hour, perhaps tomorrow." Red Pony went on grooming the brown Thoroughbred. "*Rajah*—what does that mean?"

"It means ruler," said Russell. "Gryphon is the name of a mythical beast."

"I learned what a gryphon is from the nuns," Red Pony said.

"Portia is a woman's name," Russell finished.

"Perhaps I will come to the hotel when I have taken care of Rajah, Gryphon, and Portia."

Liam Cauliffe returned to Charity between the first and second snowfall. He brought with him a supply of books he had purchased in Denver, and announced his attention to establish a school in his church as Padre Antonio had in his.

"There are more than twenty children in Charity who ought to be in school and aren't," he declared to a town meeting held in the hotel. "There are more families moving in every year, and it's time that we made sure that there is a place where the children can learn their letters and sums."

One of the ranchers laughed. "What's the point of it?"

"Men who can read can know their Bible and their God," said Cauliffe. This brought more laughter.

"Men who can read and figure can deal with the world," said Jason Russell from his place at the side of the room. "If you are going to make your way, you must know how to read and write and figure. If you cannot do these things, you will be entirely at the mercy of those who do, and you will be deaf and mute to all those you seek to reach."

This forceful statement caught the attention of several men in the room. "What makes you think we'll need a school? Schools cost money," Daniel Calvin stated.

"Daniel," Russell said, "you've told me you have a sister in Ohio, but you know nothing about her, even if she is alive or dead, married or widowed, or if she has children. If you could read and write, you and she could exchange letters. You would have been able to tell your family where to find you."

"There's many here who don't want their families to find them," Samuel Gall, who made boots and shoes, reminded them.

"But do they want to be cheated by merchants and lawyers?" Henry Clayton asked, taking up Russell's argument. "Do you want to rely on others to tell you what you need to know in order to do business?"

"I trust a man's word," said Arthur Mattington, Hepsibah's leathery husband. "A man's only as good as his word."

"That's fine so long as you're dealing with honorable men," Russell reminded him. "But there are those who will give their word and it will mean nothing to them. What then?"

"Shoot 'em," suggested a voice in the crowd.

Russell shook his head. "And then you would have me, or someone like me, to deal with."

George Fletcher, who had sat at the front of the room with Purvis and Olfrant flanking him, now rose imposingly to his feet. "Charity is growing. Five years ago there were less than sixty people living here and now we have more than three times that number, with more arriving. We have an obligation. If we wish to attract families of substance, we must offer them safety and advancement. We are a law-abiding town, and we mean to be a progressive one."

A few of the citizens applauded, but there were hoots as well. Fletcher regarded the assembly with determination. "I have already begun a search for a man to run a newspaper for Charity. The Town Council has discussed this and we agree that it is the next step for us. If we are to be a town with a newspaper, we must also be a town with a school."

"The Padre already has a school," Calvin said.

"Do you wish your children to be taught by Catholics with Mexican and Indian children? I say that we must protect our children from Catholic influences, and we can only do that if we have our own schools." Barton Purvis had risen beside Fletcher. "I have three children of my own and another coming. My wife cannot run the household and teach our children at the same time. I say that it is time we had a school. And a proper schoolmaster."

"Preacher Cauliffe can be schoolmaster," said Hosea Olfrant.

"Preacher Cauliffe," said the minister, "is a circuit preacher, and come spring, I have others who will need me."

There was an uneasy murmur of conversation among the men gathered in the hotel.

"The Town Council," said George Fletcher in a loud voice, "has already approved a school and the eventual hiring of a teacher. For the time being, we have decided to run the school by subscription, with allowances made for those who cannot afford the full price."

Jason Russell, leaning against the wall at the side of the room, watched Fletcher and his two cronies. From time to time he shook his head, sensing the resistance the men themselves were creating to their plan. He had said what he wanted to say, and had felt that the citizens were with him. Now Fletcher was botching it. Reluctantly Russell stepped forward, interrupting a pompous statement Purvis was delivering.

"Excuse me," he said to the Town Council. "I would like to suggest that all of you with children consider what it will be like for them as the country expands westward. It looks as if all the land west of here will be part of the United States in a year or so, and that will bring more settlers. Do you want your children to be able to participate in the development or not? I began my work in London, and I learned one thing as a Bow Street Runner, and that is that illiteracy breeds poverty. Even among the very poor, those who could read and write fared better than those who could not. They had more orderly lives, were less often before the Bench, had fewer criminals in the family, and more often than the others were able to rise above their origins." He nodded to the Town Council. "I'm sorry to have interrupted you."

"Sheriff's right," said Arthur Mattington. "At least about the Mexican Territories."

Hiram Mattington, Arthur's oldest son, got to his feet to address the gathering. "I want to say that if I'd had the chance, I would have learned to read. It bothers me that I can't look at the menu over on Widow Schmidt's chalkboard and know what's for supper, or what it'll cost me. If there's a school in Charity and you can pay to go to it, well, I might be twenty-six years old, but I can tell you, I mean to go."

The room was quiet when Hiram was through, and for once George Fletcher had the good sense to keep his mouth shut.

"If anyone would like to subscribe to a school," Cauliffe said to the quiet men, "I would appreciate it if he would leave his name and the number of children he would like to enroll. I would like to have some notion of how many students to expect. And if there are those of you, like Hiram, who want to learn to read and write, then I'm sure something can be arranged. It is part of our obligation as citizens of this country to be able to discharge our duties." He straightened up and was about to propound further when the side door of the room opened and Dorabelle Schmidt bustled into the room.

"I have been listening," she announced, her voice penetrating and strange in the room filled with men. "I wish to say that if Preacher Cauliffe does not want such classes in his church, then I would welcome them here." Her accent was heavily Germanic and there were those in the room who could not understand her because of this. "I know my own language, but in English I am not . . . I am not easy. I want to know more. I will happily let a teacher use the dining room after the evening meal, or in the morning when we have finished with breakfast."

"An excellent notion, Frau Schmidt," said Liam Cauliffe. "It would please me to find more persons in this town who were as willing as you are to come to the aid of those who wish to better themselves." He looked over the assembly.

Once more Russell stepped forward. "For those who might have to spend a night in jail for drunken disorder or disturbing the peace, I'll let them off for school." It was the only sensible thing he could offer, and he noticed that this proposal was not liked by George Fletcher, who at last reasserted his control over the meeting.

"Those who break the law must pay for it!" he thundered.

"Of course," said Russell. "But there is a world of difference between getting drunk and trying to roust the girls over at Lorinda Dooley's"—he ignored the embarrassed hush that came over the men at the mention of the town brothel—"and those who try to shoot up a store. The first is inconvenient and requires little risk to stop; the second is dangerous for everyone."

"We will discuss this later, Sheriff Russell," Fletcher vowed.

"As you wish, Mayor Fletcher," Russell said, stepping back to his place at the side of the room.

After the second snowfall there were four days of blindingly clear weather, and during that time Jason Russell rode out to check with the farmers and ranchers and miners living near Charity. He had learned from his years in Australia that such isolated persons were more vulnerable than those in town.

"Sheriff," said Cloris Bell as Russell approached the log-and-sod house she shared with Maude Rossiter. The women had come to their land four years before. They were known as the Cousins and were content to be left alone.

"Just out checking," said Russell as he got out of the saddle. "Do you mind if I give Rajah a rest? He's been carrying me for hours."

"You're welcome to a cup of coffee, if you like. I could pour a little brandy in it, if you'd like."

"It'd be very welcome, Miz Bell," said Russell as he led his horse up to the door of the three-room house.

"Tie him up at the rail by the barn," Cloris suggested. "There's water and I'll put out a handful of oats for him, if you like."

"That's good of you," said Russell, and went into the house, where Maude Rossiter was busy repairing harness for their two big grey draught horses. "Good afternoon, Miz Rossiter," he said as he closed the door and pulled off his fur cap.

"Good to see you, Sheriff Russell," said Maude without looking up. She was a spinster, unlike Cloris, who was a widow with three grown children living in the East; she had a small inheritance that funded the farm, and at thirty-eight it was assumed she was willing to be an old maid.

"I've been riding the rounds of the outskirts," said Russell, dropping into a straight-backed chair. "There's two sick children at the Snowdon place, but other than that, so far there's no bad news."

"It's good of you to take the time to do it," said Maude without giving him more attention than she had to. "I've got to finish this."

"Go ahead," said Russell, letting a little of the stiffness ease out of his bones. "I have a couple of other questions to ask; I hope you don't mind."

"Depends on what they are," said Maude, still concentrating on the harness.

Russell moved a little nearer the hearth, where two good-sized logs smoldered. "I heard that there've been armed men spotted near here. Estimates are that there are nine to fourteen of them. They've been raiding herds and stealing supplies. Have you had anything taken recently?"

"Not that I know of. You ought to ask Missus Bell. She tends to the stock. I take care of the house." Her needle moved more rapidly.

"I thought she might have—" He stopped as the door opened and Cloris Bell came into the room.

"It's ferocious cold out there, and going to get worse tonight," said Cloris, pulling off her gloves and tossing her cap across the room. "I'm that glad you gave me an excuse to stop work for a while. My bones were starting to turn to ice." She went to the stove. "Coffee and a little brandy. I'll have the same. What about you, Cousin?"

"The same, if you don't mind," said Maude, finally putting her work aside.

While Cloris poured the coffee into large white mugs, Russell said, "I don't want to alarm either of you ladies, but I do think it is wise to be prepared. I wouldn't like to think of you trying to fend for yourselves with men as desperate as these are rumored to be."

"I wouldn't be too fond of that myself," said Cloris. "Who are these desperate men, do you know?"

"The rumor is that they're part of the Mayhew gang," said Russell, making no effort to minimize the impact of his words.

"I thought Mayhew was near Denver," said Maude, her face showing more alarm than was in her voice.

"They're moving south, it would seem. I was warned over a month ago, but thought little of it at the time. Now, it seems that there are good reasons to be concerned. I don't think it would be wise to underestimate this gang. And I don't want you assuming that you can deal with him in your own way. Where Mayhew is concerned, there is no easy way to deal with him."

"Shotgun blast between the eyes might do it," said Cloris, and brought three mugs on a tray. She gave the first to Maude, then offered one to Russell. "Tell me, Sheriff, do you think we're in any real danger?"

"Yes," said Russell as he felt the warmth of the mug seep into his hands. "I don't want to cause you worry, but I truly think you have every reason to be on guard. These are not simply thieves, they're murderers."

"And you think they might come here?" Cloris asked.

"I think they might come to any isolated house. Yours is one, but there are quite a number of others."

"What about Don Maximillian?" Maude suggested with a hint of rancor.

"I haven't spoken to him. From what I have been told, he has a large number of hands working his land and he maintains a regular patrol of his boundaries. I am assuming that he is able to protect himself, at least for the time being." He took a sip, and although the coffee was almost scalding, it was welcome as sunshine going down.

"I see." Cloris chose one of the other three chairs and sank into it. She was dressed in buckskin trousers and boots, and she almost shocked Russell by resting one ankle on her opposite knee. "So we have to watch out for strangers. What do you want us to do if we see one? There's just Maude and me here. Do you want one of us to leave here, exposing the other, or have you something else in mind?"

"Actually, I was hoping that I could persuade you to come into town if you're concerned." He stared into his coffee.

"We've got cattle and goats and we're not going to leave them for robbers to slaughter." Cloris did not raise her voice but there was an implacable note that Russell heard clearly.

"Better to lose a few head of cattle than your lives." He took another sip of coffee. "And Mayhew—if it is Mayhew—rarely makes it simple. I had a report from Denver three days ago describing what his gang has done to their victims, and I would not like to think of that happening to you." He drank the rest of his coffee while the two women sat in silence.

"We'll think about it, Sheriff," said Maude after a short silence.

"Thank you. And thank you for the coffee." He rose and put his mug on the mantle. "I'll be by from time to time. If you have any reason to need assistance, don't hesitate to ask. I can't emphasize that enough."

Maude smiled for both of them. "We appreciate the visit, Sheriff."

"And the warning," added Cloris, rising and escorting him to the door. "You better head back to town soon," she advised as she squinted up at the sky. "There's a storm coming tonight or tomorrow. You don't want to get caught out when it hits."

Russell looked up at the open sky. "It's fine."

"Not when the sky's white around the edges and the sun goes glarey like that. When you've been here another winter or two, you'll learn to recognize the signs. The storm's coming." She glanced toward the barn. "And the goats want milking. I'll walk over with you, Sheriff." Without waiting for him to speak, she fell into step beside him. "That's a fine-looking horse you have there."

"Yes, I think so," agreed Russell as he untied Rajah and reached for the stirrup iron.

"And a mighty peculiar saddle." She watched him mount.

"It's a hussar's saddle," said Russell automatically.

"Whatever, it's peculiar." She waved to him and went into the barn, whistling "Mary Hamilton" as she walked.

4

"Señor," said the man in the doorway of the jail. He had a wide Mexican hat in his hands, and his bulky clothing marked him as much as his accent.

"Yes?" Russell said, looking up from a number of packets and letters Smilin' Jack had brought by earlier that day.

"Señor, I am from Don Maximillian." He bowed slightly, as if the name alone deserved a show of respect.

"Yes?" Russell repeated, setting his papers aside. "What can I do for you?"

"Don Maximillian has sent me to bring you. He has need of you." The man spoke English well, but in a stilted way, as if uncomfortable with it.

"Truly?" Russell pushed back his chair. "Do you know what the reason is?" He reached for his heavy jacket and cap as he spoke.

"He did not tell me," the man said.

"But you can guess?" Russell suggested.

"I think . . . his daughter is . . . troubling him." The rim of the hat twisted in the man's hand.

"All right," said Russell, deciding against bringing his shotgun. "I will have to leave word at the hotel and my horses are at the livery stable. It won't take long to be ready." As he started toward the door, he asked, "What's your name? You haven't told me."

"Paco," the man answered. "I am . . . like a foreman. I am in charge of running the rancho but not the hacienda." He followed Russell out the door and into the muddy slush of the road. His horse, a leggy pinto, was tied to the hitching post in front of the church across the street.

"If you like," Russell offered, "I could join you here shortly. That way if you have something you'd like to say to the Padre, you can do it in peace." He strode away before Paco could respond.

By the time he returned on Gryphon, Padre Antonio and Paco were in deep, private conversation on the church steps. Both men looked up with alarm as Russell came up to them. "I didn't mean to startle you."

"We're nearly through," Padre Antonio said to Russell, then added a few hurried words in Spanish to Paco. "Thank you, Sheriff," he went on, now addressing Russell. "I hope you will be able to assist Don Maximillian. Go with God." He gave Paco his blessing and went back into the church.

"I am ready, Sheriff," said Paco as he hurried to his horse, vaulting into the saddle and gathering up the reins in one smooth move. He pointed to the west. "We take that road."

"Yes," Russell said politely. "I know."

There had been several times when Russell had skirted the edge of Don Maximillian's land, but he had never ventured onto it. Riding beside Paco, he took full advantage of this opportunity to observe the vast holdings of the Spanish landlord. "I understand that Don Maximillian's family was given this land by the King of Spain," said Russell, as much to have something to say as to gain information.

"Si; three generations ago. It was his . . . grandfather's father—"

"His great-grandfather," Russell supplied.

"That is it! He was the one who came here first; the family has never left but to bring home brides since that time." He indicated the rise of the mountain. "Everything to the crest, along that ridge, and then two valleys beyond, are part of the rancho."

"Impressive," said Russell sincerely.

"There were some much bigger, but the Arreba y Corre family has done well with that el Rey gave them." Though the snow on the ground obscured the actual road, Paco was following what was to him a well-known path. Here and there footprints of his horse from earlier could be seen, but for the most part the snow was as smoothly undulating and unbroken as the surface of an ocean.

The hacienda, when they came in sight of it, was more spread out than Russell had anticipated. The main house enclosed a large courtyard; beside it two large buildings flanked a large arena.

"For the horses; Don Maximillian's family has been breeding horses for more than a hundred years," Paco announced with pride.

"And the rest?" Russell asked, indicating the other buildings.

"Housing for the . . . hands, you would call them. A chapel; you see the cross? Three barns for cattle, and those last buildings are for the pigs.

Grain is stored there"—he pointed to three hive-shaped structures—"and there is hay in the barns and the stables."

"Very impressive," said Russell as he and Paco drew nearer the hacienda.

Two servants took Russell in tow as he tied Gryphon at the front of the house.

"I'll see he's fed and watered," Paco informed him, and did not wait for a response.

"Venga conmigo," said the older servant, smiling and bowing.

"I'm afraid I don't speak Spanish. I don't comprendo," he said very slowly, shaking his head.

The two servants bowed and smiled and indicated a hallway toward the back of the house. Sighing, Russell went with them, hoping devoutly that Don Maximillian knew some English.

Apparently the room was some sort of study, for the walls were lined with bookshelves and there were two massive writing tables in carved dark wood near the windows.

At the larger of these sat a middle-aged man, whip-thin and sharp-faced, dressed in leather and wool garments, all embroidered. He closed the book he had been reading and held out his hand as Russell was brought into the room. "You must be Sheriff Russell," he said in very educated English, tinged with the soft lilt of Spanish.

"Jason Russell," he said, taking the long, thin hand in his.

"British, they tell me." He released Russell's hand and indicated a chair near the hearth. "Please. Sit down."

Russell did as he was told, draping his jacket over the back of the chair and straightening his collar. "I understand," he said when Don Maximillian said nothing more, "that you have a problem."

"That is true," Don Maximillian said.

"And you would like my help?" Russell prodded, wishing he knew how best to get information out of the formidable Spaniard.

"I must have it; I do not like it at all." He glared toward the fire. "I hope that you are a gentleman."

"I was raised to be," Russell said stiffly. "Does that matter?"

"In this case, since it concerns my daughter's honor, I must pray that what you say is true." He stared down at the tabletop. "Did you know I have a daughter?"

"I believe I'd heard something of her, yes," said Russell carefully.

"She is my only remaining child. I had four once, but the others, and their mother, died of putrid lungs, five winters ago." He crossed himself. "Only Elvira was left, and now she is gone." The words came out quickly, as if he were afraid that if he did not say them in a hurry, he might not be able to speak at all.

"Gone?" Russell repeated.

"Yesterday. Her duenna . . . her maid went to her room, when she had not come to breakfast. We feared that she might be ill, for the nights have been so cold." He folded his hands and looked at them as if he had never seen them before. "She was not in her room. We searched the hacienda. She was not here. There were two horses gone from the stables, neither of them hers; her own mare was still in her stall . . ."

"And what then?" Russell asked when Don Maximillian did not continue.

"I organized a search. There were a few prints in the snow from the horses, or so we think, but we could not follow them. They had been crossed by many cattle, and then the snowfall began again, and—" He shook his head in helplessness. "I have had my men out looking for her, for any sign of her."

"I see."

"I am certain she was taken against her will, that she was kidnapped and that there will be a demand for ransom. I have heard that there are desperate men in this area. They would not hesitate to seize such a prize."

"You mean the Mayhew gang?" Russell asked.

"That is the name!" For the first time there was wrath in Don Maximillian's eyes.

"Have you noticed strangers on your land recently?" Russell asked.

"Of course not! If I had noticed them, my men and I would have run them off." He got to his feet and began to pace. "But from what I have been told these are dangerous and subtle men, who are not easily found if they do not wish to be."

Russell nodded. "Have you noticed anything missing? Was anything taken from your daughter's room?"

"Very little, other than she herself. There were two pair of shoes gone, and her maid thinks that some of her nightclothes are gone. Her brushes and her jewelry case. I am not surprised that they have taken her jewelry." He said this last with great contempt.

"Neither am I," Russell said, but kept his impressions to himself. "Her brushes as well, you say."

"That is why I fear they will hold her for ransom. Her nightclothes and her brushes—that must mean that they intend to keep her alive for a time." He turned toward Russell, and for a moment there was a desperation in his eyes that was truly pathetic. Then it was gone and haughty ire took its place. "I want my daughter back, Sheriff. I would use my own men, but since it is likely that I would have to search beyond the rancho, I require your assistance."

"That you do," said Russell.

"And so I have sent for you. Now you may begin your investigation. I have told my household and all my . . . hands that they are to cooperate with you. If they do not, you are to inform me of it at once so that they might be reprimanded." He stared out the window into the leaden afternoon. "This is my land. I am Patron here, and my people know that they must do as I tell them."

"Your fiefdom, in fact?" Russell said, rising. "I will do my best to bring you daughter back, because, Don Maximillian, that is my job. That is what the Council of Charity hired me to do. If there is a way to find your daughter, she will be found." He paused to let Don Maximillian consider his words. "I will need to have a portrait of your daughter. You have one, I trust?"

"She sat for one only last year," said Don Maximillian heavily. "It is in the dining room. I will ask Inez to show it to you before you go."

"I will also want to see her room and to talk with her maid." He could sense Don Maximillian's urge to be rid of him, but he was not prepared to leave. "If she does not speak English, then I hope you will send Paco along to translate."

"Paco cannot go into her room!" Don Maximillian was shocked. "If someone must translate, then I will."

Russell was not sure he wanted Don Maximillian to do that, for he was reasonably certain that most of the staff would not speak candidly in front of him. "I do not want to take you away from your responsibilities, Don Maximillian."

"My first duty is to find my daughter," he snapped. "Tell me what else you need."

"I am not certain yet," Russell said. "It will depend on what I find, or what I do not find when I look at her room and talk with your staff." He indicated the door. "The sooner we begin, the sooner it will be over."

"I will have my man bring you coffee. You will be able to work while you take it." This grudging hospitality did not fool Russell, who knew that Don Maximillian thought of him as little better than a servant.

"That's very kind. After the ride, I could do with a cup of coffee." He had to walk behind Don Maximillian, and as they climbed to the second floor, he asked, "Are your doors all locked at night?"

"Most are, but the cook's door is not. That is in case of a fire, the servants in the kitchen would be able to get out. Otherwise there is danger they would be burned alive." He indicated a heavy door. "That is her room."

"Has it been disturbed?"

"Certainly not. Her maid keeps everything in perfect order." Don Maximillian opened the door, revealing a chamber that was the closest thing to luxurious that Russell had seen in the West. Every article, every piece of furniture was polished and neat.

"And her maid? has she cleaned, or moved anything, since your daughter disappeared?" Russell asked, already knowing the answer.

"Naturally. Everything was restored. I insist that the house be kept properly at all times. Even when my wife and children were dying, I insisted that the house be run correctly. I cannot accept excuses." He watched with ill-concealed distaste as Russell walked about the room, now pausing to examine the contents of a drawer, now opening the closet, now glancing out the window.

"Are these draperies closed at night?" Russell touched the heavy velvet hangings.

"Certainly."

"And is there a candle or lamp in the room?"

Don Maximillian indicated the prayer stool in the corner and the small votive candle that burned there even now. "Always there is a candle to the Virgin."

"So the room was not entirely dark. And did you notice whether or not the draperies were open or closed the morning she disappeared?"

"I . . . I don't know. Inez did not mention it, that I recall." Don Maximillian hesitated. "Would it matter?"

"It might," said Russell. "And the vigil candle was still burning?"

"Of course."

"Did you see it?" Russell persisted.

"Inez . . ." He stopped. "I assume it was still burning."

"But you aren't sure." He walked around the room. "Did the shoes come from the closet?"

"That is where her shoes are kept." Don Maximillian was clearly offended at the questions. "Why do you ask these things? What can they matter?"

Russell regarded Don Maximillian patiently. "I realize you are worried for your daughter's welfare and you want me to take quick action. But before I do that, unless I am to waste my time and possibly increase her risk, I must find out all that I can about the circumstances of her disappearance. Now, you say that her own horse was not taken."

"That is correct." Don Maximillian was very stiff now.

"Which horses were taken? I believe you said there were two of them?"

"Yes; my old grey gelding and a black mare." He considered what

Russell had said and added, "The mare was new; I purchased her less than a year ago, in Mexico."

"Is she a highbred horse?" asked Russell, as much for his own information as for anything to do with the investigation.

"Andalusian," said Don Maximillian. "Very fine bloodlines." He lifted his chin. "You know about Andalusians?"

"Not a great deal. I've seen some, but I have Thoroughbreds." He looked around the room. "Your daughter was aware of the value of the mare, was she?"

"As much as you might expect a girl to be. She said the mare was beautiful, which is true. I do not expect more understanding from her."

"I see." He indicated he was through with the room and as Don Maximillian closed the door behind them, he said, "I would like to see her portrait now. And if you will give me your candid opinion on how good a likeness it is, it would be most helpful."

"She is a striking young lady," said Don Maximillian, not entirely pleased about that, from the tone of his voice.

Russell considered the answer. "Does she have a tutor?"

"She had two when she was younger, but now there is only her music master. She has said that she was bored with playing the piano and the harp, but one must expect these little rebellions from sixteen-year-olds, I suppose." He led the way to the dining room, and nodded toward the large painting at the far end of the room. "That is my daughter: Elvira Carmen Isabel Arreba y Corre."

"Very pretty," said Russell as he strolled up to the portrait. He noticed the proud angle of the head and the determined set of her mouth, as well as the way her delicate hands gripped the corners of her mantilla. She would be a temperamental handful, he decided, and the man who tried to win her would have an uphill battle.

"She is considered so. Her confessor has had to warn her of the snare of vanity more than once." Don Maximillian had not moved from his place in the door. "The likeness is excellent."

Russell nodded and turned away from the picture. "Thank you, Don Maximillian. I hope this will speed her return."

"You must punish those who have abducted her." It was a blunt and emotional order, made without apology.

"I have to find her first. Once she is safe, then the law will determine what should happen next." He paused. "I would like to speak with her maid and others in the household."

"I will translate for you," Don Maximillian declared.

So Russell spent the better part of two hours listening to his host repeat what the servants said. He considered this largely a waste of time, for he was aware that none of the servants would speak his mind when el Patron was in the room. The time was spent being assured that Elvira was a gifted, attractive, devoted girl, one who was occasionally hot-tempered, but what could be expected of so aristocratic a child? The story was always the same, and Don Maximillian was satisfied, though Jason Russell was not.

"You can see that my daughter has need of your help," said Don Maximillian when the last of the servants had been dismissed.

"Yes." He had taken a number of notes, more to convince Don Maximillian that he was serious about the investigation than to record any significant information. "I will keep you informed of my progress."

"I require that," Don Maximillian agreed.

"But I warn you that investigations of this sort take time. I will have to proceed with caution so that she will not be endangered by my investigation. When a person is abducted, it is difficult to take them back without injury; I don't believe you want that to happen, do you?"

Don Maximillian stood even straighter than usual. "I want my daughter returned to me unharmed and I want those who kidnapped her executed for their outrage."

"You've made that very clear," said Russell. "I will do what I can to find her. After that, we will see about the rest."

"I will not tolerate more insults than I have suffered already." He was about to launch into a tirade—Russell knew the signs—when he remembered himself and stopped the avalanche of words that he was about to release. "I rely on you to do your work properly, Sheriff."

"I'll do my best," said Russell sincerely as he swung into the saddle.

"I will, of course, provide you a reward for your service." He made a gesture of dismissal, the same he had given his servants earlier.

"That's not necessary; I get a salary for my work." He tugged Gryphon back and was about to head off when Don Maximillian added a last comment.

"That is a very good horse you're riding."

"Thank you; yes, it is." He held Gryphon steady.

"You have papers on him?" Don Maximillian's expression said that he doubted it.

"He's from the stable of the Earl of Mindenhall in England," Russell said, taking secret delight in the surprise in Don Maximillian's eyes. "I have the documents in my office, if you wish to see them."

Don Maximillian said nothing more. He turned on his heel and went into the house.

*   *   *

"William," Russell said to William Red Pony the next morning. "I need your help."

"What could I do for you, Sheriff?" he asked, continuing to measure grain into small metal buckets.

"I need you to find a horse for me." Russell was going on a hunch now, and the more he considered it, the more confident he was.

"You have three horses and more coming. Why do you want another one?"

"I don't, not for me." Russell picked up two of the buckets and followed William into the stable.

"Tell me," said William, raising his voice a little over the excited nickering and stamping of the horses.

"A black Andalusian mare." Russell fed his own horses first, then turned his attention to two others.

"Andalusian?" repeated William Red Pony, permitting himself to sound surprised.

"There is one missing from Don Maximillian's stable."

"I see. And I gather that is not the only filly he's lost in the last week." William did not laugh out loud, but his eyes crinkled.

"Best to keep that to yourself. Don Maximillian is convinced his daughter was kidnapped and I would not want her to be endangered by rumors." He finished graining the horses on the west side of the stable. "Do you want me to bring more grain?"

"No, I have enough. What rumors might endanger her?"

"Her father is afraid that she might fall into the hands of the Mayhew gang." He was able to say this without any emotion whatever.

"And you do not," William said, reading the sheriff correctly. "Why the questions about the horse?"

"I think she might have taken the mare," said Russell. "And that is to be kept between the two of us. Understand me, William. I do not want it known that I doubt what has been said by Don Maximillian. He would not accept the idea, and there is every reason to think that if she was not in danger before, she could be in danger later."

"I won't say anything. Not that anyone would listen to me. What do I know?" He gathered up the buckets and went back to the feed room. "Tell me more about this black Andalusian mare."

"I don't know very much. There were two horses missing the morning after Miss Arreba y Corre disappeared. Don Maximillian thinks that the kidnappers also took the horses. I would be willing to believe that his daughter and a friend left together." Russell sighed. "And since an expensive horse and her jewels are missing, I have to assume that eventually someone will see the horse."

"Makes sense," said William. "All right, I'll listen and make a few inquiries. That's the best I can do without raising questions." He pulled out a rickety wheelbarrow and began to load it with oat hay. "I'll let you know what I learn. If I learn anything."

"I appreciate that, William." Russell held out his hand and was pleased when William took it.

"Pleasure, Sheriff." He went back to his work, ignoring Russell.

By the time Russell got back to the jail, he decided he was satisfied with the beginning of his investigation. A few more careful questions and he would be prepared to begin his hunt in earnest.

5

Sister Mercedes appeared almost as white as the snow that was falling at her back. "You must come at once," she said to Russell as she hung onto the door frame. "It is the Dooley child; she is very . . . ill."

Russell was already out of his chair and reaching for his heavy coat as the nun held out her hand in supplication. "Take me to her. How old is the girl?"

"She is barely seven," said Sister Mercedes, her teeth chattering from the cold.

"You say she is ill? Have you sent for Doctor Clayton?" He was aware that whatever was wrong with the child, it was not just sickness.

"Sister Anna Maria has gone for him. Oh, please, hurry." She all but dragged him across the snow-blown street and into the chilly confines of the church. "We have her here, out of the classroom." She indicated a small chamber across from the single confessional. "Don't alarm her, Sheriff. She is troubled enough without that."

"I'll try not to." He stepped in front of the nun and took off his cap.

There was a low cot against the wall, and a small child huddled there, blankets drawn up to her chin. She paid no attention to the nun or Russell, preferring to suck on her knuckles. There were dark circles under her eyes and three bruises marked her face.

"She was like this when she came to school this morning. Her mother warned us that she was not feeling well. If I had seen her—"

"This is Lorinda Dooley's child?" Russell interrupted.

"Yes." Sister Mercedes crossed herself. "It is not my place to judge her mother, but the way she lives . . ."

Russell nodded, bending over the cot. "What's the girl's name?"

"Rosemary." Sister Mercedes remained in the door, watching closely as Russell gently touched the girl's shoulder.

"Rosemary? What happened to you? Who did this to you? Did your mother . . ."

"Not her," muttered Rosemary.

"Then someone at her house?" He waited, but there was no response. "Rosemary? Will you tell me who hurt you? And why?" He did not want to interfere in family matters—the disciplining of children was a matter for the parents, not the law—but if Lorinda Dooley had not done this . . .

"She has refused to speak," said Sister Mercedes. "I have tried to discover who mistreated her, but so far I have learned nothing."

Russell waved her into silence. "Rosemary? Won't you tell me what happened?"

"No." She rolled away from him and brought her knees up near her chin.

Russell had seen children from the manufactories who looked better than this little girl. He had seen bonded servants with more hope in them. He put his hand on her shoulder again. "I want to help you, Rosemary."

She did not laugh, but the smile she gave was filled with despair.

"If someone did this, you must help me. I will keep it from happening again." He wondered if Lorinda Dooley knew what had happened to the girl, and if she did, what she planned to do about it.

"No one did it," was the child's stony reply.

"If you don't tell me, there's nothing I can do to stop it happening again. Please help me." He waited again, and was discouraged by her silence.

"Jason?" said another voice in the door, and Henry Clayton, his bag in hand, came into the room. "Sister Anna Maria came for me. What's going on?"

"It's Lorinda Dooley's little girl," said Russell, straightening up and speaking softly. "By the look of her, she's been beaten."

"How badly?" asked Clayton in his resigned way.

"There are bruises on her face. I don't know about the rest of her." Russell moved aside so that the doctor could have a quick glance at the little girl.

"What can you expect of a whore's girl?" Clayton murmured to the air, shaking his head.

"The law protects children from such mishandling," said Russell with determination. "I am under obligation to try to stop this happening again."

"And if the mother did this?" Clayton asked. "Who knows what a whore does when she gets drunk or when she has customers who ask more of her than she usually gives."

"If Lorinda Dooley did this, then there's nothing more to say, but if she did not, she may want the girl protected as much as I want to be certain that she is not hurt again." Russell folded his arms. "Tell me how badly she's hurt when you're through and I'll go have a talk with her mother. I don't want it said that I've shirked my duty simply because this girl's mother runs a brothel."

"If you insist," said Clayton, shooing Russell out of the room with a wave of his hand.

"I think that one of her ribs is broken—it feels broken, in any case," said Clayton half an hour later.

"Anything more? The bruises are terrible." Russell sat behind his desk, regarding the physician with impatience.

"Possibly," Clayton said, then made a quick gesture. "Jason, do you want to get mixed up with this? Lorinda Dooley isn't worth the time. This brat of hers . . ."

"According to the law, everyone is worth the time. That is the basic precept of your Constitution. It doesn't matter if the entire town would rather forget Lorinda Dooley and her house, but the law—" He stopped.

"All right," Clayton sighed. "I will give you a written report and you can present it to the circuit judge when he comes to town next. The way the weather's been, that might not be for some time."

Russell nodded slowly. "Thank you."

"But the judge might not . . . Jason, she's a whore's bastard. You have to expect that she will be . . . she will be a—" His confusion grew with each word.

"I am a bastard, Henry, and there are those who see little difference between a mistress and a whore." He had risen, and though his voice was low, the words fell like blows. "I was fortunate—my father looked after my mother and me. This little girl isn't quite so lucky."

Clayton was truly embarrassed now. "Jason, it's hardly the same case."

"Because my father was rich and had a title?" Russell shook his head. "Because I'm English? What is the difference, Henry? Or is that she is an Irish whore's brat, bound to turn out like her mother?"

"Stop it, Jason," Clayton said. "It's not your place to make judgments about—"

"I might have agreed with you, twenty-five years ago. What's one poor kid, more or less? Might even be a blessing in disguise if she died young. And a girl, too. You can't expect much for her, can you? She won't find anyone to marry her, not with her past, and you know what that means." He folded his arms and stared at the wall, though the sight he had fixed his eyes on was more than fifteen years in the past and thousands of miles away. "Why don't we just do what the Hindoos do, and burn the leftover woman. I saw that, in India. More than once. The wives and concubines of a man would go living to his funeral pyre and burn with him. We weren't allowed to interfere. There was one time . . . the man was old and rich. He had three wives and a whole slew of concubines. The youngest wife couldn't have been more than thirteen, just a slip of a girl, with eyes like a doe, the way some of them . . . They let her get on the pyre with the others, and then they all burned. Some of the other company men laughed about it, and one of them said that so long as the Hindoos wanted to get rid of their excess women, he'd be willing to buy a few. I think he was half serious. The worst of it was that I caught myself laughing with the others."

"For God's sake, Jason. These were Hindoos, man. You aren't talking about civi—"

"Good European Christians, you mean?" Russell cut in. "No, not about them. For which I am heartily thankful. When you think of how we conduct ourselves abroad." He deliberately changed the subject. "How long will it take this child to heal? I mean heal properly?"

"It's difficult to tell. If she were in good health, that would be one thing, but look at her—she's thin and so pale that it's hard to say what else might be wrong with her." He took a turn around the room. "Say a minimum of six weeks. The worst should be over then, and if she's fed decently and there isn't anything more to go awry, she—" He stopped. "With winter coming, what chance is there that she can have that kind of care? You aren't saying that you expect her mother to give it to her, are you?"

"No; I was hoping that Sister Mercedes and Anna Maria might." His expression was speculative. "I don't think that the nuns would refuse, and I don't think that Lorinda Dooley would object. Any other suggestion might be disastrous, but given the circumstances, I might be able to persuade them all to agree." He reached down and touched the sleeping child. "Wish me good luck, Henry."

As Russell started from the room, Clayton called after him, "Aren't you exceeding your authority, Sheriff?"

"Not if no one protests," Russell said, a note in his voice that was almost jaunty.

* * *

"I've heard . . ." George Fletcher said in his most ponderous way as he addressed Jason Russell over the expanse of his desk at the bank, "though, of course, I do not entirely believe it, that you have taken a hand in some highly questionable doings."

"That's what you hired me to do," Russell said, unphased by Fletcher's admonitory attitude.

"But to remove the child of a . . . a certain sort of woman, and . . ." He had turned a dark plum color and the ends of his imposing moustache quivered with emotion.

"I have arranged for her child to be with two nuns while she recovers from illness," Russell said, simplifying the truth with a clear conscience. "It seemed to me that having illness spreading through the town—and given the nature of the girl's background, it is fair to assume the illness would have a chance to spread—at the onset of winter would be far more dangerous than arranging for the child to go to the nuns without the assistance of the circuit judge." His eyes crinkled at the edges. "Illness in a place as isolated as Charity—forgive me, Mister Fletcher—can be as dangerous as the cholera in an overcrowded slum."

Fletcher's color was a little less alarming, but there was still a strong air of disapproval about him. "You're a damned high-handed fellow, Russell."

"If you say so, Mayor."

"You know it's true." He squeezed his big hands into fists. "Before you undertake anything of the sort again, I hope you will come to me so that the Council might have the opportunity to discuss it."

"If you like." He hesitated, and then went on as if he were puzzled. "Does that include instances of private concern?"

"Private concern?" Fletcher echoed suspiciously.

"Yes; occasions when there are two parties who require matters not entirely in law." He let the words sink in. "As in the case of Don Maximillian's missing daughter? Do you think that the Council needs to discuss the matter? It could embarrass Don Maximillian and—"

"That requires discretion, and well you know it, sir." Fletcher glared at Russell. "Have you made any progress on that front, by the way?"

"I believe I have some useful clues to hand, Mayor. But it wouldn't be discreet to discuss them at this time." He waited in case Fletcher needed to erupt again, and when this did not occur, Russell permitted himself to relax. "Listen to me, Mayor Fletcher; I will do my work better if you do not try to interfere. I will observe the law as much as possible when and wherever possible. I will not expose this community to anymore hazards than necessary if they are within my power to prevent. I gave you my word on that before, but apparently you must hear it again. Very well. As Sheriff of Charity, I have no intention of abusing my position or the law. Even if there were something to gain from it, I would not want to. Are you willing to accept my word on that?"

Fletcher grumbled an answer that was neither yes or no.

"Mayor Fletcher, do you want me to continue as Sheriff?"

"Of course." Fletcher was more astonished than indignant. "Whatever gave you the notion that I didn't?"

"Then you will accept my word as I've offered it?" His manner was deceptively mild; his light eyes seemed to fade from blue to grey.

"Oh, you British, with so much attention to form. Out here, sir, a man's word is his bond and there's nothing said about it. The acceptance is understood." His bluffness fooled neither of them, but Russell let that pass.

"There must be some British influence in you, Mayor Fletcher; you have a British name." That had little meaning in this part of the country, and Russell did not truly expect any comment.

"True, true," Fletcher said complacently. "But it's thinned down some. The family came over in 1697. They settled in Virginia. Family tradition has it that they were yeomen from the area of Somerset." He waved his hand to dismiss such distant events. "Hardly has bearing on what happens now, Sheriff." He nodded in the direction of the door. "If you insist on continuing this Dooley business, I trust you'll be more cautious than you have been."

"If that's necessary," said Russell, letting himself be dismissed. "By the way, I'm going to ride the perimeter holdings again tomorrow if the weather holds. I should be gone for no more than two days. I'm asking William Red Pony to stay at the jail while I'm away. He's also agreed to search for me if I'm not back in three days, and he will find me in an emergency."

"Red Pony? The man's nothing more than a savage."

"He also has lived here longer than anyone else, he can read and write, and he speaks Spanish as well as English. He is also willing to do the work, which is more than most of the men his age in this village."

"They are gainfully employed," blustered Fletcher.

"That's a factor. I've also arranged with Sun Fan-Li to have meals provided for prisoners if there are any who have no relatives in the town and who must remain in jail for more than a night." He smiled faintly. "I have the costs worked out and I'll see that the Town Council has it for review before your next meeting."

"I suppose that some such arrangement was inevitable," said Fletcher miserably.

"No doubt," Russell agreed. He put his fur cap back on and reached for the door. "You don't want prisoners to starve, do you? And we can't have them stepping out for a bite whenever it takes their fancy."

"But the hotel cook . . ." Fletcher nodded in aggravation, as if his jowls were suddenly much heavier.

"Who else has the time? Who has the equipment? Missus Schmidt has said that she does not mind the hotel kitchen being used, and during the winter, there are many who would begrudge a few extra logs to a man in the lockup."

"This isn't what I anticipated," said Fletcher, more to himself than to Russell, as the sheriff closed the door.

Lorinda Dooley was more impish than pretty, with a pert nose and bright red hair that formed a messy halo around her pale face. The rouge on her cheeks made her pallor more apparent and the circles around her eyes more prominent. She wore a sensible flannel wrapper and sat in one of the overstuffed chairs that cluttered her parlor. "I can have my cook make you some chocolate," she offered to Russell after she had taken his overcoat and cap. "You might want a dram in it, as well."

"That would be welcome," said Russell, sitting down on the largest chair and glancing around the room. "I take it you've thought about my suggestion."

"I want my girl here with me," she declared, her chin up. "I know what they say about me in town. Everyone knows what I am and what kind of house this is. They all cry shame, but they're pleased I'm here. They say it keeps the drifters from bothering their wives, but if I did business only on drifters, I'd be by myself in a hut, not in this house." She looked up as May came into the room. "We'd both like chocolate, with a little something extra. And if Sammy has any of those cakes left, put them on the plate as well."

May, who could not have been more than eighteen, nodded, gave a roguish wink to Russell, and left the parlor.

"The nuns will take good care of her, Miss Dooley." He looked around the room. "You already send her to the church for school. You can let the nuns keep her there, surely."

"Because you're afraid of what happens here?" She had meant this to be defiant, but it came out on a sniff.

"I'm not afraid, but I am not a little girl, and I do not have two broken ribs," Russell said, his tone neutral.

"I didn't break them!" She had started to play with the sash of her wrapper, tying knots in the tassel that hung from the ends.

"I didn't think you did. I think that one of your . . . guests decided that he was not getting what he wanted—whatever it might have been—

and he found a way to punish you for it." He knew from her guarded expression that he was right, but he did not say so.

"He should have hit *me*." Her green eyes shone with tears.

"That would not have punished you," Russell said gently. "I suppose he'd beaten you before—Henry Clayton has told me that he has treated you for bruises." He saw her straighten in her chair. "I was curious about the town. I did not ask specifically about you."

"Be damned to you, Jason Two-middle-names Russell," she said without heat.

"I hope that when your guests get out of line like that you will send for me. Disturbing the peace is disturbing the peace no matter where it's done." He looked up as May came back into the room carrying a tray.

"And then you'll calm everything down by putting us all in that jail of yours. And how will I make a living then? And when it's learned that Lorinda Dooley will put you behind bars, how many customers do you think I'll have?" She motioned to May to put the tray down. "And bring the whiskey."

"Do you want it for this?" Russell asked as he took up one of the large, expensive cups. "Very nice."

"I got them in Boston, before I came West. I had a little money put by, so that I could start out proper when I found a good place. I tried Kansas first, but there were too many Baptists there. I came here three years ago. Not bad for a fisherman's brat from Bantry Bay." She regarded Russell with a speculative grin. "Word is you used to be a Runner."

"For once word is right," said Russell as he sipped at the whiskey-laced chocolate.

"And now you're in America."

"And I was in India and Australia," he said blandly, wondering which of the town worthies had offered these tidbits to Lorinda Dooley along with two dollars for an hour of her company.

"You travel a lot. All nice and soft-spoken and toffy in your ways."

She was being deliberately provocative, and Russell put his cup and saucer down. "Miss Dooley, your daughter is in danger from someone who comes here. I think it best for all concerned that she remain with Padre Antonio and the Sisters until we can be certain that her health has improved."

"Poor Padre Antonio," said Lorinda with a languishing sigh. "He has to listen to my confession. It's not supposed to matter who the priest is, or who the penitent is, but there's only one priest in Charity. He's never able to think of anything to say. He's shocked, but he's not supposed to be." Her giggle belonged to a younger woman. "Are you certain that Padre Antonio wants to talk to me?"

"Yes; he and I have talked over your situation already. We understand that you have your work to do. If you have your daughter here, not well, there is a good chance that you will put both her and yourself in danger. That's the only reason I've suggested she remain at the church. I think that you will agree if you give it your consideration again. Go and talk to Padre Antonio; arrange times when you can be with her without putting her in danger." He paused. "I take it that she's still . . . that no one has . . ."

"I wouldn't let anyone touch her," Lorinda said with heat. "Not anyone, not ever." She was sitting quite straight now, and the rouge on her cheeks looked like fever spots. "I won't let her be harmed. God is my witness."

"I believe you," Russell said, knowing that now Lorinda was wholly sincere. He picked up his cup again. "This is excellent chocolate. Where do you get it from?"

"From New Orleans. It comes along the Santa Fe Trail and then Smilin' Jack brings it up special." She finished her cup in one long drink and clapped her hands. "May. More of the chocolate and something to eat. Lord love you, you'd think that we were paupers here."

While May brought in four little buns filled with fruit compote, Lorinda indicated the two large prints on the wall. "I got those in Boston, too. The larger one cost three dollars and I've had to get a new frame for it twice."

The print showed a pretty girl in Empire-style clothes sitting on a low bridge and dangling her bare feet in the water.

"Very nice," said Russell.

"Everyone likes it. They say it's better than all those naked goddesses most houses have. I liked it, and it . . . oh, I don't know." She got up and brought the whiskey decanter to the center table. As she poured some into her empty cup, she went on. "I know you're right about the Sisters. They'll take care of her and they'll keep her safe, which is all I want. I just don't want it to seem that she was taken away from me, that the priest wouldn't let me keep my own child. Though that might not be a bad idea, either, when all's said and done." She filled the china cup halfway with the whiskey and then, as an afterthought, poured some into Russell's cup as well. "I know how things are, Sheriff. Damnation; I'm almost twenty-nine, and in this work, that's a lot of years. I've got three, four more at the most, and then I'll have to have my own place free and clear, and girls to staff it, or I'll end up in the workhouse. My daughter should have a better chance. Though why I should trust a priest, I'm blamed if I know—it was a priest fathered my child, wasn't it?" She downed her whiskey and poured more.

Russell listened without comment. He did not touch the drink she gave him, though he took one of the buns.

"You tell them, Sheriff, all right? They'll believe you. You tell them that I want my girl with the priest and nuns, away from this place. You tell them that I'm for it, and that the priest doesn't mind. Will you?"

"If you like," Russell said.

"Yeah." She tossed off the whiskey. "Fine. That way I'll go along with it. Probably just as well." She looked at him. "Is there anything I can do for you, Sheriff? After all you're doing for me, that is?"

Russell brushed the crumbs off his fingers. "Now you mention it, there is something that would be of use."

Her features changed, becoming world-weary and knowing. "Of course. And no charge. Isn't that the usual way?"

"I've been looking for a girl." He ignored her innuendo. "I think that you might be able to help me find her. The trouble is, it must be done very discreetly, very secretly. If it's learned how and where she was found, it would be very hard for her. Do you understand?"

"You mean there's one of the good ladies who took off for a taste of the gay life?" Lorinda mocked. "I've seen it happen, now and again. Who is it this time?"

"Unfortunately, it is Donna Elvira Arreba y Corre. And I do not want a word of this to go beyond the two of us." His warning was sharp and Lorinda took it to heart.

"The Spanish lady? Has she gone off, then? Saints-and-angels!" She crossed herself. "What makes you think that I'd know where to find her?"

"Call it a hunch," said Russell.

"You are a downy one, no question," said Lorinda, and did her best to bend her slightly muddled thoughts to the problem. "So you want to know where you might look for this girl?"

"I'm going to be gone for two or three days, visiting the outlying farms and ranches. If you have some idea where I might look to find her—"

She sighed, then yawned. "God, the drink's got to me."

"Lorinda—"

"I'm trying, I'm trying," she said, motioning him to silence. Finally she steepled her fingers together and frowned over them. "Mind you," she warned at last, "there's no saying that this is any help, but there is a roadhouse, a big one, near Pueblo on the Taos Trail. There's a Dutch couple runs it, and they say there's more to get there than a hot meal and a pot of ale. A girl I used to know, in Kansas, had been there for a year or two. She said it was busy all through the summer. In winter, not so much, but they didn't starve and they weren't bored."

"Near Pueblo on the Taos Trail," said Russell, in case Lorinda wanted to change her information.

"Don't say you heard it from me," she told him. "And what in the Devil am I to do with this second pot of chocolate?" This last was directed to May who had returned with the drink.

Russell was already on his feet. He reached out and took Lorinda's hand. "I should drink it all myself, if I were you." He bent and kissed her fingers. "Thank you very much. You've been a great help."

"Sure," Lorinda said sarcastically.

"You have been," Russell insisted as he went to get his overcoat and cap.

6

"Hallo! Hallo the house!" Russell shouted, cupping his mouth with his hands against the first whistles of the storm. He was on the farthest reach of his journey, and had been searching for the better part of the morning for the Vreeland farm. Under him, Gryphon shifted uneasily, whuffling at the wind.

There was smoke coming from the house that had been built back into the hillside. It was fronted with rough planks, but most of it was dug into the flank of the mountain. The chimney leaned at a precarious angle and there was a large overturned barrel on the rickety platform that served as a porch.

Russell swung out of the saddle and pulled his old-fashioned volley-gun out of its leather sheath. He knew it was not loaded, but he was willing to bluff with it. Little as he liked it, he had an Adams revolver as well as his baton holstered to his side. Leading Gryphon, he approached the house slowly, holding the gun with its formidable multiple barrels pointing to the clouds.

The door was flung open without warning and a thin, frightened woman lurched out, bringing an old carbine to her shoulder. "That's far enough!"

"Missus Vreeland?" called out Russell, stopping in the snow and feeling his feet turn cold.

"You just get back on that horse and ride on out of here!" Her voice was strident and ended in a long, hacking cough.

"Missus Vreeland," Russell yelled, trying to be patient. "I'm Sheriff Russell from Charity. I've been trying to reach all the ranchers, to make sure everyone's all right."

"Sheriff, you say?" the woman shouted, and once again gave way to coughing.

"From Charity. Jason Russell. Missus Mattington might have mentioned me." He lowered his volley-gun, now pointed the barrels down and to the side.

"Bess sent you here?" The unsteady aim of the carbine faltered even more.

Although it was not entirely accurate, Russell said, "Yes. I wanted to make sure you and your family are all right."

Cora Vreeland hesitated, then lowered her weapon. "Come on closer. Let me get a look at you."

"I have a badge," Russell said, doing as she ordered. "And letters from Mayor Fletcher—"

"Him!"

"—and Liam Cauliffe, if you'd like to read them." He had reached the porch. "Is there somewhere I can put my horse? I have oats for him, if that's a problem."

"There's a shed out back," said Cora Vreeland, indicating two or three tumbledown buildings at the side of the house. "There should be some water, as well."

"Thank you." He led Gryphon around and took him into the most substantial of the sheds that appeared once to have housed sheep. As he emptied the sack of oats into the manger, Russell said to his horse, "Sorry about this, friend. I'll make it up to you later." He unfastened the girths and pulled the saddle off, leaving it propped on end against the wall. There was a pile of old sacking in one corner, and he helped himself to three sections of rough cloth to provide Gryphon a blanket before he went into the house.

It was by far the most dreadful of any Russell had seen: the walls were little more than packed earth; what little furniture there was showed signs of being ill-used; the stove was little more than a heavy tin box with a pipe to take the smoke out. There were no dogs or cats. In a hollowed-out alcove there was a box bed where a pathetically weak child lay.

"Sorry there's nothing to offer you, Sheriff," said Cora Vreeland, gesturing toward the stove. "We got beans for tomorrow and the next day. Matthew's out hunting. He's good at finding game, snow or no snow."

It was an effort for Russell to keep his distress from showing. "I'm . . . I'm sorry I haven't stopped by here before now."

"No one comes here, Sheriff." She said it without bitterness or complaint. "What can I do for you? I'm Missus Vreeland." She held out her hand, and when Russell took it he felt the roughness of it, and its frailty.

"With winter coming on," Russell began, launching into his usual talk, "I was hoping it would be possible to establish some sort of regular contact with you ranchers and farmers, in case of trouble. There are gangs said to be in the area, and for your protection and the protection of the whole area, it might—" He broke off as Cora Vreeland began to cough again.

She waved him away as he moved to help her. "I can manage. It's just a cough."

"You ought to have that attended to," Russell said.

"Doc Clayton won't come out here for nothing," she told him, and tossed her head. "And we don't take charity."

In spite of himself, Russell smiled. "But that's where you live, Missus Vreeland, in Charity."

"That was for the church," she said, dismissing it. "You won't say that we took from others." She forced back another bout of coughing.

"Missus Vreeland, forgive my asking, but how old are you?" Russell knew that hard work aged women—especially slight, graceful girls like this one—uncompromisingly, but he was not prepared for her answer.

"I'll be eighteen, next March." She drew herself up. "That don't mean I'm not grown up. I've had three babies already, and I've been a married woman for four years."

"Good gracious, Missus Vreeland, I didn't mean—" He broke off. "What about your other two children?"

"Fever took 'em, last year." She coughed again, and this time it was a sob. "Whatever it is you want, get on with it and leave me to my work. I got chores to do." Her fierceness gave strength to her words.

"I'd rather help, if you'd allow."

"No call for that." She put her hand to her head. "You brought word that there might be robbers. I heard you. You want us to send word if something happens, is that it? If we can we will. That's all I can promise, Sheriff. Will you leave us alone now?"

For an answer, Russell asked, "Where have you stacked your wood?"

"What does that matter to you?" Her defiance was growing desperate.

"It doesn't, but I thought so long as I'm here I'd help you get your fire built up. It gives me a chance to get warm, too. I've been in the saddle for three hours, and I'm glad of a chance to rest." He was not certain that this ploy would work; he tried not to watch her as she considered what he had said.

"I can't give you anything," she warned.

"I wasn't expecting it," he replied. "But if you'll tell me where the wood is . . . ?"

"Out back," she said, capitulating. "But see you don't bring too much. We got to make it last all winter."

As he went out the door, Russell bent over and righted the barrel, taking care to balance it so that it would not fall again.

Half an hour later he had brought in three sections of wood and had the room warm enough that the child in the bed had stopped fretting and fallen asleep. He went out to the well and drew enough water to fill two buckets and brought these into the house as well.

"I thank you, Sheriff," growled Cora Vreeland.

"Think nothing of it," he said, glancing again at the child. "What are you doing for . . ."

"Mark," his mother supplied. "Been giving him broth when he'll take it, and borage tea. Same thing I do for myself."

"I'd be happy to leave a little brandy with you," Russell volunteered.

"We don't have spirits in this house," Cora Vreeland announced sharply. "Don't hold with it."

"As you wish." Russell did his best to bank the burning logs in the stove to preserve its heat the longest. "Tell your husband that I was here, will you? I will be back from time to time, and if you require help, you have only to send word. You need not come all the way into Charity; you're closer to the Mattington's, and Missus Mattington can spare a hand to go to town."

"We don't like to impose on our neighbors," said Cora Vreeland as if reciting in class.

"Who among us does?" Russell said mildly. "But there are times it is helpful to have neighbors, don't you think? You can be of help to Missus Mattington as well, for you can send warning to her if you see strangers in the area. A gang might not stop here, but the Mattington place would draw them. Your warning would mean a great deal to her." It was a careful argument, worked out while he stoked the stove. "Surely you're not too proud to warn an old woman of danger, are you?"

"Of course not." She was indignant, her jaw set and belligerent.

"Good. Then you can arrange between you how to proceed." He gathered up his coat and looked around the room. "Are you sure there is nothing more I can do while I'm here." Before she could speak, he added, "I wish you would reconsider having Henry Clayton out. Your son is very ill and he is quite young. The doctor can help him."

"God will help him, Sheriff." She raised her head; then she began to weep.

"Missus Vreeland . . ." Russell said, feeling helpless. He sensed she would not accept his comfort and he knew she was not willing to take anything more from him.

"You get out of here, Sheriff. I got things to do. I got to tend to Mark here. Go on. It was kindly of you to . . . do what you did, but . . ." She wiped her eyes with the flat of her hands. "Go on with you."

Russell permitted her to shove him out, and once on the porch he pulled on his coat again. It was growing colder—not even the warmth of the Vreeland house could disguise that—and Russell felt the arctic breath of the storm at his back. He went to the shed for Gryphon, saying to his distressed nicker, "Don't worry, we'll be home before it gets bad."

He was as good as his word. Night was just coming on, and the storm was quickening when Russell dismounted in the livery stable, calling out to William Red Pony for help.

"How'd you know I'd be here?" Red Pony asked as he came to take the bridle.

"I didn't," said Russell. He tugged up the stirrup and threaded the leather through before he unbuckled the girths. "I hoped either you or Calvin would be here. The way the weather's backing up, though, I wouldn't have blamed everyone for staying indoors with the shutters up and the doors bolted." He had set the other stirrup before swinging the saddle onto an empty rack. "That pad ought to be burnt."

"I'll do it, if you like." Red Pony indicated the stalls. "Your other two are tired of being indoors."

"That's what they think," said Russell. He was tired and sore and hungry. His hands hurt and his eyes stung and there was a twitch in his neck. "Can I get into the hotel?"

"Missus Schmidt said to come to the kitchen door. Sun will let you in." He had reached for brushes and was going over Gryphon's coat. "Any instructions?"

"Extra grain, pull the shoes and trim the feet. Leave him barefoot for a week, if possible. Check his nose and throat—we both got chilly out there." He slung his gun over his back and put his saddlebags across his arm. "Anyone in jail?"

"Not right now," said Red Pony.

"Have you kept the place warm?" Russell was almost at the door.

"Not like this, but not icy." He began to clean Gryphon's hooves.

Russell paused. "Do you know where I can find Henry Clayton?"

"Doc's in his room," Red Pony said, suddenly unwilling to talk.

"Something wrong?"

It took a moment for Red Pony to answer. "Smilin' Jack brought him a package the day you left. Doc's been . . . keeping to himself."

"Be *damned* to him!" Russell swore quietly.

"Give him a day or two, he'll be fine." Red Pony left off his task and came over to Russell. "You got to go easy with Doc, Sheriff. It's not his fault. He didn't . . . you just have to understand."

"About what?" Russell countered. "I need him to help a woman whose child is probably dying, and he is smoking opium. He's lost in his dreams." He said the last word with such scorn that William Red Pony was shocked.

"Sheriff—"

"Do you know what that pernicious stuff does, man? Have you any idea how unspeakable it is? Have you?" He turned on his heel and wrenched the door open. "I'll wait until morning, and then I'll have his help and his sanity if I have to drag him mother-naked through the snow."

Red Pony stood quite still. "A man does not say such things among my people unless he intends to bind his spirit."

Russell nodded once. "It's the same with me," he said before he went out into the blizzard and the night.

Henry Clayton's skin was taut and pale; he had not shaven for two days, nor changed his clothes. There was a smell about him, a lingering sweet odor that in a subtle, searching way filled the room. He stared at the figure in the door as if Russell were an apparition brought on by the storm and his drug.

"You might as well let me in and get it over with," Russell said, shouldering his way into the room and shoving the door closed again. "You'll freeze if you don't."

"Jason." His voice sounded rusty and unused.

"Good; good. You haven't forgot who I am—that's something." He stopped and leaned back against the door. "Are you going to tell me about it?"

"What?" Clayton returned to the bed in the corner of the room and dropped down on it as if those few steps had exhausted him.

"Sun Fan-Li is coming over with breakfast for you. I am going to watch you eat it." Russell's tone was light but there was an underlying implacability that nothing could disguise.

"There's a storm."

"He's doing me a favor." Russell drew up one of the three wooden chairs and straddled it. "How long have you been using opium?"

Clayton opened his mouth twice before he could bring himself to answer. "Too long."

"We're agreed on that." He waited, studying the doctor. "How did it start?"

This time it took a little while for Clayton to answer and when he did, it was in bits. "After medical school . . . that was in Boston . . . I wanted adventure. Do you mind getting me a glass of water? my throat's parched."

"All right." Russell did as Clayton asked.

After he had drunk the water, Clayton went on. "I signed on a ship . . . a big China trader . . . Lisbon, Martinique, along Africa, the Cape, Zanzibar, Arabia, Persia, India. You aren't the only one who's been in Bombay. Rangoon in Burma. Then Canton. Some of the sailors went to the dens, when they were through with the whores and drink. One old Scot said he'd rather spend the time with his pipe because the dreams were better than anything a woman could give you, and no dream ever gave you the pox." He fell silent.

"And you went with them, is that it?" Russell stared at Henry Clayton, willing him to speak.

Clayton yawned, once, twice, grotesquely. "I need some sleep. I'm worn out." He stretched and his joints cracked.

"Is that what started you on opium?"

"Um?" His eyes were glazed. "China. It was China." He leaned back, vision fixed on the middle distance.

"Henry!"

This time the response was a long time in coming. "It's so wonderful. You have no idea."

There was a loud banging on the door and Russell went to answer it.

"Breakfast, Sheriff. I brought for two." Sun Fan-Li was dressed in an amalgam of Chinese and local clothes; his heavy, long jacket was quilted silk, but his trousers were stout twill and his boots had been made by Jock Bruder, whose shop was a street away.

"Thanks." Russell took the covered tray and was about to close the door when Sun bowed and stepped into the room.

"Not to intrude, but I have some experience of this." He indicated the doctor, now leaning back, lost in the vestiges of his dreams.

"I'll manage," said Russell.

"You are sheriff," Sun reminded him politely. "You have duties to perform. I have nothing to do for two hours, and Frau Schmidt"—he pronounced the words perfectly but with difficulty—"has told me to aid you."

"Thank you." He paused. "I don't know how many people in town know about this, but the fewer the better."

"Of course." Sun put the tray down on the dresser and went to the bed, looking down with curiosity. "It is a pity he does not have a tub here—a hot bath can be useful."

"So can food," said Russell. "We had a Company man in Delhi who had got the habit from an old China hand. Food helped."

"Truly." Sun touched Clayton's forehead, fingered his hair. "He has smoked at least two pipes. Where does he keep his supply?"

"I don't know," Russell admitted. "If I did, I'd bury the stuff."

Sun went back to the tray and removed the lid. He chose one steaming mug of spiced beef broth and brought it back to Clayton. "This is a beginning. There is some breakfast for you, Sheriff. You might as well eat it while I tend to this."

Russell started to object, then shrugged. He could tell that Clayton was in more competent hands than his own, and he resigned himself to remaining on the sidelines.

A day after the storm the sky burned blue and the mountains, engulfed in white, were fresh and crisp as gigantic sails against the sea.

"You'll have to tell them that you had another call to make on the way, or I don't think Missus Vreeland will let you look at the child. I only hope the boy is still alive." Russell looked up at Clayton. "Can you manage?"

"I'll manage," he vowed grimly. "I don't know what to say to you. There's no excuse, no reason for it." He glanced toward the church at the top of the street. "I tried to talk to Cauliffe about it once, but he doesn't know what it is to have this need. He talks about drink, and it's not like that at all."

"Henry—" Russell began.

"Every time I tell myself that it won't happen again, that I won't ask for it, and if I get it I won't use it, and if I use it, I'll have only one pipe and then put it away." He jerked on his horse's reins and the gelding shied.

"You don't have to say this to me. And on the main street of town, it isn't wise to discuss it, is it?" Russell patted the horse's rump. "Off you go. Bess Mattington will give you a place to sleep for the night if you need it. I didn't meet the husband, but if Missus Vreeland is like him, you'll get little hospitality there. Remember they haven't got enough food."

"I'll remember." He tugged the horse around, calling over his shoulder, "Brute's got a mouth hard as granite."

Russell waved and stood watching while Henry Clayton rode up the slushy street toward the heart of the mountains.

7

All the way from Charity to the Taos Trail, Jason Russell wondered if he had been mistaken—what if Don Maximillian's daughter had truly been abducted and had not run off as he suspected? If that were the case, he had lost precious time in the search for her and every hour reduced his chance of ever finding her.

Few travelers were on the trail in November, and by the time Russell found the roadhouse, he fervently hoped he would not be one of them again. "Sorry to bring you out in this," he said to Rajah, repeating the apology for perhaps the fortieth time. As he led his Thoroughbred into the stables, he found himself longing for the stamina of his youth. When he was still a Runner, a journey like this would not have been wearing and exhausting. "Except for you, old fellow," he added to his horse.

The roadhouse was more extensive than others Russell had seen, with accommodations for up to fifty guests. Since business from settlers, coaches, and drovers could not account for prosperity or extent of the roadhouse, Russell guessed that Lorinda Dooley had been well-informed about the place.

"Good evening, sir," said the landlord as Russell came into the main room. "You need a meal and a room, sir, I can see that."

"It would be," Russell agreed.

"Excellent." He gestured toward a curtained-and-swagged archway. "The dining room is right this way. Unless you'd prefer a drink in the bar first?"

"That won't be necessary." He dropped his cap on the hat rack and removed his overcoat. Vaguely he noticed that there were carpets on the floor, so old and soiled that it was hard to see what they had been like before they were dragooned into service in this place. A desperate gentility was apparent in every aspect of the building, from the worn velvet upholstery to the china on the tables.

There were eight other men in the dining room, most of them as anonymous as Russell. Two stood out: a preacher with a paunch and spade beard, and a flashy young man in a brocaded waistcoat and cravat.

"The table by the fireplace?" suggested the landlord.

"Thank you, yes." Russell took his place and looked around for a chalkboard to tell him what was being served that night. He was puzzled when he did not find one.

"There's just two choices here," explained the young woman who came to his table. She was dressed modestly enough if the neckline of her satin gown was the standard for modesty, but the tight bodice and the heavy scent she wore indicated clearly what her purpose was. "There's fowl and there's beef, and that's it."

". . . uh, fowl, if you please," said Russell, regarding the young woman. "I wonder, is there someone I might talk to about . . . a person who might be here?"

The woman laughed. "Not to your taste?" she asked, her hand on her hip.

"You're very attractive; this is nothing to do with your charm." He sat back in his chair and regarded the other men in the room, especially the fellow in the flowered waistcoat. "It isn't terribly urgent, but if I might talk to one of the . . . managers before the end of my meal?"

"If you like," she said with a shrug that was intended to show him how indifferent she was to his request. "I'll mention it in the kitchen."

"Thank you." He took out a dollar coin and put it in her hand. "Thank you."

She looked at the coin in surprise. "You're welcome," she responded with more feeling than she had shown earlier. "The fowl and the manager coming right up."

Russell suspected that the fowl meant any bird that they could shoot, and that beef could be from cattle, buffalo, or almost anything with hooves. He felt safer with the fowl—the worst he would have to contend with was shot in his teeth.

"I want a girl at the table with me," said the fellow in the flowered waistcoat more forcefully as he reached out and seized the wrist of the young woman standing at his table. "For the prices they charge here, it's the least they can do."

"Let go," the woman said.

"I said, I want a girl at this table. Is that understood?" His accent was an odd mix of upper-class and Cockney English.

"And I said *let go*," the girl insisted, trying to pull out of his grasp.

The other men in the dining room were watching, some in chagrin, some with amused interest. Russell rose and started toward the table, his hand closing on the head of his baton as he went.

"I'll be back; just let me go now," the girl said, her cheeks bright with emotion. "Please."

"I'm paying for your time, woman," the man snarled.

"Excuse me," Russell said diffidently. "I believe the young woman would prefer to be left alone."

Both turned to look at Russell, and the man started to rise. "This isn't any of your business."

Russell rested the baton on the table. "The woman does not want your company at present."

"For Chrissake, she's a whore. She wants any man's company," the waistcoated fellow scoffed. "You're fair and far off with your gallantry."

"Let go of her."

"Please, Mister . . ." the young woman protested. "I'll get into trouble for this."

Before the young man could get out of his chair, Russell had snagged one leg with his toe and pulled it out from under its occupant. The young man went over, bellowing obscenities. Before he could get to his feet, Russell had grabbed one of his arms and pressed a foot against the man's neck. "Now then," he said, "suppose we begin again. The young woman would rather not remain with you just now. Whatever arrangements you make for later is another matter." With his free hand he took his baton and shoved its end once—hard—against the young man's ribs. "For the time being, conduct yourself like the gentleman you are pretending to be." He stepped back sharply, out of range of the sudden lunge the young man made at his knees.

A large figure filled the archway to the kitchen; the man lumbered into the dining room. "Anyone giving you a bad time, Amelia?"

"Not now," said the young woman, regaining some of her composure. "This man"—she indicated Russell—"helped me out."

"That's good of you," said the enormous man. He turned a disinterested stare on the young man huddled on the floor. "What was the trouble, Mister?"

"Nothing," muttered the young man.

"Good." He reached down and casually lifted the young man to his feet. "And there won't be any, will there?"

"No," was the sullen answer.

"Good," he repeated, and left the young man alone, ignoring him as he gave his attention to Russell. "Thanks."

"Pleasure," said Russell. He put the baton back in its holster and started toward his table again.

"Norah was saying that you wanted to talk to the managers. What about?" The big man trundled after him, moving lightly for all his size.

"I'd rather discuss that with them." Russell took his place at his table and was amused that the other men in the dining room were carefully avoiding looking at him or at the young man who was meticulously and conspicuously dusting off his lapels.

"I'll send one of 'em out." The man hesitated. "Why'd you do that?"

"The woman was being manhandled," said Russell in his most matter-of-fact way.

"There's most'd say that's what she's here for." The big man folded his arms and waited for answer.

"Possibly, but not during supper, I hope." Russell took his napkin and fastened one end over his belt.

"And that stick?" He pointed to Russell's holster.

"It's properly called a baton," Russell said, making it plain that he was being patient.

"Whatever it's called. You look handy with it."

"Thank you; I hope I am." He looked up. "Is there anything else?"

The big man shrugged and went away.

A few minutes later, just as two black servants brought out trays of hot bread, a small, motherly woman approached Russell's table and dropped a little curtsy to Russell. "You wanted to speak to me?"

"If you're the manager here, I do," said Russell, rising and holding a chair for her.

"How kind," she murmured. "I understand you assisted one of my . . . nieces. I appreciate that."

Russell had seen these sweet-as-treacle madams before and he distrusted the breed. "Glad to be of help."

"But there was something more?" Behind her soft words there was a hard edge of avarice. "What was it?"

"I'm looking for the daughter of an important man," said Russell, deciding to tackle the question head-on.

"Here?" The madam put her hand to her ample, puce-swathed bosom.

"So I believe," said Russell. "He very much wants her back. No questions asked, price no object." He let these last, promising words sink in. "No object at all."

"No object?" she said archly. "How fortunate for . . . someone. Assuming that the child will ever be found." Her eyes were averted, but Russell could see the eager light in them.

He cleared his throat. "Should the girl be found, there would be few questions asked. It would not be likely that there would be repercussions for . . . whomever has aided her."

"Interesting," said the woman softly, looking up as Norah brought a plate to Russell's table. "My dear," she said to the young woman, "please be good enough to bring a cordial glass for this gentleman."

"Of course, Missus Smith," said Norah quickly and without any inflection.

"You needn't," said Russell.

"You were so helpful earlier," said Missus Smith. "It's only fitting that we do something for you." She indicated the plate. "Have your supper, Mister . . ."

"Russell," he told her.

"A pleasure, Mister Russell." She made no sign of leaving, and after Russell had had a few bites of meat, she said, "Not that I can be of any assistance in your search for the daughter of this man, but perhaps if I knew something about the girl, I could be alert . . . ?"

Russell concealed a sigh. "Of course. The girl is of Spanish heritage, very attractive and impetuous. I have been told that she might have put herself at a disadvantage . . ."

He got no further. *"Her!"* exclaimed Missus Smith with vehemence. "That hellcat."

"Missus Smith?" Even as he said the name, Russell wondered what the name had been before.

"You need not trouble to look for her. I will be delighted to turn her over to you. I have wanted to get that creature off my hands since she arrived. Donna Elvira. I'm sure I've never found any female harder to hand than she." Missus Smith took the glass of cordial that Norah had brought on her tray, and tossed it off. "At another time, I might have found someone to deal with her, to render her tractable, but—"

Russell had seen many of the girls who had been—as Missus Smith described it—rendered tractable, and he was thankful that Donna Elvira had not suffered that fate. "She is here, then."

"Upstairs. As soon as you are finished with your meal, have Norah inform me and I will be happy to get her out of here." There was a slight sly shift in her expression. "Of course, I expect compensation for the time and effort she has demanded of me and my staff."

"Naturally," Russell said with a resigned gesture.

"And a little something for my . . . discretion. I do not imagine Donna Elvira's father would like it known that his precious daughter had spent time under my roof." Her manner was as saccharine as before, but now there was no disguising the greed that possessed her.

"I will see you have compensation," said Russell. "But we can discuss it less publicly if you please."

"How kind," murmured Missus Smith as she rose. "I'll leave you to your meal, then. And thank you again, Mister Russell."

*   *   *

Donna Elvira had been kept in a low-ceilinged room at the back of the roadhouse, over the pantry. There was a narrow brass bed, a small chest, and a chamber pot for furnishing. Donna Elvira herself was shackled to the bed, with enough chain to permit her to walk three or four steps away from it.

"Who are you?" she demanded of Russell as he came into the room.

"Your father sent me," said Russell, thinking that this information would reassure her. He was mistaken.

"What does he want? Why won't he leave me alone?" She was dressed in nothing more than her shift and a wrapper. The room was cold and undoubtedly she was chilled, but her manner was imperious. "What right does he have to send you in pursuit of me, as if I were a common criminal?"

"He is your father," said Russell, and glanced around the room pointedly. "And he is concerned for your welfare."

"Rot! He is looking for a filly to bargain with." She tugged violently at the chain that held her. "He is as bad as these vermin are." With sudden emotion she kicked over the chamber pot.

"Donna Elvira . . ." Russell came nearer. "You and I must leave here tonight."

"You and I?" she repeated, mocking him. "Leave here tonight? Why?"

Russell blinked. "Your father has asked me to find you and return you. He thinks you were abducted and must be ransomed."

"He would." She threw back her head and laughed defiantly. "How like him."

"I've given him my word to find you."

"And you have." She glared at him. "Go home and tell him that. Tell him where I am and he won't bother me again."

Russell stood still, regarding her with somber concern. "If you want, I will. After you hear me out."

"Madre de Dios," she expostulated.

"And you will hear me out," he said quietly. "If I have to wait for an hour for your attention."

She reached out and gathered her pillow under her elbows. "Very well. Go ahead. Say whatever you have to and leave."

He did not speak at once, and when he did, it was in a calm, conversational tone. "You are bored with your life, aren't you? That's why you ran away. You thought that this would be a more exciting way to live."

"My father thinks he's living in Spain." She pouted.

"And you decided that you wanted adventure. You saw yourself forgotten and overwhelmed if you remained on the rancho. So you looked for the most opposite life you could find. You think that you will become the belle of the Texas Territories. You think that men will come thousands of miles to shower gifts and affection on you. You imagine yourself rich and jeweled and sought-after. Don't you?"

She did not answer, but there was a defiance in the arch of her brow that was eloquent.

"Do you know what becomes of women like . . . the ones who work here? Have you seen Lorinda Dooley in Charity? Have you asked the women who work here what it is they do, and how they are rewarded for it? You think your lovers will be handsome and rich and young and will thrive on your caprice, don't you? They will be any man who can afford to pay Missus Smith the price she asks for the use of your body, and they will do whatever they wish to you. Do you understand that? These women live hard lives, and they are exhausted by it as fast as a homesteader is exhausted by working the land."

"You're trying to scare me," she accused him.

"I'm trying to warn you—if you're scared, then so much the better." He rested his hand on his baton. "Your family would disown you if your father ever learned you have slept under this roof. Do you want that?"

She nodded.

"Truly?" Russell asked her. "I have already given Missus Smith the money she requires to release you."

"I don't want to go."

"You want to remain here all winter? They will starve you eventually, you know, unless you are earning your keep." He paused. "There were several men downstairs when I arrived. Only one had any pretensions to style or elegance, and they were just that—pretensions."

"I am a virgin. Missus Smith won't let me go for a low price."

"And who will be paid that price, do you think? It would not be you. And how would you claim damages? What judge would listen to your claim, since you would accuse yourself and be cast into prison. As hellish as these houses can be, prison for women is more vile than you can imagine." He studied her face. "And when you were released, penniless, without employment, possibly diseased, possibly pregnant, what would you do then?"

"It isn't going to be like that," she insisted.

"It isn't?" Russell shook his head. "Who has promised you otherwise?" It was only a guess but a shrewd one, and as she flushed he knew he was correct. "So. You are intending to meet someone here. Where is he?"

"He will come," said Donna Elvira.

"When?" Russell came a step closer. "You have been here more than a week, haven't you? And he has not yet arrived."

"There are problems," she argued.

"No doubt. But what problems keep a man from removing his beloved from a place like this?"

"It's not like that at all," she said.

"Then how is it?"

"He has to get money before . . ." She stopped herself with difficulty.

"What is he planning to do to get money?" Russell asked. "Is he going to commit a crime? That would certainly be an auspicious beginning to your life together, wouldn't it? You hide in a whorehouse"—he saw her flinch at the word—"and he robs someone. It would have to be robbery."

"No, it wouldn't," she declared. "His family—"

"Ah, an inheritance. How can he be certain that he will have the funds soon enough?" He stood at the foot of the bed and looked down at her with aggravation and sympathy. "What sort of a fool are you, child? You are about to throw away everything in your life that makes it worthwhile. How can you do this?"

"You're being horrid," she said, but with less conviction than before.

"If you have a suitor, have him address your father," Russell suggested.

"We've tried that. My father ran his father off the land. He would not even speak with him, said that he would not tolerate his daughter associating with Protestants." She sobbed once and then mastered herself.

"A Protestant, is he? And that is his objection?" He knew that a difference in religions was sufficient for any family to end an engagement and he did not think that such decisions were unreasonable, but he said nothing of this. "Surely if your attachment endures for a year, there might be—"

"In a year he will have sent me to Mexico and arranged for me to marry one of those hideous men he admires so. I will be nothing more than a bond to seal a bargain, I will never do more than live in a hacienda and produce heirs for the family. I don't want any of that." This last was a wail of outrage.

Russell had held up his hand to slow her stream of words. "Donna Elvira, I can't leave you in this place. I have said that I will bring you back to your father, and I will keep my word, if I have to truss you up like bagged game."

She threw the pillow at him.

"But I give you my word that I will urge your father to reconsider your situation. I will ask him to discuss an engagement with the young man in question, and I will do everything I can to aid you in pursuing that engagement." He put his hand on her hair. "You must not throw your life away in this fashion."

"You mean I should throw it away in my father's fashion instead? He thinks it is still the Middle Ages." She tugged once on the chains that held her. "I'll escape again, you know I will. If you take me back, I will be gone again before the winter is over."

"I hope not." He took the key to her shackles from his vest pocket and unfastened them. "I would have to come searching for you again, and frankly, I have better things to do with my time."

She watched him free her with sullen eyes. "You won't find me."

"Don't challenge me, Donna Elvira. I've been finding people who want to stay lost for more years than you've been alive." He held out his hand and helped her up from the bed. "Your clothes are in the next room, and I have taken the liberty of bringing along a coat for you. Since we must travel now that it is dark, I have a lantern to help us."

"How thoughtful," she said acidly.

He held his tongue, making a point of showing his respect as she moved toward the door.

"I could say you attacked me."

"Missus Smith would not believe it, but she might use it as an excuse to keep you here and lower your price." He opened the door and waited for her to step through it. "If you will?"

"You're hateful."

He waited while she dressed, and once she emerged from the second room, he led her toward the stairs.

"Keeping the best for yourself?" suggested the young man in the flowered waistcoat as he saw Russell come down the stairs with Donna Elvira in tow.

"Nothing so romantic," said Russell, and tried to hurry Donna Elvira past the young man.

"He's bought me," she said grandly. "He is taking me to his own establishment. He is debauched."

"A nice prize for a tussle," said the young man with a nasty laugh.

Donna Elvira was shocked. She turned on Russell. "I don't want to go with you."

"Say anything more, and you will not. And I will tell Missus Smith what your plan was. Would you like that known, for when your friend arrives here?" He had pulled on his overcoat and held out a bulky wrap to her. "Put this on, please."

"My tutor was French, and he said that all gentlemen assist ladies with their wraps."

"Doubtless they do," Russell said. "And in a time and place where there are ladies and gentlemen, I might do as you suggest." He waited while she tugged the garment on, then went to the door, signaling to Missus Smith. "I appreciate all you've done," he said.

"I'm glad the whole episode is behind me," she told him, then looked at Donna Elvira. "You were lucky to come to me, you wanton. Another might have done badly by you." She turned her back and returned to the dining room where three of the men were now playing cards at the largest of the tables in the room.

Outside it was bitterly cold, and as Russell and Donna Elvira made their way toward the barn, their breath wreathed them in helmets of mist.

As Russell saddled two of his horses, Donna Elvira asked, "How much did you pay her?"

"One hundred dollars," said Russell, buckling the girths on Rajah's saddle.

"One hundred dollars?" Donna Elvira repeated. "I'm worth more than that."

"Are you?" Russell asked as he offered his joined hands to toss her onto her mount.

8

Don Maximillian greeted his daughter with a mixture of relief and suspicion. "You were missed, my child," he said as he kissed her hand.

"I was safe enough," she responded, directing an angry glance at Russell. "Your hound there has—"

"He is not my hound, Elvira, he is the local sheriff." He turned to Russell, saying, "I will settle with you later, once I have had some time with my daughter. I appreciate all you have done." This was clearly a dismissal, and Russell did not linger to hear more. He was almost out of the hacienda when Don Maximillian added, "One of my workers brought me word that a gang of desperados are taking shelter in a line cabin on the upper slopes of my land. It might be worth your while to investigate."

Russell regarded Don Maximillian narrowly. "Who saw them and when?"

"Andreas brought me word two days ago," Don Maximillian said, irritated by the questions which he regarded as impertinent.

"And is Andreas available? I would like to speak with him." Russell stood by the door, ignoring the servant who waited to open it for him.

"He may be in the . . . bunkhouse. He is a man about my age, with two fingers missing from his left hand." He bowed. "I must attend to my daughter."

Russell still did not leave. "I gave her my word I would speak with you on her behalf. When would it be convenient for me to call and discuss her situation with you?"

Now Don Maximillian looked vexed. "Next week, Thursday or Friday. Call upon me then." He indicated Donna Elvira. "I have a few things to say to her myself."

"I will be here Thursday, in the afternoon," Russell promised, as he left the house.

Andreas did not speak English well, but he listened to Russell's questions attentively. "It was seven, eight days."

"Since you saw them?" Russell asked, confused by the answer.

"Where they camped. They were gone. The casita was . . . no one was there." He waved his hand as if to indicate that the desperados had vanished by magic.

"How long had they been gone, can you guess?" Russell pursued.

"Two days, maybe three." He held up fingers to support his words. "The bones. They were not . . ."

"You mean that the bones of what they had cooked and thrown away had not rotted yet?" suggested Russell. "It has been very cold—surely the bones would not rot quickly."

"There was a stove," said Andreas. "I will show you."

"I'll be back in a few days. If your Patron will permit, I want you to show me this cabin and where you found these bones. All right?" He hoped that Andreas understood most of what he was saying.

"Si. All right." He appeared relieved not to have to answer more questions. "If the Patron says it is all right," he added, then made a strange gesture. "You will not say this to others? You will not let the desperados find out that I was the one who saw them? I do not want to be . . . known to them."

"That's very sensible of you; and I think that it would be best if you say as little as possible to the others about this. I don't want everyone getting nervous and taking shots at innocent travelers because they're afraid of desperados." He left Andreas in the bunkhouse and returned briefly to the hacienda to inform the housekeeper that he would appreciate the loan of Andreas.

"I will inform the Patron," said the housekeeper, and Russell had to be content with that.

* * *

Henry Clayton came to the jail less than an hour after Russell returned. "I don't think the Vreeland child's going to make it," he said after the tersest of greetings. "I didn't get there in time."

"I'm sorry," said Russell.

"So am I; more than you know."

"Why's that?" Russell asked, knowing the answer already and having no notion of how to offer solace.

"If I hadn't been lost in an opium dream, I might have been able to do something." He looked toward the stove.

"And perhaps it would have been the same," Russell suggested. "Perhaps the child would have not had a chance no matter what you, or I, did. If you were too late, maybe I was, too. He was pretty sick when I first saw him."

"His mother wouldn't let me bring him into town, no matter what I said. She won't be beholden to anyone. And I think that husband of hers has run out of money, and neither of them can admit it." He shoved his hands deep into his pockets. "With winter getting worse, I don't see what I can do that will make that much difference now. Without constant care and nourishing food, the child is going to die. They haven't enough to eat, they haven't any help, and from the look of Missus Vreeland, they're all worn to the bone. I've run out of ideas, Jason. I hope you've got something in mind."

Russell leaned back in his chair and studied the ceiling with concentration. "You know, I think there is something I can do, after all," he said after a while. "Well, not me specifically, but it might help."

"What's that?"

"Bess Mattington has said that she's willing to take on a few of the tasks—Hiram's learning to read and write enough to satisfy her, and half her hands are coming in to take class at the church, so she wants to do something in return. I think maybe she could help Missus Vreeland out— they're near enough to be neighbors." He indicated the pot of coffee on the stove. "Pour yourself a mug and get one for me."

Clayton did this without comment, handing the thick white mug to Russell before pouring his own.

"I'm almost out of coffee. I hope that Smilin' Jack remembers to bring me some."

"There's coffee at the general store," Clayton pointed out.

"And Lord knows what they make it from," Russell sighed before taking a cautious sip. "Hot coffee on a cold day."

"Warms the heart," Clayton said, his words sardonic.

"I don't know about the heart—it certainly warms up the rest of the body." He rubbed at his badger-grey hair. "I went to Kabul once; I thought I'd freeze to death just breathing the air."

"What was it like? I didn't get inland while I was on the ship, just saw the ports and the dives."

"Kabul or nearly freezing to death?" Russell inquired sweetly.

"I know more than enough about freezing to death; every year we find some poor devils after spring thaw. What was Kabul like?"

Russell thought, frowning a little. "It's a fierce place; the men, the women, even their donkeys, are all . . . hot-headed isn't the word for it. They carry knives and they're willing to fight over anything. I was glad to leave the place." He shook his head. "I think tomorrow I'll go over to the Mattington place and have a talk with Bess. I think she's more likely to help us than the Cousins are." He had taken to calling Cloris Bell and Maude Rossiter by the same collective nickname that the rest of Charity used.

"Missus Vreeland wouldn't have anything to do with the Cousins in any case." Clayton shrugged. "Even the Vreelands hear gossip and they know what's said about the Cousins."

Russell nodded. "I have to go to Don Maximillian's on Thursday. That means Tuesday or Wednesday I'll go to the Vreelands, unless you think it needs—"

"Tomorrow might be too late," Clayton interrupted.

"All right, then; I'll attend to it tomorrow morning. I'll have to inform the Mayor; there's a Town Council meeting tomorrow at noon and I don't think I'll be back in time."

"If it's still snowing, you might not be able to leave," Clayton conceded somberly.

"Well, ask Liam Cauliffe to have a word or two with God. Or Padre Antonio, for that matter." He could sense he had shocked Clayton. "Sorry, Henry. I didn't mean to offend you. The trouble is that I lost my capacity for religion years ago and now I forget to keep my mouth shut."

"It's all right," said Clayton, more from friendship than truth.

"Is it: if you say so." He lifted his mug. "And if prayers will work, I'll be as thankful as the most devout. I do not mean that the least insincerely."

Henry Clayton said nothing.

Don Maximillian bowed to Russell, but gave no sign of wanting to have the Sheriff in the house. "I do not think that we have anything more to discuss. You are free to speak with Andreas, and if you must take him to the cabin, I will agree."

"I told your daughter I would speak with you on her behalf," Russell said with a stern expression.

"You had no right to do that, for I am her father. There is no reason to talk. My daughter has gone for a prolonged visit to relatives in Mexico." Don Maximillian regarded Russell with obvious lack of interest.

"She did not want that to happen, sir," Russell informed him stiffly.

"She is a headstrong child who has no idea of what is best for her. I am her father and I know that she is unwise and her mind is unformed. She requires guidance and the strong hand of a grown man. For too long she has been permitted to do whatever she wishes; I am a too-indulgent father." He stared at Russell. "I have been more than forthcoming in telling you this. It was impertinent of you to offer to interfere in this family."

Russell knew that the rebuke was justified, but he felt a galling anger toward the man. "I said I would speak with you on her behalf, and I will do that. She did not want to go to Mexico."

"I must remind you that I am her father; I will do whatever I wish with my own child." He started to close the door. "You have not been repaid for your pains. I will see that you have the full sum as soon as you present an accounting to me."

"I am Sheriff; I do what I must for the town, not because it pleases you." He straightened up. "I will send you an accounting of what was spent on ransom, and that is all." He stepped away from the hacienda, trying not to hear the slam of the door at his back. He knew he was being watched as he went to the bunkhouse, but he did his best to ignore the whispers and quick covert glances that were directed his way by those working at the ranch.

Andreas was waiting, his horse already saddled and a bedroll tied to the cantle. "I am ready, Señor," he said, touching his hat in a suggestion of a salute.

"Let's be on our way, then; I've no reason to tarry." In spite of his best intentions, he looked back toward the hacienda, wondering if there was any way he might have been able to help Donna Elvira without overstepping his—admittedly limited—authority.

"Ya lo creo," said Andreas as he climbed into the saddle. "Many of us have seen things—"

Russell cut him off. "There is nothing I can do; it wouldn't be proper even if there were." He shifted in the saddle, letting his legs go almost slack, for it would be a long ride and he did not want to wear himself or his horse out.

It was more isolated than most line cabins, set in a small hollow with trees around it. There was a creek dividing the hollow that cut the cabin off from the trail, and unless a man knew where to look, he was likely to miss it.

"That is the place," Andreas said, drawing in his hard-breathing gelding and pointing.

"It's quite a place, isn't it?" asked Russell of no one in particular. He was cold and sore, and the last hour in the saddle had been more of an ordeal than he liked to admit. "Show me what you saw, and where."

They crossed the creek—it was frozen over now, but they used the bridge—and drew up in front of the cabin. Since the hollow was protected and in the lee of the wind, there was less snow here than might be expected. As Russell came out of the saddle he sank to the tops of his boots.

"Where can we put the horses?" he asked after he had taken the time to check Rajah's hooves.

"There is a shed. It is behind the cabin." Andreas dismounted reluctantly. "I do not like this place, Señor."

"Nor do I," said Russell, reaching under his long oilskin coat and taking his baton from its holster. He had a pistol in the pocket of the coat, but did not want to use it. "There's no sign that anyone's been here recently."

"They could be watching," said Andreas miserably. "They could be"— he gestured to the peaks around them—"and they could see us."

"If they're up there, you can be certain that they are not interested in what we are doing here; they're too busy trying to keep warm. Is there any wood left to burn, do you think?" He squinted at the long purple shadows that fell along the flanks of the mountains. "There'll be more snow come morning." He had not intended to be away from town more than a day, but he began to fear that it would take him longer to return than he wished to admit. "Let's get a fire going and take care of the horses. Other than the creek, is there water?"

"No, Señor. There is no need." Andreas had gone to the door of the cabin and stood there, unwilling to open the door for fear of what might be inside.

"Go ahead. The worst you'll find is an animal, and I doubt you'll encounter that. Animals make noise when they're trapped." To emphasize his point, Russell went and shoved the door open, then stopped on the threshold.

"Madre de Dios!" exclaimed Andreas, crossing himself and staring with huge eyes.

"Sodding wogs," Russell muttered as he stared at the body on the floor of the cabin.

What was left of the man's clothes was in tatters around him. Dark pools of frozen, dried blood framed him like a huge, malign halo. His hands and feet, still tied to spikes in the floor, were almost blue. There was no part of his exposed flesh that had not been burned or cut.

"This is a bad place, Señor," Andreas whispered.

"Bad people have certainly been here," Russell said grimly as he went to look at the body. He holstered his baton and drew a small notebook from his inner coat pocket, then pulled out two sharp pencils and set to work sketching the scene.

"What are you doing?" demanded Andreas when he saw what Russell was drawing. "This is . . . You are not right to do this."

"I am making a record of the scene. If ever I find witnesses, I need some record of what was here." He kept up his work, trying not to think about how the body came to be there.

"Señor . . ."

"This man, Andreas, was murdered. More than that, he was systematically tortured. Whoever permitted this, let alone who did it, is a dangerous criminal and if I am to find him and stop him, I require as much information as I can find." He began to list the extent of the injuries beneath the sketch of the body.

"Let me cover him at least, Señor." Andreas had crossed himself again as he listened to Russell explain. "It is not right he should be this way."

"In a moment," said Russell. "Take the horses to the shed while I finish this. Then you can cover the man. There must be sacking here somewhere." He did not want Andreas to see what he was going to do next.

"It is a shame to do what you do," Andreas said, accusing him with his sad, dark eyes.

"Possibly," Russell responded distantly. "Make sure that they have water. With the kind of climb they've had, they will need it."

Andreas did as he was ordered, though the stiffness of his posture and the angle of his head revealed his reluctance and disapproval more eloquently than his English.

Russell knelt down beside the body and began a thorough examination. The extent of the bruises was not significant—the victim had bled heavily and had been dead for a time. It would not be easy to establish when he was killed, for the cold preserved the body before any tell-tale decay could set in. With care Russell looked at the knife-cuts, inspecting the cuts for depth and angle. Two knives had been used, he determined, and one of them was a heavy knife with a wedge-shaped blade. The other was a more standard hunting knife that anyone in this part of the Texas Territories could be expected to carry. Russell finally looked at the face: the victim was young—not more than twenty-two or -three at the most. He wore a beard and his cheekbones stood out sharply above the matted hair. His staring blue eyes were set under firm brows. With a jolt Russell realized that the dead man was probably young enough to be his son. "It's such a dreadful waste," he said to the body, knowing there was nothing anyone could say to him anymore.

By the time Andreas returned, Russell was searching for two more sacks to cover the body.

"There are some in the shed."

"Good. Bring them when you bring in wood for the fire." He said this in as ordinary a voice as he could manage.

"Surely . . . we will not stay here, Señor." Andreas shook his head repeatedly. "No, Señor. No."

"But it is growing late. Do you want to find your way down the mountain in the dark with snow coming?" Russell was being as reasonable as he could. "We will put the body . . ." Where would they put the body? he wondered. Andreas would not tolerate keeping it with them in the cabin, and once they started to warm the air, it might cause a problem. They could not put the body in the shed with the horses, for the scent of death would make them nervous and hard to ride in the morning. If the body were put outside, animals might try to eat it in the night.

"Where will we put it?" Andreas asked, coming as close to insolence as he ever would in his life.

"We will wrap it in sacks, and tie them well. And then we will put it on the roof," said Russell. "If anything tried to reach it up there, we would hear it."

"Who will do that?" Andreas asked, making it clear he would not.

"I will," Russell said, and bent to take up the spikes from the floor.

Snow was falling steadily by mid-morning. Andreas, in the lead, had difficulty finding the familiar landmarks in the obliterating whiteness. He insisted that he ride well ahead, so that Russell, with the body slung over Rajah's rump, would not be contaminated by it.

They went slowly, the horses straining and cold, the chill penetrating clothing and tainting the air so that after the first hour each breath sliced through the chest like steel.

Finally, some time after noon, the hacienda of Don Maximillian came into sight. Andreas pointed, then directed Russell to the road leading to Charity.

"Sagrada Caridad is that way," he said, using the name of the Catholic church instead of the town.

"Yes; thank you. Gracias." He might have offered Andreas payment if he could have reached into his pocket without a major effort. "You were most helpful."

"I will pray for el muerto." He crossed himself again and then set his gelding down the slope toward the hacienda.

Russell accepted the unstated refusal to have him and the gruesome bundle on his horse come any nearer to Don Maximillian's home. He had been warned that the Don did not look kindly on discourteous actions: bringing a corpse to the hacienda would be the height of discourtesy.

It was dusk by the time Russell reached Charity. The snow was thickening, and though there was little wind, the weather would quickly render travel impossible.

"Good to see you back, Sheriff," said William Red Pony as Russell led Rajah into the livery stable.

"It's good to be back." He indicated the covered bundle. "Careful how you handle that."

Red Pony glanced uneasily at it. "A dead man?"

"Yes, worse luck. I hope someone can tell me who the poor fellow is." He went into the nearest stall. "Make sure Rajah has extra grain, will you, William? He's been shivering with cold and I ran out of rations for him. It's fortunate that we did not have to stay out very long."

"You were gone two days." Red Pony avoided Rajah.

"That's what I mean; had we been gone longer, it would have been much harder on my horse. I think I'll see if I can get my half-brother to send me some horse rugs—God knows I could use them." He busied himself taking the body off his horse. "Pull Rajah's shoes; he needs a trim, and I think that there's a bruise of some sort on the onside rear hoof. Keep him barefoot as long as he's tender." His voice was rough with cold and fatigue.

"All right," said Red Pony. "If you'd put turpentine on the hooves, then you wouldn't have this trouble."

"Is that what you Indians do?" Russell asked without any hint of condemnation. "I've wondered."

"No, that's what the drovers do, and the coachmen. Indians hardly ever shoe their horses, and they trim their hooves only at the start of winter." Now that the body was off the horse, he took Rajah's bridle and drew the reins over his head. "He looks worn out. I hope you're not planning to use him again for a few days. He needs rest."

"He *is* worn out, and he isn't the only one who could do with some rest," said Russell. "Do you happen to know where Doctor Clayton is?"

"He's been having his supper at the hotel these last few weeks. I don't think that's changed." He unfastened the girth and pulled the hussar's saddle from Rajah's back. "What are you going to do with the dead man?"

"Ask Doctor Clayton if he knows him, first off. I'll be able to decide more once I know who he is."

"Are you going to leave him here?" The tone of Red Pony's voice was more eloquent than the question itself.

"Not if it distresses you," said Russell, realizing that William Red Pony was upset.

"I would prefer you remove it. The door is in the wrong place for a dead man."

Russell had seen more unfamiliar practices with the dead than most men, and now he accepted Red Pony's reluctance without question or too much disapproval. "I'll carry him away myself right now. I'll take him over to the jail, if that's satisfactory?"

"Very," was Red Pony's succinct answer.

With a sigh, Russell struggled to sling the wrapped body over his shoulder. He had never liked such tasks, and now that he was well into his forties, he found it harder to do than when he was a young man. He was not sure if it was simply a loss of strength in his body or the too-present reminder of his own mortality. He left the livery stable and started up the street toward the jail, his head bent against the weight of his load and the gently falling snow.

9

"The poor devil," said Henry Clayton softly as he drew back the sacking over the dead man's face.

"That's the least of it. The bloody scum that did this took his time about it." Russell folded his arms and watched the doctor. "Know who he is?"

"I think so," said Clayton after a short pause. "Mind you, I can't be sure for I only saw the man once, two years ago, and he didn't have so much beard and was heavier, but I'm afraid that this is Matthew Vreeland." He said the name heavily and then he moved away from the impro-vised table the body had been laid upon.

"Cora Vreeland's husband?" Russell asked with unhappy surprise.

"I think so," Clayton answered guardedly. "I think he's the . . . vic-tim. But as I've said, I can't be sure, really sure. It's been two years, and . . ." He was unable to finish.

Russell sighed. "I suppose I'd better plan to ride out to the Vreeland place as soon as the weather clears. Don't take this amiss, Henry, but I hope you're wrong. I hope that this is some unfortunate drifter with no family and few to miss him. It would be sad for the man, but dear God, what's going to become of that poor woman if her husband's dead?"

"Did you talk to Bess Mattington?" Clayton asked, having no words of consolation to offer. "She could be of help, or so you said."

"I sent her a note, with Hiram," said Russell. "I was planning to call on her after I got back . . . which I must do now, I guess."

Clayton cleared his throat. "You'll need an examination of the body, won't you?"

"I'm afraid I will," Russell said, apology in his tone. "And anything you can tell me about how the wounds were made, and over how long a period of time."

"The flesh is frozen," Clayton pointed out.

"I know; just do what you can," Russell requested. "I'll put the body in the woodshed for the time being, so that it won't thaw until there's a place to . . . to bury him." He moved toward the stove, seeking its warmth.

"Sensible," Clayton agreed. "They used the poor man hard," he added as if the words were hard to say.

"Very. You haven't seen all of him."

"And I don't want to until morning, if you don't mind. I already have half my dinner inside and I don't want to ruin it entirely." He rocked back on his heels. "Do you need any help getting him to the woodshed?"

"Are you willing?" Russell asked. "It would be much appreciated."

"Very well, then." Clayton took the body's feet and Russell the shoulders; between them they carried it to the woodshed and closed it in, putting the heavy wooden brace firmly in place.

"Not that I expect anyone to take it," Russell said, as the two men puffed their way back to the jail.

"But you can't run the risk, can you?" Clayton finished for him.

"No, I can't." He held the door for Clayton and followed him into the small front office. "You know, my father had some excellent brandy, from the time of Napoleon. He probably got it from smugglers—that's what most of his cronies did—and kept it in the cellars. It was simply superb. He poured me some on three different occasions, and I still remember it. I think I'd give up a couple of fingers for a dram of that brandy now."

"Widow Schmidt has brandy, and schnapps, if it comes to that." Clayton jammed his hat down on his head. "Speaking of the Widow Schmidt, I intend to have the rest of my supper. Will you come with me, Jason?"

"I suppose I should eat," Russell allowed. "But the brandy and even the schnapps are nothing compared to what my father served."

"Memory can be like that," Clayton pointed out as Russell wrapped his muffler around his neck and the lower part of his face.

"You mean that I remember it as better than it was? No fear, Henry; that brandy was like nothing else I've ever tasted. It isn't simply that my father gave it to me, or that those were happier days—it was remarkable brandy, that's all."

"If you say so," Clayton remarked, unconvinced.

Cora Vreeland's face was the color of whey and she swayed on her feet as she looked down at the uncovered face. "Yes," she said faintly. "That is my husband."

Henry Clayton put his arm around her shoulder, making a murmur of apology for the familiarity. "I'm very sorry."

"What happened to him, Sheriff?" Her voice was thready and tears shone in her eyes, but she did not flinch from the answer he gave her.

"He was murdered, I'm afraid." Russell shook his head slowly. "I will do everything in my power, Missus Vreeland, to bring the criminals to justice."

"I pray you will," she said without meeting his eyes. "And I pray you will show them no more mercy than they showed him."

"You have my word that I will enforce the law to its full extent, Missus Vreeland." He glanced at Clayton, hoping that the physician might give him a clue as how best to proceed with this young woman so burdened with tragedy.

"I will not ask for more, Sheriff," she said, and then collapsed in Clayton's arms.

"Get me my salts," Clayton ordered, pointing to his bag which sat on the Sheriff's desk. "Quickly."

Russell did as he was ordered, and stood beside Clayton as he brought Missus Vreeland back to consciousness. "I must tell you how—"

Cora Vreeland was crying now, in sudden deep sobs that shook her all through her body. She was not able to speak; her hands were clenched and her face was mottled.

"Later, Jason," Clayton warned. "I will see Missus Vreeland to the hotel and ask Frau Schmidt to look after her."

"No," Cora Vreeland protested with such vehemence that both men were taken aback. "I have no money to bury my husband," she burst out, the words mixed with weeping. "I cannot stay there."

"I will pay for it," said Clayton in his most reasonable and soothing tone. "You cannot think of returning to your house tonight. It is snowing."

Her tears increased and though she attempted to protest again, the words were nothing more than a few broken phrases, hardly more than fragments. She reached out and covered her dead husband's face.

"I'll take you to the hotel, Missus Vreeland," said Clayton, this time with more authority. "And I will see that you are comfortable before I leave."

"Thank you, Henry," Russell said softly as the doctor escorted the weeping woman to the door.

He made no answer, his attention taken wholly by Cora Vreeland's grief and despair.

My Dear Nephew, Russell wrote as he studied the letter that Smilin' Jack had brought to him in a lull between snowstorms. *I am very appreciative*—he crossed the last words out and wrote in their place—*pleased to hear from you, and I want you to know that I am grateful you are curious about what has happened to your father's half-brother. There are many families where I would be worse than invisible, and I hope you can value your father for his affection and concern as much or more than I do.* He trusted that these remarks would quell any objections that might arise from Reginald's letter to him.

You say that you are curious about the Far West and want to know more about it. You imagine that there are Red Indians covered in tattoos and paint whooping through herds of wild bison. While there may be places this is true, the town Charity is not one of them. Charity began roughly a century ago as a Spanish mission. Then it was called Sagrada Caridad. Caridad is Spanish for Charity. It was on the road to San Esteban de los Viajeros, which at that time was by far the more important church and mission. However, Charity boasts six natural wells that have water all year long, and in time the wells made this place a crossroads; inevitably it became a town.

"Sheriff?" said Frau Dorabelle Schmidt from the other side of the lounge.

"Yes?"

"They are going to be having another reading class in here in a little while. Do you want to remain or go up to your room? I can clear a table for you in the dining room, but you know how noisy these classes can get, and with the weather closing in, some of the men will be staying over." Her accent was strong but she had made it a point to speak English as well as she could, trusting that one day she would not sound like a foreigner.

"I'll go up to my room, then. Call me if you need me, won't you?" He gathered up the papers and headed for the stairs.

This place is not at all like India, which is a very ancient land with a way of life that has ruled its peoples for thousands of years. This is much more like Australia in many ways, except that it is a haven for new-comers, and the forces of the government are few and far-off. Here at the edge of the Texas Territories, it is often necessary for communities such as this one to become very self-sufficient. The cavalry is the only arm of the official government of the country that can easily be reached, and the nearest fort is more than three days away in good weather. Now, with snow blocking the roads, it would take at least a week to reach, assuming one could get through at all.

Russell set his pen aside and gave some thought to what he had written. He doubted that his half-brother could object to what he had said, but he measured his words, looking for a possible turn of phrase that might result in all connections with that part of his family being severed. What could a bastard uncle safely say to the twelve-year-old heir to the title?

There was a knock on the door, and Russell was glad of it. He set his letter and his doubts aside for the time and called out, "Who's there?"

"Henry," said the doctor. "Can you spare me a little time?"

"Certainly," said Russell, opening the door to the man who had become his friend.

"I've arranged for Cora Vreeland to stay here for the week. Frau Schmidt has said that she will look after her—there's work to do, if Missus Vreeland insists on working." He sat on the edge of the bed, for there was only one chair in the room.

"She probably will; she's that sort of woman." Russell kept his voice even and his expression neutral, for he was not yet certain why Clayton had come.

"She's lost two children and a husband in the space of a year. The second child and the husband were gone in a month." He paused. "A few years ago there was whooping cough and diphtheria to contend with, and there were whole families lost. I remember seeing yellow fever and cholera. But this poor child has suffered more than she ought."

"Yes?" said Russell.

"I'm too old for her, and I . . . . I am enslaved by opium. I have nothing to offer her, nor would I if—" He stopped and looked at Russell. "I want to help her."

"I'll talk to Missus Mattington." He folded his arms. "You could offer for her, you know. She's a sensible girl and she would make you a good wife, I think. She would not expect more than you could offer her."

"That is what concerns me," said Clayton. "If I were younger, then I believe it would not be improper to speak with her, but at my age, and with her youth, well—"

"Considering her husband's body is still in the woodshed, I think it would not be sensible to ask anything of her just yet, and I think that perhaps in a month or two, you will know your own mind better." He stopped, feeling uncomfortable.

"I hope I could give her solace." Clayton lowered his head. "You're right; it is much too soon to consider such an offer, if not for me, then certainly for her. Good conduct as much as her own grief would make it impossible for her to—" Again he broke off. "I shouldn't have said anything to you, either."

Russell shrugged. "I don't know what to say."

"No, of course not." He plucked at the drooping edge of his moustache. "Forgive me for the imposition."

"It's hardly an imposition, Henry. You may decide in time that you wish to offer for her, and you may decide that you do not. I hope that you will not think that it was wrong to broach the matter, whatever the outcome." He paused as an outburst of laughter came from below.

"I am surprised," said Clayton, changing the subject abruptly, "that so many have continued with their studies."

"It is something to do," said Russell. "On these long winter evenings, I would rather they master the alphabet than drink and gamble, or pass the time at Lorinda Dooley's house."

Clayton nodded in agreement. "I have seen Lorinda Dooley recently; she's not well."

"What's the matter?" Russell asked sharply.

"Not pox, if that is what concerned you. No, I think it may be consumption. Poor creature, to have her life cut short that way." He knotted his hands. "It is always difficult to know what to do in such a case, for a woman who has fallen so far must already be worried for the welfare of her soul. To have her health taken, and with it her beauty must be very hard."

"Has she said anything to you about this?" Russell asked, thinking of the little girl in the nuns' care.

"No, of course not. And Padre Antonio would not speak to me under any circumstances. Those Catholics are very private about their rites. I cannot approve when the well-being of my patients is in question, as it must be." He got up and began to pace. "If it is only an inflamation of the lungs, she might improve, but there are those who could take the contagion from her. With seven women in her . . . employ, I am uneasy."

"Have there been other cases?" Three times before Russell had had to enforce a quarantine and he did not want to have to do such a thing again.

"There has been one family—the Howes—who have had putrid sore throats, but I have given them laudanum and they are improving. I've told them that they are not to make cheese for at least a month, but who knows if they will do it or not." He slapped his hands together. "And who is to stop them selling to travelers, in any case? As it is, they must milk their cows, whatever else they do, for dairy cattle, you know . . ."

"Do you know anyone who might be willing to assist them for a short while?" Russell suggested, trying to think of possibilities himself.

"If it were not winter, then most certainly there would be no difficulty, but as it is winter, who knows?"

"Do you think Missus Vreeland would be willing?" It was a reckless idea, but Russell spoke before he could stop himself.

Clayton stopped pacing. "You may have a notion there, Jason." He cocked his head to the side. "I ought to have thought of it myself, but I've been so caught up in other things that I . . ."

"You would have thought of it," Russell assured him.

"They could use all the assistance available now, and it is just the sort of thing that Missus Vreeland knows how to do. It would be more familiar to her than any work that Frau Schmidt might find for her here, and then she would not feel that she was taking . . . charity."

"And given where she is . . ." Russell said, letting himself smile.

"There is that, isn't there?" Clayton came to rest beside the door. "I'll speak to the Howes first thing in the morning. With the milking to be done and the family feeling so poorly, it would not astonish me to have an offer for Missus Vreeland before noon."

"Will that relieve you, Henry?" Russell asked, certain he knew the answer.

"A great deal," said the doctor. "And doubtless it will also relieve the Howe family. If they were not so new in the town, it would be another matter, but they have not been here long enough to make themselves known . . ."

"Most of the people in town have been here less than four years, from what Mayor Fletcher tells me," said Russell in a quiet way. "That would tend to make it difficult for anyone to rely on others."

"Yes; I think that is the case," said Clayton, opening the door. "Thank you, Jason. You've taken a load off my conscience and I am grateful for that."

"I've done nothing," Russell said, dismissing the matter. He waited until the door was closed again before he resumed his letter.

There are roughly five hundred men, women and children living within ten miles of Charity and the town itself. That may not seem many, com-

pared to the thousands you see every day on the streets of London, but in this part of the world, it is quite a considerable number, and one that is growing rapidly.

Nathaniel Howe took Cora Vreeland on as temporary help in the family dairy just as Henry Clayton had hoped he would. Russell heard about it while he dawdled over breakfast two mornings after Clayton had spoken with him.

"It is better this way," said Frau Schmidt with ponderous good-will. "She has tended cows most of her life. Not that she does not clean well, because she does, but she is not used to a place like this, and she would not be happy."

Russell had another fried trout and half a cup of his own precious coffee. "Why was she unhappy?"

"She misses her man and her children. She could not forget their loss here, with people all around her. But a family like the Howes, that is another matter."

"I would have thought it worse," said Russell, giving the question his consideration.

"Ach, no, my friend. They are like . . . pretend cousins. She can imagine that they are distant relatives, and that she is part of them. It is good for her to think that. She has been so taken with loneliness. There she has work and there are many to . . . to gather around her." Dorabelle Schmidt sat down opposite Russell, her muscular arms braced on the table. "She does not have to be reminded."

Russell nodded and finished his coffee.

"And she does not have to worry about Sun."

"Why would she worry about Sun Fan-Li?" Russell asked as he expertly removed the bones from the trout.

"She . . . doesn't like foreigners, at least not Chinese ones. She found him much too strange, and she did not understand that he is not stupid or dangerous." She clapped her hands, calling out, "Sun! Bring me some of your tea."

"Would you like some of my coffee?" Russell offered without enthusiasm.

"I would love some of your coffee, but you have so little left that I won't touch it. I thank you, of course." She looked around the room where four other men dined. "Here it is late November and we still have travelers. Remarkable."

"Why?" asked Russell with little more than idle curiosity.

"Last year we had almost no one through the town after the middle of November, and certainly not so many at one time. It shows that things are changing. And the year before almost no one came through in the winter at all. From October to May we had no strangers through Charity. Look at the register, and you'll see. Smilin' Jack was here all winter long, and he was about the only guest I had, most of the time, except for part of the Bevis family early in the spring when they made the tannery larger." She chuckled. "Poor old Bevis. He came up here ten years ago, when only the Padre and the Sisters were here. The trappers brought hides to him. And the next you know, there are sheep farmers and pig farmers with hides to be tanned, and a shoemaker and a saddler buying the tanned hides, and Charity isn't just a little valley with good springs anymore."

"Bevis is a strange one," said Russell, speaking his thoughts aloud.

"Bevis is a sour man, and that's the truth," said Dorabelle with solid emphasis. "That wife of his is little more than a shadow and his children . . . well!"

Sun Fan-Li came to the table and poured scalding, fragrant tea into a large mug for his employer. "I have almost no cabbage left, Frau Schmidt." He had great difficulty in pronouncing the last, but did not apologize for his lack of ability.

"What about canned goods? What have we there?" Dorabelle Schmidt shook her head. "Don't tell me; I didn't order enough. Well, how was I to know we would have so much business through the winter?"

"I have spoken to the Dooley cook, and I think perhaps I can arrange for some goods from there. Also, the Pueblo Road Tavern might be convinced to sell some of their stores. They have a very good root . . . cellar?" He bowed to Dorabelle and to the Sheriff. "I have made a venison curry for tonight, sir. Most of these guests won't like it, but as you've been in India . . ."

Russell's years in India had, in fact, given him a pronounced dislike of curry, but he said, "I look forward to it. I don't think I've ever encountered a venison curry."

"Nor I," said Sun. "It is . . . curious." He bowed again and withdrew.

"You ever wonder what he thinks of this place, Missus Schmidt?" Russell asked when the Chinese cook was gone.

"Often and often," she answered. "I know that he worked in an English household and shipped to the Sandwich Islands when he was little more than a lad, but it can't have been much like the Texas Territories, can it?"

"And you?" He lingered over his last precious sip of coffee. "Do you miss Germany?"

"Mein Gott!" she exclaimed. "I cry for Hannover. I long to hear my own language spoken around me, and see the river and the ocean and the castles, watch the parades, hear songs. There are times it is worse than pain, missing my home. When Gustav died I thought I would never miss anything in this world more than I missed him, but now, I find that homesickness can be more lasting than grief. Don't you pine for London?"

"Sometimes," Russell admitted. "But for the most part, I am glad I left. There was no place for me in London, or in England, for that matter." He threw his napkin onto the table and rose. "I have to attend to my duties."

"You mean Mister Vreeland," said Frau Schmidt. "Ach, ja, that sad little woman." She sighed and rose to her feet. "I will look for you at supper."

Vaguely Russell recalled Liam Cauliffe's warning about the German widow, but he put it out of his mind. "I'll look forward to it."

"Tell me," she called out as Russell reached the dining room entrance, "were you ever in Germany?"

"I was in Vienna once. I remember seeing the Dampierre Cuirassier Regiment on parade in full kit, black horses, black tack, sky-blue saddlepads, black boots, white uniforms with sky-blue collars and cuffs and those Roman helmets all in gold and black. It wasn't a royal escort, so they didn't use the red saddle pads with the royal crest in gold on them. All the officers had gold sashes with gold-and-blue tassels. It was a treat to see them."

"I never went to . . . Vienna." She laughed. "Strange to call it that."

Russell nodded and went out into the lobby to pick up his cap and coat.

"Sheriff," said Martin Corley from his place behind the counter, "there's a man came into town last night, late. He's asleep upstairs in room 8A."

"Oh?" Russell said as he pulled heavy gloves onto his hand.

"Another Englishman, like you."

"Like me?" Russell repeated, polite doubt in his voice.

"Fancy accent, clothes nicer'n yours." Corley was annoyed that his news had not been more enthusiastically received.

"What name did this fellow-Englishman give?" asked Russell, strolling over to examine the register.

The signature was hard to read and the hand was uneducated: *Eugene Randolph Exeter.*

"Mister Exeter arrived last night, you say?" Russell said, turning the register back to Corley.

"Yes; it was after ten o'clock. Red Pony showed him the way from the livery stable." He was somewhat mollified by the increased interest Russell showed.

"Where had he come from, did he say?"

"All I know is he came in from the south and he gave his address as

London." He hesitated before going on. "He was looking for a place to winter."

"And he chose Charity," Russell mused. "How curious." He met Corley's eager gaze. "Perhaps you will be kind enough to introduce me to this Englishman when I return this evening, assuming he is here?"

This was more than Martin Corley had hoped for, and he beamed. "Sure. You can bet I will, Sheriff."

"Thank you, Martin," said Russell as he went out of the hotel.

10

"That fellow is no Eugene Randolph Exeter," said Russell to Mayor George Fletcher at the next meeting of the Town Council. "I concede that he is British, but he gave himself that name, he was never born to it."

"Aren't you being a little unfair, Sheriff?" the Mayor inquired. "He has already deposited four hundred dollars in the bank—you will allow that it is a handsome sum, more than many of our depositors see in years."

"I won't argue that, Mayor," said Russell. "But the man is a gambler and I can promise you he is up to no good. When I was a Runner, we were taught to recognize a Captain Sharp on the prowl for flats, and Exeter is a Captain Sharp if ever I saw one." He looked at Hosea Olfrant. "He's taken a room at your house, hasn't he?"

"The Missus is taken with him; calls him a sweet boy. He's mighty soft-spoken and helpful to her." His expression was troubled even as he spoke in praise.

"Well, of course," Russell said in exasperation. "Find me a Captain Sharp who isn't a smooth talker. He's probably said something pleasant to Missus Fletcher, too. I wish I knew which fish he's hoping to land." He looked around the bare walls of the community hall, his hands thrust deep into his pockets. "And I wish I could convince you gentlemen that Mister Exeter, as he calls himself, is out to pluck pigeons."

"You're being too cautious, Sheriff," Fletcher chided him. "You are determined to demand perfect conduct of all Englishmen and this one is no exception. I won't remonstrate, but let me say that I would not want to think that you had acted hastily where this young fellow is concerned. He has shown himself to be an excellent influence on my son Frederick already, and that is more than anyone else has accomplished in the last three years."

Barton Purvis rubbed at his eyes. "What troubles me, George, is that the Sheriff might be right. Oh, I concede that it isn't very likely, but with his experience, it might be wisest to permit him—"

"That is the point!" Mayor Fletcher pounded his hand on the table. "I allow that the experience Sheriff Russell has had until now has stood him —and all the rest of us, of course—in excellent stead. But this time, he is seeing bogeys in the dark." He pushed his thumbs into the watch and fob pockets of his vest. "You are permitting yourself to be blinded, Sheriff."

"Blinded, is it?" Russell challenged. "All right; I will not make the inquiries I had intended until spring, and I will not issue till then the warning I had planned to. But I am telling you that someone in this town is going to be sorry that you held me back, and whoever that person is, I will refer him to you gentlemen and you will explain how it came about." He took a deep breath to steady himself. "I intend to watch that young man, however."

"You are not to interfere with him," warned Mayor Fletcher.

"I won't. Since you will have it that way. If it were left to me, I would have asked him to move on the day he arrived."

Olfrant shook his head. "It might be a very bad business, Sheriff. Suppose that you are wrong, and the young man is everything he says he is—"

"He claims to be," Russell corrected stiffly.

"Whatever the case," Olfrant went on with an uneasy glance from the Mayor to the Sheriff and back again. "If he has as much to offer as he . . . purports to, then it behooves us, as the Town Council, to give him our full attention and encouragement. If you, as Sheriff, are making his way . . . difficult for him, we might have cause to regret our . . . reticence at a later time." At the end of this, he cleared his throat and hunched his shoulders, like a tortoise attempting to retreat into its shell.

"And if I am proved correct?" Russell asked. "If this is a Captain Sharp? What then? I say that if this man is everything he has told you, then he will welcome my inquiries and my questions, for it will show him to advantage. He will request that I take every opportunity to find out that what he has offered to you is genuine and that he is a legitimate man of business." He stopped. "I can see it is useless to cavil."

It was the first time he and the Town Council had had so blatant a clash of wills, and Russell found it upsetting. He looked to the Mayor, waiting for George Fletcher to speak. "I allow that some questions should be asked," he said at last. "It would be lax for me to assume that everything I have heard this far is as sure a thing as Mister Exeter believes it is, for that would be folly. I'm not like you, Russell. I do not suppose that Mister Exeter is preying on an unsuspecting citizen of this town, but I am aware that there are those who are not familiar with the difficulties we in such remote areas must contend with. When the time comes, I will take it upon myself to pursue the references Mister Exeter has presented, and I will see that he is not over-extending himself in any way. That's reasonable, isn't it, Sheriff?"

The other two Town Council members nodded in sage agreement, both of them relieved to have the unpleasantness behind them.

"I hope for all our sakes that I'm wrong," was Russell's equivocal answer. He cleared his throat and changed the subject. "About the lookout station for South Knoll?"

"Oh, yes." The Mayor relaxed. "I'm pleased you mentioned that, for it is very much along the lines I have been thinking for the last several months. It could make a significant difference to our safety, I agree."

"Mayor?" asked Olfrant, "why on the South Knoll? Why not on the East Knoll?"

"I rather preferred the East Knoll," said Mayor Fletcher, but he was looking at Russell as he spoke, inviting comment.

"The East Knoll does not provide the view encountered by the South Knoll location," said Russell. "It is true that the East Knoll is somewhat higher, but the town and both the Hacienda Road and the Pueblo Road are visible easily from South Knoll. Also, while the East Knoll blocks line-of-sight from the South Knoll of Lorinda Dooley's house and the new house that the Carter family built, its position gives a clearer view of the slope from one side of the town to the other. From the top of the East Knoll, the western-most spring cannot easily be seen, and such buildings as the wagon-maker's shop and the jail, for that matter, block the view of, say, William Red Pony's little house and part of the Bevis tannery as well as most of the Howe dairy." It had been Russell's intent to offer more than enough argument to make his point, but he sensed that he had achieved his ends more completely than he had anticipated.

"Have you climbed both Knolls, then?" asked Olfrant.

"Certainly. I believe that South Knoll suits our purposes most effectively." He looked toward Mayor Fletcher. "And you? Have you climbed the Knolls?"

"Not recently," mumbled Mayor Fletcher. "At the time, I had not yet formed a notion of a lookout station."

"May I make one other observation?" Russell asked, determined to press the advantage he had gained. He did not wait for permission, but added, "I have noticed that where the mountains steepen to the west of the town, there are a greater number of rockslides and avalanches. Jack

Johnson has told me that the west side of the town always has the greater number of rock-and-snow slides. From East Knoll it is difficult to see the shoulder of the mountain on the west side of the town, but from the South Knoll the vantage point is excellent."

"All right," said Mayor Fletcher. "All right. I see your reasons." He looked at the other two. "We have set aside money for improvements of this sort. I believe it would be worthwhile to provide funds for such a lookout station to be built next spring."

"Fine with me," said Olfrant.

"Good idea," said Purvis.

"We'll work out what is to be paid and who is to do the work at the next meeting," said Mayor Fletcher, establishing his authority once more.

Russell smiled slightly. "Sounds good to me." He dragged one of the wooden chairs a little nearer the stove. "My feet are like slabs of ice," he declared as he sat and thrust them toward the stove.

"You've been working very hard, Sheriff," said Olfrant. "I understand you are the one who arranged for the burial of Matthew Vreeland."

"It was a poor solution, but it was better than waiting for spring thaw. The excavation for the new building at the corner of West and Spring Streets was the only worked ground in the entire town that isn't a midden." He sighed. "I wish there was something that could be done for the widow."

"She's working for Howe," Purvis pointed out. "Doctor Clayton has paid her debts—a most irregular thing to do—and Missus Mattington has said that she will take Missus Vreeland on as her housekeeper at any time. I'd say she had more good fortune in adversity than many another."

"And she has her health and her good name," added Olfrant. "That counts for something."

Russell sighed. He stretched his legs and wiggled his toes in his boots, enjoying the painful tingle of returning sensation. He listened to Olfrant and Purvis toady to Mayor Fletcher, but he could not bring himself to participate. Finally he heard reference to Linus Cooke, the saddler who had a new house near the dairy and the tannery. He turned his head to listen.

"And what I say is that he will want to bring in more and more of his family, and what then?" Purvis demanded.

"They might be worthwhile citizens in their time," suggested Olfrant. "Cooke is a good man. He deals fairly from all I have heard, and he makes good saddles and harness. He buys from Bevis and the wood is bought from Ritchards out near Cowley Pass."

"But how long can he continue if he brings in an enormous and indigent family?" Purvis insisted. "From what I have heard, his brother has no less than twelve children, and aside from the work that is being offered, he has none."

"It may be that what he needs is the company of his brother and the promise of work. We have given opportunity to many others with less promise." He looked toward Fletcher. "Are you going to advance him the funds he has requested?"

"I have not yet decided." He turned toward Russell. "Do you have an opinion on this as well as everything else, Sheriff?"

"I think it would be a good idea to build a school and hire a schoolmaster." Russell heard all three men take in a surprised breath. "And if Cooke has more business than he can handle, then who better to approach than his own brother."

"With all those children?" said Purvis.

"So much the better, if they are given an education, for if Charity is to grow, it must look not only to new families moving in from other places—after all, you have all remarked that most of the people who live here have arrived in the last six years—but to the generations to come." He dropped his feet and stood up. "But you will do as you think best."

"Are you leaving, Sheriff?" asked Olfrant, a little affronted at the thought.

"I want to take advantage of the weather; we won't get snow for another day or two and I want to ride the perimeter, to see if there are any difficulties. Ever since I saw Matthew Vreeland's body, I have been concerned for those on the outlying ranches and farms." He reached for his fur cap. "I'm taking Gryphon. My other two horses will remain at Calvin's."

"Why don't you arrange to use the private stable we have?" suggested Mayor Fletcher in his most mellifluous tones. "I'm certain that something could be arranged."

Russell smiled faintly. "I thank you, Mayor. If I weren't looking to establish a horse farm of my own, I'd be tempted; as it is, I'd rather keep the horses where they are until I find what I want."

"Do you have anything in mind?" Fletcher asked, caught off-guard by Russell's candor.

"Actually, yes, I do. There's land on the Denver Road, near the eastern spring. I've been told it gets boggy in the spring because it lies low, and East Knoll blocks some of the drainage. But it isn't as steep as most of the land here, and it doesn't have the tannery for a neighbor. I'll talk to you about it before the New Year," he added, smiling faintly. "And if I buy it, you know there is enough money in my account to cover it."

"And what," Fletcher could not resist asking, "if your contract with the town isn't renewed and we hire another Sheriff come August?"

"Why, then I'll tend to my animals and raise horses, as I intend to do in any case. My father saw to it that I would be able to run a breeding stable; when I was younger I didn't find the idea much to my liking, but now that I am nearer fifty than forty, it has a genuine fascination." He smiled again, this time more openly. "I should be back tomorrow. I'll go out the Old North Road and return on the Denver Road."

"To see your land as you come into town?" Purvis sounded angry.

"I suppose I could do that. But actually I want to see how many of the women at Lorinda Dooley's are still ailing, and find out if they are generally on the mend." He went to the door. "If Liam Cauliffe arrives while I am gone, please tell him I want to speak with him while he's here, will you?" He gave a little bow and stepped out into the bright, crisp cold.

"Sheriff," said Cloris Bell, as she saw Russell ride into their yard. "Maude is in the barn. How good to see you."

"Good to see you too, Cousin Bell." He had taken to calling them by the same titles as the rest of the people in Charity. "I hope you're both well?"

"Nothing that worries us," she replied. "We're not so young anymore that our bones don't hate the cold, but that and a little sore throat is all." She indicated the barn. "We have a cow with an untimely calf due. I was getting my bag of tricks when you rode up." She stepped onto the porch and held up a small satchel. "Care to come with us? In general my cousin doesn't like the farm chores as much as she likes the house chores, which is just as well, since I've done more than enough housekeeping in my time." She let Russell follow her toward the barn, talking over her shoulder as she went. "Poor Maude—I've had her making up britches for me and she isn't happy about it. But she knows as well as I do that I can't take care of our stock in a sidesaddle. Those are for sweet ladies in parks and Duchesses on fox hunts who never take anything over three feet." She turned back to him. "Aren't they?"

"Aren't what?" Russell asked, then continued without waiting for her comment. "In this country sidesaddles aren't very practical. Missus Mattington rides in britches." He recalled that twenty years ago he would not have been able to say this to a woman without acute embarrassment, but his years tracking down criminals and working in India and Australia had blunted his sensibilities. "Why not have a talk with her—she could make some suggestions."

There was a slight pause. "I don't think that Missus Mattington approves of my cousin and me. She doesn't think it right that two women should live alone and work a ranch together." They had reached the barn, and Cloris Bell stood aside to let Russell lead Gryphon into the barn. "You can use that stall over there." She pointed to the far side of the double line of stalls. "There's grain and hay, if you need either, and water in the back trough."

Maude Rossiter looked up from the cow. "You brought reinforcements?"

"The Sheriff seems to be making one of his periodic checks," said Cloris Bell, then called, "That is what you're doing, isn't it, Sheriff Russell?"

"Yes. Doctor Clayton is concerned about the possibility of illness spreading, and I've heard that there may be a gang of outlaws operating in the area. I want to warn you about them, if I may. Should you find anything unusual or suspicious, please send me word—"

"How?" asked Maude as she got to her feet, brushing off her hands and then her skirt fastidiously. "It would mean that one of us would be left alone. You're not recommending that, are you?"

"Not specifically, no," said Russell as he watched Cloris settle down beside the cow with her bag open. "But there may be an opportunity— and there is no reason you cannot both come to town if you are genuinely concerned."

"And leave the ranch to outlaws!" Cloris asked. "No, thank you. We've both worked too hard to let this place fall into the wrong hands now." She leaned over, her ear pressed to the distended abdomen of the cow. "Something's wrong in there; I can feel it." Straightening up, she put her hands on the cow's neck. "Too bad you can't talk, 'Vangie. It'd make it easier for us to know how to help you. As it is, I don't know . . ."

"Who are the outlaws you're concerned with?" Maude Rossiter asked. "Is there some group you think is involved?"

"There are a few, but a body was discovered a short while ago who had been killed by one of these gangs, and I would not like to have that happen again in my jurisdiction."

Cloris had got to her feet and she shook her skirts vigorously to get the clinging straw off them. "Do you mean killed or murdered?"

"Murdered, not that it makes much difference." Russell looked at the two women. "I hope you won't take this amiss, but the two of you, living here alone, clearly prospering, are more likely to be the target of such gangs than those with . . . less to recommend them."

"If by that you mean a man with a shotgun," said Cloris in her bluntest manner, "both of us know how to shoot, and we have four guns, two pistols and a good supply of ammunition in the house."

Russell nodded. "All right; if you are satisfied with your own protection, there's little more I can say."

"You might work out a plan to have us contact you from time to time.

That way if we miss a time . . ." Maude faltered. "But, of course, that could be a matter of weather as much as anything else, couldn't it?" She cleared her throat. "If the weather keeps us housebound, I am sure that it does the same for men on horseback."

"I hope you're right," said Russell. Then he rubbed the back of his neck. "I can't stay if you don't require me. I want to get around to all the outlying ranches by tomorrow night."

"I hope you do," said Cloris. "There's a God-Almighty blizzard—"

"Cousin!" protested Maude.

"—building up in the sky. If you don't make town by tomorrow night, you probably won't get back for a week." She turned back to the cow, who was thrashing feebly. "I hope we don't lose her. We've only got three more."

"I hope you don't lose her, either," said Russell. Then he went to the stall where Gryphon was making the most of his opportunity to have something to eat. He led the horse out of the barn and swung into the saddle after checking the girths. "I want you to know that I'm concerned about you," he told the two women who stood together in the wide barn door.

"We appreciate that, Sheriff," said Cloris.

"I won't take any request for aid from you as an imposition. And I know better than to assume that you're suffering from the vapors." He pulled the reins in and started out of the yard. "I'll be back as soon as I can."

"Thanks." Maude Rossiter raised her hand and waved.

Cole Ritchards moved about from one to another of his three line shacks, selecting timber, stacking it for curing, and then, through most of the summer, hauling it down to Charity to sell for building. "I tell you, Sheriff," he said to Russell when he found him at the largest of the three shacks, "I don't know what to make of it. Time was the only people for forty miles around was Bevis, Don Maximillian, the Padres at Sagrada Caridad and San Esteban and Smilin' Jack coming through. Now, I can't go ten miles without seeing a house or some such." He was knotted and grizzled, and he stank worse than a shambles in high summer. His beard was kept fairly short with irregular hacks with a knife and he walked with a permanent stoop.

"Getting a little too crowded for you?" Russell suggested, not quite amused.

"Crackers, yes. I come up here to get away from people, not to find 'em under every rock." He spat and looked back at Russell. "You gonna tell me what you come up here for, or you gonna babble?"

"I was hoping you could tell me about some of the people you might have noticed in the area," said Russell with growing amusement.

"You mean Coffin Mayhew and his bunch?" Ritchards asked. "Sure, I seen 'em. They took over one of my cabins for a week or so—fair to wrecked the place and then burned it when they left. They had a kid with them and they killed him up there. I think they throwed the body in a ravine. Wolves'll find it before you do." He half-sat on the edge of a massive table. "That what you wanted to know, Sheriff?"

"Not wanted to know, Ritchards—*needed* to know." Russell braced his arms and cleared his throat, noticing that he was a bit hoarse. "When was this?"

"Two, three weeks back. I disremember." Ritchards spat again, more copiously.

"Why didn't you send word about it then?"

"Because I had work to do, and those varmints—" He could find no adequate words to express his feelings so he struck the table with the palms of his hands three times.

"They burned your cabin. I suppose they burned the wood you had stacked as well?" Russell hoped he sounded sympathetic for Ritchards was noted for the quickness with which he took offence.

"I don't leave my stacks by the house. I'm not that dumb. I keep 'em some distance away." He gave a crafty smile. "But they didn't know where to look, and neither do you." He rubbed his hands together. "And with all the fools you got coming into Charity, they're gonna be paying my price come spring."

"They certainly will," said Russell, wondering why a man who so disliked the company of other people was so eager to gain riches. "And if Mayhew and his gang leave you alone . . ."

"They better, if they know what's good for them." He folded his arms. "If I'd known what they were up to before they got inside, they would never have done it. I got traps all around my places, and I know how to make 'em work, which is more'n the rest of you do." He laughed, the sound more like a bark.

"And what then, Ritchards?"

"They'd be gone, that's all, just gone." He shook his head, chuckling at the thought. "Don't you worry, Sheriff. I can take care of myself. You don't have to trouble yourself."

"I hope you're right," said Russell, then went on, "because there are so many who aren't as prepared as you are and who are running much greater risks."

"Fools shouldn't be here if they can't take care of themselves," growled

Ritchards. "I got no intention of helping 'em out if they can't manage for themselves."

Russell nodded. "But you understand, don't you, that I have to know as much as I can about what is going on? The law has warrants out on these men and I have a duty to—"

"Duty! Law! Warrants!" Each word was more condemning than the last. "I'll tell you about duty and law and warrants, Sheriff. You let those varmints come near me again and you won't have to trouble no judge to give the word to hang 'em. I'll deliver 'em up the same way I deliver my wood. You can take your oath on that."

"All right." Russell sighed.

"You don't worry none about me, Sheriff. I know what to do and you can be sure I'll do it. That Mayhew! Thinks he's the only man in the Texas Territories knows how to get things done. He's being a horse's hinder-end." He scowled. "If that was all you was wanting, Sheriff, I want to get back to my work. I got things to do. You go on and check on the other folk."

"I'll be back again when the weather permits."

"Suit yourself," said Ritchards. "Don't make no difference to me." He reached to gather up his various axes and saws, his huge, hard hands moving with so habitual a skill that they had an unexpected grace.

"Mayhew can be dangerous, Ritchards."

"Thunderation, Sheriff," Ritchards objected. "So can I."

"Both Arthur and Hiram are away," said Bess Mattington as she poured coffee for Russell. "You're welcome to have your supper here and spend the night, if it won't bother you."

"If it won't bother you or your family, it would be welcome to me," said Russell, admiring the house that the Mattingtons had built. Unlike most of the other ranches in the area, this place already felt substantial and established, as if it had been there almost as long as Don Maximillian's hacienda. There was a settee in the parlor and a china cabinet in the dining room, and the most recently acquired treasure—an enormous, flowered carpet—covered the floor of the front hall, so grand that most of the visitors and hands were afraid to walk on it.

"I'll be glad of the company, Sheriff. My menfolk are fine company, but variety now and then is a welcome thing." She poured coffee for herself and leaned back in her high-backed upholstered chair that had been shipped all the way from St. Louis. "Now that everyone's learning to read, it's made a change."

"Are you pleased with the change?" Russell asked, curious to hear what she would say.

"Mostly, yes. But every now and then, I miss the days when they all had to come to me to write letters or to get letters read." She eyed him over the rim of the cup. "You didn't ride all the way out here to get my opinion on the schooling in town. What's on your mind, Sheriff?"

"Am I that obvious?" Russell inquired with a faint smile.

"We're both practical people, Sheriff—it figures you have some purpose other than passing the time. The weather's not right for that." She lifted her mug and settled back, prepared to listen to whatever he had to say.

"Well, you're right." He looked around the room. "You might have heard that a body was found in one of Don Maximillian's line shacks?"

"The Vreeland boy. What a sad thing that was. And that wife of his, losing him and their babies—how's she doing? You tell her there's a place for her here, did you?"

"Yes, but for the time being she's content to work at the Howe dairy. And they do need her; there's been sickness in the family and Doc Clayton has refused to let them make cheese while they're poorly." He had some more of the coffee and accepted one of the heavy, sweet buns she offered him.

"So what was it about the body that worried you?" Bess Mattington asked in her direct way. "Don't think you have to beat about the bush for me, Sheriff. I been around long enough and I seen enough not to need soft soap."

"All right: according to Henry Clayton, Vreeland was tortured to death, probably by the Mayhew gang, which means that they are probably still in the area. Those are the facts without varnish." He read dismay in her face. "That's the reason I'm going to the ranches and farms in the area, to let everyone know that they'll have to take precautions for a while."

"Mayhew," she said. "I heard about him, nothing good and nothing I'd wish on anyone I liked." Her lined face grew more stark. "You need any help I can give, or my hands can give, rest assured it's yours."

"Thank you," said Russell, certain she meant it.

"I got a young hand, Mexican, names Luis Guerra. Padre Idos at San Esteban sent him over about a year ago, said that he needed work and was in some kind of trouble in the Duke's Town. I said I'd take him on providing he didn't get into any mischief, and so far he's been fine." She broke one of her sweet buns in half. "The reason I mention him is that you might want someone to fetch and carry for you. I'll keep him on my payroll, but loan him out to you, if you like."

"That's very generous," said Russell, taken by surprise.

"Well, you can't be everywhere at once, and unless I miss my mark, George Fletcher won't part with a single penny for help for you. So someone's got to lend a hand until the Town Council gets a little starch in its backbone and stops licking Fletcher's boots for him." She dunked her bun into the coffee and chewed on it eagerly.

"You don't have to do this, Missus Mattington."

"Thought I told you to call me Bess," she said in a reflective tone. "It's as much for me as for you. If I need you, or I need to get a message to you, Luis will do that job, and he'll carry out your orders or answer to me and to Padre Idos. Between the two of us, he'll listen to sense, I promise you." She did not quite chuckle, but there was a rumble of laughter at the back of her throat as she spoke. "He's not really dangerous—at worst he's a thief, but he's as frightened of murderers like Mayhew as any sensible and law-abiding man would be."

"That's quite a recommendation," said Russell with unfeigned amusement.

"No use wrapping up garbage in silk, as they say," she pointed out, her attention more on the bun than on him. "I'll introduce him to you at breakfast. That's at first light, so we better not stay up all night gabbing."

Russell drank his coffee. "I'll turn in before nine," he promised her.

Bess Mattington shook her head in disbelief, then said, "It might be an idea if you make Luis a deputy or something—he's more reliable if he thinks there's something in it for him."

"Deputy it is," said Russell.

11

Luis Guerra was thin in a way that came from a childhood spent in poverty. His narrow face was almost expressionless, but his dark, restless eyes revealed his fear and his hunger. "You are the Sheriff?" he asked as Bess Mattington presented him.

"Yes; Jason Russell." He held out his hand and waited for the other man to take it. "It's a pleasure to meet you."

"Um," said Guerra. "The Patrona tells me that I am to assist you."

"That's right," said Russell, not certain that he understood Guerra at all. "I need a . . . deputy, and Missus Mattington recommended you." He caught her quick nod of approval and felt better.

"What does a deputy do?" asked Guerra, suspicion pinching his features. "Why do you ask me when there are others?"

"I need someone who is reliable and who knows the ranches around Charity. Not everyone in town has been out to the ranches and many of them haven't the time for the job, especially now that winter is here. You know where the outlying ranches are, and Missus Mattington says that she can spare you from your work here to assist me." He could not interpret the odd reaction Guerra gave: the Mexican crossed himself and put his hand to his chest.

"If la Patrona gives the word, I will do it," he announced as if he were accepting a commission from President James K. Polk to capture all of Mexico.

"That's good of you," said Russell, uncertain how to react to this promise.

"I will do all that you require of me, Sheriff," he said, and then bowed to Bess Mattington. "I thank you from the bottom of my heart and soul, Patrona, for you have trusted me and made me a man among men."

Russell did not acknowledge this effusiveness, but said in his most pragmatic way, "Can you ride in half an hour?"

"I will be ready in half that time," vowed Guerra. "You have only to give the word."

"Consider it given," said Russell, thinking that he would not be able to deal with too much of the grand style Guerra used.

"Take the pinto gelding," said Bess Mattington. "And make sure you put an extra blanket in your bedroll."

"It will not be necessary," said Guerra.

"Oh yes it will," Russell countered. "And if you have a spare cinch and a second pair of socks, you will be glad of it before the winter is over." He looked to Bess Mattington. "Thank you."

She hitched up her shoulders. "Least I can do. You're the only one in town who has any wits about him. I don't want to leave the place entirely to George Fletcher and his buzzards, for all they'll do is pick it clean—without thinking that's what they're doing, of course—and then lord it over the place. You're not cut from that bolt of cloth, thank the Lord. So I figure if I give you a little bolstering here and there, shore up the weak spots, then we all benefit." She turned on Guerra. "You remember that, Luis, when you're in town. No matter what anybody tells you, you're the Sheriff's man, and your duty is to him."

"Señora, I will do this for you and count myself blessed." He bowed to her before he hurried out the door.

"Think you can bear with him?" Bess Mattington asked when Guerra was out of earshot.

"It might take some getting used to, but I was in India for more than five years; I handled that." He paused, then went on more seriously, "I hope you'll take precautions about Mayhew, assuming he's still around. He's a very dangerous man."

"I got seven hands here at the bunkhouse and another three riding the boundaries. That should keep us out of the worst trouble." She looked up at the sky. "It's the ones out on their own who worry me," she said. "Caught out in a storm is bad enough, but if one of them runs into Mayhew and his gang, there isn't much that you or I or anyone short of the Good Lord can do for him. That bothers me. It bothers me having Arthur and Hiram gone now, too. You'd think that at my age I'd have learned better, but I haven't."

"I'll try to keep an eye out for them, Bess." He found that it was not as difficult to say her Christian name as he had thought it would be. "And I'll see that word gets passed. I hope to get to all the outlying ranches."

"You will. Let me go down to the bunkhouse and tell Luis that he rides first thing in the morning. He probably thinks that he was supposed to leave here in a half hour. So long as he's packed and ready you'll be out of here at first light in the morning."

"I have to go to Don Maximillian's," Russell said. "What do you think I ought to do with Guerra then?"

"Send him to San Esteban or on into town. No use making this worse." She closed the inner door. "I want to put a few more logs on the fire. You attend to that and I'll talk to Luis. The wood's piled in back of the pantry. Put some in the stove while you're at it." With that, she dragged a shapeless fur wrap around her shoulders and went into the kitchen, heading for the back door.

Russell busied himself with the fire and then the stove, all the while thinking of what he would be able to accomplish with an assistant—a deputy, he reminded himself.

An elderly priest with a resigned face met Russell at the door to Don Maximillian's hacienda. "Don Maximillian is ill, gravely ill," he intoned in a heavy Spanish accent.

"It's important. I'm Jason Russell—"

"I know who you are, Sheriff," said the priest. "I am Padre Idos, from San Esteban. I am attending to Don Maximillian along with his physician."

"What's wrong?" Russell asked. "What's happened to Don Maximillian?"

"He is very ill," Padre Idos insisted.

"Yes, but with what?" Russell said. He was cold and tired, he had not eaten for more than six hours, his back was sore from riding in the wind and he was not in the mood to wrangle with a priest.

"He has a putrefied foot," said Padre Idos. "He must consent to having it removed or soon there will be no remedy."

"Gangrene?" Russell said, feeling sympathy for the arrogant Don Maximillian. "When did this happen?"

"He suffered a slight wound in his foot," Padre Idos said, capitulating. "That was more than two weeks ago. He treated it and went about his work, confident that there would be no difficulty. You might as well come inside."

The hacienda was hushed. The servants moved like ghosts through the halls and the uncharacteristic smell of incense was a lingering perfume on the air. Padre Idos led the way to the library and indicated a large, uncomfortable chair near the fire. "I will ask them to bring you chocolate and brandy," he said, then issued swift orders in Spanish.

"Thank you. When did Don Maximillian send for you?" asked Russell as he opened his overcoat and removed his cap.

"Two days ago. By then there was much infection. He could not walk without pain. I ordered his men to fetch his physician to treat the wound." He took another one of the wooden chairs and drew it nearer the fire.

"Which physician is this?" asked Russell.

"This is someone you do not know. He rode all night from the village of Los Ossos, almost twenty miles from here. He has been attending Don Maximillian ever since he arrived." The Padre joined his hands in his lap, his long face somber. "There is sufficient cause for worry that I have administered the Last Rites to him."

"What does the physician think?" asked Russell in a gentle tone.

"He is afraid that Don Maximillian will not permit the removal of his leg, and if that is the case, then it is only a matter of how much time and suffering God will require of him before calling him." He crossed himself and folded his hands again.

There was nothing Russell could find to say. He stared into the fire, wondering if he should offer to send Henry Clayton to the rancho as well. He did not want to offend Don Maximillian or his Spanish doctor, but he wanted to help convince the Patron that he must consent to losing his leg or sacrifice his life. He rubbed his stubbled chin. "Will you tell him that I hope he will have the surgery and recover?"

"If it seems wise, I will," said Padre Idos.

"I came here for another reason entirely, and I have an obligation." He looked away from the flames.

"Tell me; I will do my best to assist you." The priest sighed once, as if feeling another burden on his stooped shoulders.

"There is a dangerous outlaw in the area, or so we think. The man who was killed at the line shack on Don Maximillian's property was the victim of this outlaw and his gang, or so we believe. We also fear that there may be other incidents, especially if those living in outlying areas are not warned of him." He saw Padre Idos nod. "I want to urge you to take precautions against this gang."

"I will issue the orders."

"And if there are any circumstances that are suspicious or you believe should be investigated, I want word to be sent to me at once. It is most unwise to attempt to deal with this gang on your own."

"There are many servants here, and the men who work the range are not unused to trouble."

"Padre, forgive me for saying it, but this trouble is more than they are—"

One of the maids, silent as a shadow, came into the library with a tray in her hands. She curtsied to the priest and left the tray on the table before backing out the room and leaving the two men alone once more.

"Permit me to get your chocolate," said Padre Idos, rising without waiting for Russell's response.

"Thank you," said Russell, continuing as he watched the priest pour out the hot liquid from a large silver pot into a good-sized china cup. "It is part of my duty to try to protect all the people living near Charity, for in almost every sense you and the townspeople face the same risks."

"I doubt that, but continue, Sheriff," said Padre Idos as he added a generous tot of brandy to the chocolate.

He accepted the chocolate and went on, "This rancho is older than the other holdings in the area, and you have the prior claim."

"That might not last if your campaign in Mexico succeeds. As it appears it will. All the land west of here will be annexed to the United States before another year passes, of that I am sadly certain." He resumed his seat. "You are the newcomers and you are the ones who seek to take charge of the land. We who have been here for nearly a century are now being cast aside. It may be just as well if Don Maximillian refuses to be saved, for he would not want to be stripped of all that is his and see it parceled out." Though he spoke softly, Padre Idos' voice was fierce with emotion. "So, tell me why it should be of any interest to us that there is an outlaw whose men are preying on the invaders we have resisted for so long?"

"It should be of interest because Mayhew makes no distinction between Mexican and Spanish and Indian and American. He would treat every man the same—as dog meat." To keep from losing his temper, Russell drank the bitter chocolate, though it scalded his mouth and made his tongue burn.

"We have not had any trouble here, or at San Esteban," said Padre Idos as if this was sufficient dismissal.

"So far. And the body of Matthew Vreeland was found here. Ask your workers about that, Padre. And ask them, while you are at it, if they want the same thing to happen to them. Because it could happen. We don't know where Mayhew is, or what he is doing. We don't know when he will strike again, or where."

"Or if," added Padre Idos.

"Yes, or if. It may be that he has taken his gang and gone toward Taos or Denver, or over Cowley Pass into the Mexican Territories. But we do know that wherever he is, he is going to be committing crimes, and those crimes include murder." He drank more of the chocolate. "Is it correct for you, with your calling, not to do all that you may to prevent more bloodshed and suffering?"

"If it is the Will of God, then men will suffer and die," said Padre Idos.

"As Don Maximillian is doing?" It was deliberate and cruel, but Russell could see that he had finally pierced the old priest's angry indifference.

"It is not the same," Padre Idos whispered.

"No; Don Maximillian was not hurt by men determined to kill him. He was not held by them and maimed. He was not tormented by others, only by his own pride." He finished the chocolate and set it aside. "I thank you for your hospitality in Don Maximillian's place. I hope you will extend that hospitality to warning those men who work for him that they are at greater risk now than they were before Mayhew came here." He stood up, feeling his muscles object. "I hope that Don Maximillian will let them take his leg. Gangrene is a terrible way to die."

"Most ways to die are terrible. Faith alone will give courage and tranquility." He rose and went to the door with Russell. "I will convey your information to the workers, Sheriff, and if there is reason to notify you, I will." He opened the door. "I must return to my duties and you must return to yours."

The few words of thanks that Russell began to express were cut off by the closing door.

"Where'd you pick *him* up?" asked Liam Cauliffe, hitching his thumb in the direction of Luis Guerra where he sat in the hotel dining room over supper.

"Bess Mattington loaned him to me. She thinks I need some help and she doubts the Town Council will give it to me." He kept his voice low but not so low as to be obvious. "She told me that she would pay his wages."

"Very sensible woman, Missus Mattington," Cauliffe approved, his sober expression changing; he looked up with a smile as Dorabelle Schmidt came toward their table with a small tray in her hands. "What's this?"

"I have made a torte, just to keep my hand in," she said, color staining her cheeks. "I do not have many guests who would like a torte. This is with apples. In the spring, when there are berries, I will make better ones." She gave one piece—the larger one—to the minister, and the second to Russell. "You have tortes in England, Sheriff?"

"We have trifle and pudding, Missus Schmidt," he said. "I have enjoyed tortes before—years ago." He lifted his fork, watching the covert way that Frau Schmidt studied Reverend Cauliffe. He remembered the warning Cauliffe had offered so many months ago about the Widow Schmidt, and wondered if he might have better saved the warning for himself.

"There is a little of your coffee left. If you would not mind, I will take some and brew it. Tortes are better with good, strong coffee."

Cauliffe took a bite of the dessert and actually smiled. "It's a proper treat, Widow Schmidt, and God bless you for it."

Dorabelle Schmidt beamed and Russell raised his eyebrows.

Russell and Cauliffe were on their second cup of precious coffee when Henry Clayton came into the dining room, his face drawn and eyes sunken.

"You wish something to eat?" Dorabelle Schmidt asked, filled with more goodwill than she had shown in months. "The kitchen is closed, but there is enough to make up a cold plate and some—"

"No; Christ no, but thanks," Clayton said, waving her away. "Jason, may I have a minute with you in private?" He did not bother to sit down or to offer apology for his interruption, and that alone caused Russell some alarm.

"Certainly. We can go to my room, if you like, or into the parlor off the lobby." This little chamber was rarely used and probably lacked both heat and light, but it would provide the privacy Clayton required.

"Anything. It's urgent." He made a gesture of excuse to Cauliffe. "Sorry, Liam. If there's a chance, if I can, I'll discuss this with you later."

"You follow your conscience, Henry, and I'll be satisfied at whatever you do." He was almost finished with his torte and a little smear of cooked apple clung to the edge of his lip.

"Good of you," he said as Russell indicated the door to the parlor. "I didn't mean to interrupt, but you were gone all day, and . . ." He stopped with an effort. "Sorry. I didn't mean to babble."

The parlor was indeed chilly and it took a few moments for Russell to find one of the lamps and strike a lucifer to get it lit. "What is it? You look like you've been up all night."

"All last night, yes." He dropped onto the settee by the window. "I'm worn to the bone."

"What is it?" Russell repeated, prodding.

"You know the family who have the little poultry farm off of Old North Road? The name is—"

"Louis and Dorothy Kinsman," said Russell. "Three children, I believe."

"No children and Dorothy won't last much more than two days and for her own sake, I hope it's sooner." He sighed heavily, his breath shaking.

"Good God, what is the matter?" Russell said, the spectre of an epidemic looming ahead of him.

"They said it was tainted food. I'm afraid it's flux, and that could mean that one or all of the wells are contaminated." He said this last in a rush, as if the enormity of it demanded that he be relieved of the burden of it.

"Are there other cases?" asked Russell, so calmly that Clayton wondered if he understood what the trouble might become.

"I haven't seen any, but I have been at the Kinsman house." He straightened up. "Don't you see, if they have flux, there is no one who is truly safe from it. Even if it isn't the wells, it might be some other contagion just as important. It's a terrifying prospect."

"I've seen flux, in India and in Australia. I know what it can do." He leaned back. "We will need to put up notices. I wish I had more help." His face was somber. "We will also have to keep you at your house in town and not rambling all over the countryside. People have to be able to find you."

"But if they are ill—" Clayton protested.

"If there is flux, there will be many ill, and that means they will have to come to you. You will have all you can do to deal with those who can reach you. In your house you have most of your supplies and materials. If you venture, out into the country, you could be caught by snow or—"

"Or take the disease myself?" Clayton suggested when Russell fell silent.

"That could happen." Russell walked down the center of the room. "I'll talk with Red Pony and with Sun. They might have heard or seen something. Often those who are outsiders for a town see and know more than those who . . . And then I suppose I'd better speak with the Mayor. If you believe that we need to establish some measure of quarantine."

"How do you mean—some measure of quarantine?" Russell asked carefully. "How great a measure?"

"I don't know yet," Clayton said thoughtfully. "I haven't worked that out yet. I can't imagine that it would be easy. For the time being, I've ordered Kinsman to keep to his house; he wouldn't leave in any case, not with his wife failing and the children yet to be buried. But the most important thing now is to see how many other cases might have developed without anyone mentioning it."

"What about Missus Vreeland's child? Was that flux?" Russell demanded.

"No; that was a putrid sore throat and an inflammation of the lungs. Flux is another matter." He joined his hands together and pressed them against his forehead. "I don't know what to tell you. I don't know how great the danger might be, only that there is danger."

"All right," said Russell, striving to keep from sounding distressed or apprehensive. He knew that Clayton was at his limit and would need very little to overburden him. "I will have Guerra find out if there are others who are ill, and once we know we can proceed from there. Is that satisfactory, Henry? Will it be enough protection for a few days?"

"I hope so," Clayton muttered.

"It will have to be, I think," said Russell. "I doubt that the Mayor will allow anything more until we can show him how much illness, or how little, we are facing." As he said this, he thought that no matter how great the spread of illness, George Fletcher would probably not want an official quarantine in his town, for it would reflect badly on his office.

"It might be—"

"It might not be as serious as you fear, Henry, think of that. It could be that the Kinsmans were more harmed than the others. For the time being, we will order water taken from the wells and—"

"And what?" Clayton burst out. "Do I drink it myself? Do I find out if—"

"You feed it to some of the runt piglets from the Durante farm, and you see if they suffer or show signs of flux. You can get the piglets for a penny apiece." He could see Clayton ease back from the panic that was threatening to take hold of him.

"I suppose I could do that. We'd know in a day or two if the wells are safe. That's something." He got to his feet. "If we have contaminated wells, what do we do?"

"Let us determine if we have, and if we have, which ones are contaminated. Then let us determine what has to be done. When we know the depth of the problem we will then be able to make our plans."

"How do you mean?"

"I mean," said Russell with deliberate coldness, "that we had better have all our plans made before we insist on martial law, if that is necessary.

And we had better not ask for so extreme a method if it is not necessary, for if we demand it once without cause, we will never be able to get it again, even if the circumstances demand it."

Clayton looked at Russell with shock in his eyes. "Martial law?"

"That's generally part of quarantine, and if I am going to have to enforce it, I must have the approval and support of the Town Council. They aren't about to approve such a thing unless they are utterly convinced that the alternative is watching their families die around them." He was coolly harsh and he regarded Henry Clayton with only a trace of sympathy. "Get the piglets first thing in the morning. I'll help you collect the samples from the wells."

"What do we do about the wells in the meantime?" Clayton asked. "If there is flux in them . . . the more they are used the more illness will . . ."

"For the time being, we will do very little. If this town is given over to fear, the results will be worse than anything the flux can do. I know. I've seen it happen before, and in that respect, the Texas Territories are no different than India or Australia." He paced the length of the parlor once more. "If the piglets are ill in two days' time, then we will know where we stand. Until that happens, we must assume that the Kinsmans were right, and that they ate tainted food."

"What if you're wrong? What if the flux is already spreading?" Clayton challenged him.

Very quietly Russell said, "If it is, it will be on my conscience."

12

"I have called at all the houses on Park Street and all the houses on Knoll and Spring Street west of Charity Street," said Guerra when he reported back to the jail at mid-morning. "There are some illnesses, but nothing of flux. One of the Samson children has the Grey Cough, but his mother has been treating him with plasters and camphor and he is improving, or so she said." He held up his notebook. "I have written it all down, just as you told me."

"Padre Antonio has three children out of school because of illness, but it is sore throat and cough, for the most part. I've covered all of Mission Street as far as the Denver Road. There are three families on Roman Street that are sick, but only one has symptoms of flux." He showed his notebook to Guerra. "Have a look at my notes and compare them to yours, and this evening, compile the lot into a report."

"A report? But what is there to say?" Guerra was upset at the idea, and he waved his hands in protest.

"I'll show you how," said Russell. "I want you to learn how to make reports, so that when you are away, or when I am away, there will be records we both can see so that we will know what the other is doing." He sat at his desk, pulling open the lower drawer where he kept his paper. "There's ink in the top drawer, and pens. I've got half a dozen nibs and you can trim them with the penknife."

"I . . . I do not write very well," Guerra admitted.

"Then you will welcome the practice," said Russell, unwilling to be dissuaded. "If you wish to take the reading and writing lessons at the hotel or the Community Church, go ahead. I'll encourage anything that helps you."

Guerra sighed. "I will do all of West Street and Prospect Street as far as Bank Street before noon, and I will bring back my notebook."

"Fine," Russell said. "I will take care of the houses east of Charity Street as far as the Old North Road. That should give us a fairly complete picture of what is happening." He drew a sheet of paper toward him and took out his writing equipment. As he selected a nib and began to trim it, he said, "I think that you ought to plan to ride out for about a mile in every direction, just to be certain that we haven't overlooked anyone. If you find any cases of flux, you tell me and you bring the names and a report on their condition back to me at once. With any luck, we should have enough information to give Doctor Clayton tomorrow, one way or the other." He opened the standish and inked the quill. "I want to be able to tell the Mayor, the Town Council and the Doctor what the current conditions are no later than noon tomorrow."

"If you wish," said Guerra heavily. "May I go to Sagrada Caridad, to ask for the Padre's blessing before I do this? I do not want to have the flux, and if the Padre gives me his blessing, perhaps God will protect me." He crossed himself and watched Russell.

"If having the Padre's blessing will help you, by all means get it. Take Confession, too, if you must, but I need the work done and it must be done soon, for there are plans to be made." He said nothing more, giving his attention to his writing.

"Is that your report?" asked Guerra.

"No," said Russell distantly, "it is my various plans for ways to deal with emergencies. I should have attended to this months ago. I started to and then did not continue." He examined the last line he had written. "I've been lax."

"Emergency plans?" Guerra inquired. "But what is there to plan for?"

"Everything," said Russell. "Fire, flood, avalanche, bad food, sickness, all the disasters that surround us. You think that it cannot happen, but if it does, you must be prepared."

"Do you think those terrible things will happen?" asked Guerra with dismay.

"I hope they will not," said Russell. "But Luis, consider what might occur if we were not prepared, for we are the ones who are supposed to provide aid and direction during a difficult time. The townspeople expect us to help them. It's part of the work we do." He hesitated, recalling the times when his best efforts had proved futile. When he spoke again, his voice was different, deeper than before, and tired. "There are more than four hundred people living within five miles of the center of town—the figure is close to five hundred, actually—and they are all vulnerable." He went back to his writing. "I want to present a set of contingency plans to the Town Council no matter what the outcome is in regard to the flux."

"What if it is the flux—what then?" asked Guerra.

"If the flux comes from the wells, then I doubt the town could survive it, either from the water itself or from the response of others moving into the area. No one wishes to live where the water is unsafe, no matter how tempting other aspects of the place are. There will be more settlers soon, if the Mexicans agree to President Polk's proposals. Once that question is settled, then there will be more settlers than you or I ever imagined, and the increase in population we have now will seem paltry."

Guerra scoffed, but wisely said nothing.

"I also would like you, while you are out calling at the houses, to find out if there is any news about Mayhew. This is not a time for us to be caught off-guard." Russell finished his writing and poured fine sand on the ink to fix and dry it. "Well, it is a start," he said.

"How am I to find out about Mayhew?" Guerra asked, his tone sarcastic; he had one hand braced against the gun belt he carried so that he gave the impression of arrogance and a subtle threat. "Do you want me to ask them directly?"

Russell had risen and was reaching for his coat. "Of course not. Use a little sense. Tell them that you are curious about any information they might have concerning the town—do they know of those who are in need, or those who might be in danger. If you ask too directly, they will tell you nothing. Remember you must be polite and express your appreciation at every opportunity." He pulled his coat on. "I want you back here at one in the afternoon, and again by four. Is that understood?"

"If that's what you want," said Guerra, "then it will be done. Have I not given my word to serve you?"

"I don't know," said Russell softly as his deputy slammed out the door.

"Well, Henry, there are a possible nine cases of flux in town, if you put the boundaries at one mile from Spring and Charity Streets," Russell informed the doctor that evening as they met for supper.

"Only nine; are you certain?" Clayton looked a little less drawn than he had the evening before, but he was not wholly himself yet. "Have you checked everywhere? Have you spoken with Padre Antonio and Preacher Cauliffe?"

"Guerra and I have checked the town and that is what we have found. Neither Padre Antonio nor Reverend Cauliffe said anything to make me suspect that there were unadmitted cases. Lorinda Dooley also said that she has seen only one possible case of flux; she's more concerned about sore throats and possible consumption. If there are other cases, those who knew of them lied." Russell saw Frau Schmidt signal him to take his usual place at one of the tables. "I'm making a full report, both for you and for the Town Council. I think that it would be best if you spoke to all those where we have found flux and determine how severe the trouble is. How are you coming with the piglets, by the way?"

The two men seated themselves at the table and Clayton propped his elbows on the tablecloth, his expression still more hopeless than not. "I don't know what to say, Jason. I want to believe you—Heaven above, I want that!—but I am worried that we might overlook something obvious and—"

"I think that's already been done," Russell cut in, and gave a quick sign to Clayton to be silent as Dorabelle Schmidt approached.

"What do you mean?" Clayton demanded.

"In a moment, Henry," said Russell. "How good to see you this evening, Widow Schmidt."

"And you, Sheriff; Doctor. We have venison this evening, nothing very different, and there are potatoes cooked with bacon. I wish I had something better, but the way things are going, my cupboards could be bare by spring if I do not conserve now." She wagged her finger at Russell. "You will have to find your coffee elsewhere until Smilin' Jack returns," she told him.

"I thought Smilin' Jack was planning to winter here," said Clayton.

"He still intends to, but he decided to make one more trip," she said severely. "Now, with more snow falling and the worst yet to come, who knows if he will be able to make it back here? And if he does not, we will have to scramble for food before spring."

"What about the farms?" Russell said. "There is a dairy and both a sheep and pig farm in town. There are ways to arrange for meat, if you must."

"And what happens when I run out of flour?" she asked as she came nearer the table. "What happens when the winter is so hard that we cannot get through the snow to pick the wild lettuce?" She put a hand to her waist. "We will all be thinner come spring."

"And so will the rest of the animals," said Clayton. He cleared his throat. "Tell me, have you any soup?"

"Sun made a heavy broth from chickens and rabbits," she said guardedly. "We added some dried peas and onions. Sun wants to use the broth as a stock for other soups. He's an ingenious devil in the kitchen, no doubt about it."

"Bring us both some. Soup is warming and it fills the body." Clayton watched Frau Schmidt make her way to the kitchen. "She's damned sensible for a woman. If worse comes to worst, then I hope she'll be willing to help us out."

"You keep anticipating disaster," said Russell without much feeling in his voice.

"I can't help it," Clayton said. "I think I want to consider all the dreadful things I can and then I want to make myself get used to them. Otherwise I will not be able to face them and—" His face darkened and he looked away.

"You mean the opium?" said Russell in a level voice. "It is up to you, to use it or not."

Clayton swung around so that his face was less than a foot from the Sheriff's. "You don't know what it is to have that hunger, Sheriff. You don't know what the pain is like, or the longing, or the need. You haven't any idea. No one can who has not been in that particular hell. There is nothing in the imagination that permits you to know." His words were little more than a whisper, but their force was tremendous.

"You don't have to succumb to it, Henry," said Russell when Clayton was silent.

His laugh was cold and mirthless. "That is like telling a man with his foot in a trap that he need not break his leg. It has already happened, Sheriff. It happened in China. Oh, I can resist the damned stuff so long as I cannot get my hands on any. But as soon as there is opium within my grasp, then I am worse than any Lotus-Eater in Homer." He leaned back in the chair. "So I make myself realize that the world is a dangerous place and that those in my care need what I can do. That way the longing is not as fierce as it is at other times, and I can almost bring myself to believe that I will not fail this time; that I will be able to do what must be done without giving way to that gnawing desire."

"You've withstood the need before," Russell said.

"I've also been locked in my room and left to scream," said Clayton bluntly. He would have gone on, but Frau Schmidt returned with a tureen in her mittened hands.

"Here is your soup. I will bring bread, and then some of the venison Sun has prepared." She deposited the tureen between them as if showing one of the lesser Crown Jewels. "Whatever else we may run short of, there is an excellent chance that we will have soup through the winter."

"That's encouraging," said Russell, sniffing the delicious steam that escaped from its porcelain prison.

"I will bring your soup plates directly," said Frau Schmidt as she looked around the dining room. There were now six men seated at various tables, and the sounds from the kitchen were growing louder.

"At your convenience," said Russell. He gave his attention back to Henry Clayton. "Well? What do you think now?"

"Let me see how the piglets do," Clayton answered, deliberately shifting the subject. "If they show no signs of flux, then we know that the wells are safe for the time being."

"What about the first notion—that the Kinsmans ate tainted food? Couldn't it be that the other cases of flux came from the same food? One of the foods got in tins at the general store, or bought from someone in the town?" He waited while Frau Schmidt deposited the wide, deep soup plates in front of him and Clayton. "That isn't out of the question, is it?"

Clayton lifted the lid of the tureen. "No, it isn't impossible, but . . ." The rest of his thoughts deserted him as he ladeled out a generous portion for himself.

"After supper, Henry, we must discuss this." Russell was mildly amused to see the transformation in Clayton.

"If that is what you wish," said Clayton.

"It's necessary, Henry. For all of us."

Padre Antonio was waiting at the jail when Russell arrived there the next morning. "May I have a word with you, Sheriff?"

"Certainly," said Russell as he unlocked the door. "Let me build up the fire and then we can talk." He indicated the priest should come into the office with him.

"I was sent word this morning," he announced gravely.

"What is it?" Russell asked as he opened the stove door and inspected the embers from the night before. He added a judicious handful of kindling before shoving three sections of log in the door.

"Word was brought from the Rancho of Don Maximillian."

Russell stood up, the cold that touched him having nothing to do with the room. "And?"

"I am sorry to inform you that Don Maximillian died last night, sometime around two in the morning. He refused to have his leg amputated and so . . ." He crossed himself and murmured a brief prayer. "We have been asked to offer Masses for the repose of his soul."

"What does this do in terms of the Rancho? Who owns it now?"

"Donna Elvira is his only child. I do not know if she was made his heir. It is more likely that her husband will inherit the Rancho, assuming your government permits anyone to own any part of it, of course." He did his best to keep the bitterness out of his voice, but with little success.

"The government of the United States is not actually my government, not yet. I am a citizen of Britain and a subject of Her Majesty Queen Victoria." He saw puzzlement on Padre Antonio's features and he smiled. "I thought you knew that."

"How can you be Sheriff here and not a citizen?" demanded Padre Antonio.

"You are a citizen of Mexico," Russell pointed out. "Or of the Republic of Texas, or the United States, depending on how you see yourself in these uncertain times." He moved a step away from the stove now that the logs had started to burn.

"I was born here," Padre Antonio stated, as if that answered all questions.

"Most of the people in this town were not. Many of them were born in Europe. Sun Fan-Li was born in China. It is a pattern of things to come, I think." Russell held out one of two extra chairs. "Sit down, Padre. I have to ask you a few more questions and I'd appreciate a little of your time."

"If you insist." Reluctantly the priest did as he was bid.

"Assuming that the Rancho will remain intact, what will become of those who work there? Don Maximillian employed many men and women; are they expected to continue on, or will they have to find employment elsewhere?"

Padre Antonio shrugged his helplessness. "I do not know, Sheriff. Perhaps they will remain. That is what has been done before, but . . . as you say, the times are unsettled."

"If they do not remain at the Rancho, what then?" Russell asked as he took his seat at his desk. The room was getting warmer and he ventured to open his coat.

"I . . . I do not know, Señor Russell," Padre Antonio admitted. "It is not certain that—" He left off.

"Very well; we will have to deal with these things as the need becomes apparent." He regarded the priest evenly. "I hope you will consider me your friend and will let me know when you learn more of Don Maximillian's Rancho."

"The Requiem will be at San Esteban and he will be buried at the Rancho. There is a family . . . what do you call it?" He made a cabin with his hands.

"A vault, perhaps?" Russell suggested, remembering the graveyard that adjoined his father's country estate. He had seen it only twice and both times his father had apologized that it would not be possible for his son Jason to be buried there.

"Yes; a vault. That is if it is permitted." Again the bitterness came into his eyes.

"Why wouldn't it be?" Russell asked. "I should think that no one would object." He paused. "Would you like me to inform the Town Council of Don Maximillian's death? I will do it if you would prefer it."

"Yes, if you don't mind." Padre Antonio gave a little shake to his head. "What of the flux? Must we prepare for the worst?"

"I don't think so, not at this time," said Russell, relief giving his tone a heartiness that was missing before. "There is flux in the town but not many cases and certainly not the number that Doctor Clayton feared there might be."

"Gracias al Dios," said Padre Antonio, blessing himself.

"I would appreciate it if you would inquire of Don Maximillian's physician if he has seen any cases of flux, or any other epidemic disease, for that matter. If we were not so isolated we would learn more, but given where we are . . ." He opened his hands on the desk. "I hope that Smilin' Jack will be able to give me a report of other towns when he returns."

"I will pray he has a safe journey. I have been told that the snow is deeper than usual for this time of year, and that could mean he will not be able to return." He stood up rather abruptly. "I must return to my church," he said with decision.

"Thank you for bringing me this sad news. Please convey my sympathies to his . . . dependents." Russell was about to put his mind to his report to the Town Council when Padre Antonio interrupted his thoughts.

"The Dooley child," he said from the door. "We believe she has consumption and if that is the case we cannot let her remain with the other children. I will speak to Doctor Clayton today, and will ask his suggestions."

"Consumption?" Russell said in disbelief. "I thought she had a putrid sore throat."

"Yes, and an inflammation of the lungs. But now she has the fever and the spots of color on her cheeks and she is getting thinner every day. We pray for her, but God has not restored her and we must revert to those devices given to us in this world."

"Poor child," said Russell. "Have you spoken to her mother yet?"

"No; we thought it best to address Doctor Clayton first, since we do not wish to give alarm where it is not necessary. Sister Mercedes' mother died of consumption, and she is almost certain that the girl has it." He lowered his head. "I will keep you informed of her condition as well, Sheriff."

"Thank you, Padre," said Russell, and when the priest had left permitted himself the luxury of a dispairing sigh.

Luis Guerra was short-tempered from cold and fatigue. He entered the bar at the hotel and shouted for hot wine before he had his gloves off his hands.

"You wait your turn," ordered Frederick Fletcher from his place at the bar. "They don't serve the likes of you before me."

"Because you are the son of the Mayor," growled the deputy as he took the stool at the far end of the bar from where Frederick sat.

"Because I am a white man," Frederick corrected him.

"And I am not?" Guerra demanded.

"God knows what you are," Frederick said in mockery. "Indian, Moor, the rest of the bastard races of Spain and Mexico." He grinned evilly. "Well?"

"You speak from ignorance," said Guerra, doing his best to hold his temper; he had given his word to the Sheriff that he would not permit insults and jibes to provoke him. Until now the order had not been difficult to follow, but he found that he could not endure the deliberate contempt of the Mayor's second son. "I want hot wine," he told the barman, not looking at Frederick.

"Don't serve him." Frederick reached out and grabbed the barman by the shoulder. "You serve him and I'll see you fired."

"Leave off, Mister Frederick," said the barman. "I got my work to do."

"Not if it means serving that Mexican half-breed." He glared at the deputy. "Fine thing, the Sheriff giving his trust to a man like that. If my father had been asked, he would have refused to allow—"

"Frederick," said Russell from the door between the lobby and the bar, "if you do not hold your tongue, I will take you by the ear and escort you home."

Frederick grew more flushed than he already was. "I don't have to listen to you, Sheriff. You work for my father, and you wouldn't dare use me that way."

"I work for the Town Council," Russell corrected him mildly. "And I will do precisely what I am mandated to do, which is keep the peace, among other things." He stepped into the bar and was about to position himself between Frederick and Guerra when another man ambled into the bar.

"Don't fash yourself over the Sheriff, Freddie," said the man who called himself Eugene Randolph Exeter. "We've got places to go and things to do." He winked at Frederick before he turned to Russell.

"He's let that Mexican in here," Frederick whined.

"Then we will not remain," said Exeter, watching Russell carefully. "How are your inquiries coming, Sheriff? Have you found out anything to my discredit?"

"Until the post arrives there is little chance of that; but don't think that means I'll be hoodwinked. That boy is half flash and half foolish, and if I find that you've been playing at foxes and drakes with him, it will be the worse for you."

Exeter achieved a smile, but it went no further than his mouth. "Fine talk, Mister Runner, but that means nothing here."

"Press me, and we'll test that," said Russell with false amiability. "In the meantime, Exeter-or-whatever-your-name-is, I expect you to proceed with caution. Is that understood?"

"Gracious, a Runner making threats," marveled Exeter. "Come on, Freddie. Let's get out of here." He took Frederick by the elbow. "I'll see to it that the lad gets home, Sheriff. No need to worry yourself about him." There was an unmistakeable Cockney twang under the upper-class accent Exeter affected, and it was stronger than usual now.

Frederick lurched off the stool. "You're right, Randolph. No reason for us to stay here with stinking Mexicans and my father's hired hand."

"Come along, laddie," said Exeter as he led Frederick into the lobby. "Get your coat."

"They'll tell his father that you couldn't handle the situation and that Exeter was the one who could," said the barman with feeling.

"They might be right," Russell said. "If keeping Frederick from getting into a fight with my deputy is what matters."

"But it isn't true," the barman protested.

"As far as it goes, it is," Russell corrected him, then turned to Guerra. "You did well, Luis. I'm grateful to you for keeping control of yourself. You managed far better than Frederick did."

"He is a foolish child," Guerra said with a trace of bravado.

"Still," Russell told him. "You did well and I want you to know that."

The barman brought out a warm mug and filled it with honied red wine from an earthenware jug. "Sorry to take so long getting this, but—"

Guerra accepted the mug and drank. "Hot wine is a gift from God." He took another long draught. "This wine is from Mexico, isn't it?"

"That's the only place we can get it from readily; the vineyards around Santa Fe are more for the Church than for sale to ordinary people." The barman looked at Russell. "What can I get for you, Sheriff?"

"Me?" Russell came out of his reverie. "Oh, brandy if you have any left." He stared into space as the barman poured out a generous tot for him.

"What is it, Sheriff?" asked Guerra, puzzled by the Sheriff's distraction.

"Where did a Cockney learn a Scots word like fash, I wonder?" Russell said as he lifted his glass of brandy.

13

Smilin' Jack was hollow-eyed and grim when he finally struggled into town at the back of a four-day blizzard. He went to the hotel after leaving his saddle at Calvin's Livery Stable. Seeing how worn he was, Dorabelle Schmidt gave orders to heat bath water for him and to prepare a hot meal.

"My horse broke his leg about ten miles back," Smilin' Jack reported that evening when he had recovered a bit. "I shot him, poor old devil, and came on."

"Ten miles on foot in this snow?" exclaimed Frau Schmidt.

"It was that or freeze," said Smilin' Jack without a trace of humor.

"How could you do that?" she asked, her face creased with worry and dismay.

"Because I had to," said Smilin' Jack, his tone cutting short further inquiry on her part.

"I think I will send Sun for the Sheriff," said Frau Schmidt as she got up from the table.

"Good; I want to talk to him. Is he at the jail?" He had finished off two large plates of soup and was working on a third.

"I'm not sure," she said. "I will send Sun to look for him."

"You tell the Chinaman to wrap up warm. The temperature's been falling all afternoon. Now that the sun's down, it's bitter out there." He helped himself to another slice of bread. "I do appreciate the food, Missus Schmidt, and that's the Lord's own truth."

"You looked so dreadful when you got here," she said, clapping her hands loudly. "Sun Fan-Li! Come here!"

There was a loud noise from the kitchen as if two large pots had been deliberately banged together. A moment later Sun came into the dining room, scowling fiercely. "What is it?"

"I want you to find the Sheriff and bring him here. Tell him that Smilin' Jack has returned and that he has mail for him." She made a shooing gesture with her large, square hands. "Go on. Get to it."

Sun bowed. "When do you wish me to serve supper, dear lady?"

"When you get back, of course," she said, undaunted by the tone Sun had taken. "It's not as if there's anything else happening in the town tonight."

"Of course, dear lady," said Sun, moving to carry out her orders.

"Aren't you being a little hard on him?" Smilin' Jack asked sarcastically.

Frau Schmidt took up his tone. "Oh, certainly. He has to be kept in line, you know." She indicated the room. "And we're so full here."

"You're fuller this winter than last," said Smilin' Jack. "You know, they say that the war with Mexico will be over by next summer and all this land, all the way to the Pacific, will be part of the United States territories." He shook his head. "Who'd've thought that Polk could pull it off. Not that he isn't feisty as a Bantam cock. Begging your pardon."

"I know the word. In Germany we are not so prissy in our words." She got up. "The Sheriff will be here shortly and then you can speak together. I will not interrupt you, and you need not worry about others listening; I will make sure that does not happen."

"Thank you," said Smilin' Jack, setting to work on his soup once more.

While Barton Purvis read the report and recommendations, the other two members of the Town Council shook their heads in amazement.

"Volunteers to fight fires as well as a lookout station—Sheriff, do you know what an imposition that would be?" Hosea Olfrant demanded.

"I know that a fire would be a greater imposition. And I think that hiring a schoolmaster is essential, since you have decided that a schoolhouse must be built." Russell did not appear to be disturbed by the indignation in Olfrant's face, nor by the slow shaking of heads from the other two Councilmembers. "I also think that it would be wise to call a Town Meeting to discuss what must be done. We've had a close call with the tainted food, and it's time—"

"Now wait a minute, Sheriff," said the Mayor. "There's no proof that it was tainted food that caused the flux."

"What else could it be? That's why I have included a request for an inventory of all foodstuffs in the general store to make sure that everything in cans and jars is safe." He rocked back on his heels. "Gentlemen, there is no reason to think that it cannot happen again. We must take precautions now or regret it later."

"You enjoy finding these items to frighten us, don't you, Sheriff?" said Purvis after he had been handed a note from the Mayor.

"Not particularly, no," Russell said in his unruffled way. "I am pleased we have averted the danger of flux, but I know it could happen. Doctor Clayton said that the piglets were all fine after drinking water from the town wells, but suppose that had not been the case? Suppose we had discovered that one or more of the wells was no longer . . . wholesome? What would you do in order to protect the people of this town?"

"It hasn't come to that," Mayor Fletcher said sullenly. "You are an alarmist, Sheriff."

"That is what you pay me to be," Russell reminded them. "And if I am to continue to serve you, I will have to alarm you again from time to time."

Olfrant looked over the neatly written pages the Sheriff had submitted. "You say that Doctor Clayton has read these?"

"Yes, he has," said Russell. "He is more than willing to discuss them with you."

"Even the suggestion that we advertise for a dentist for the town? What is the sense of that?" Mayor Fletcher inquired. "You seem to think that we are about to become a city instead of being an isolated town."

"I never said that. I have remarked that Charity is at a crossroads and therefore may expect more people passing through it as land opens up to the west of us." Russell looked at the three men. "You hired me when you realized that you needed more than a man or two to look after the town's safety. I am telling you that more is required."

"We'll consider it," Mayor Fletcher said in his loftiest manner. "And whatever our decision, you will abide by it."

"If you insist," said Russell.

"I notice also that you have copies of letters about Exeter that claim he has bilked other small towns of large sums of money," said Purvis. "Does that mean you believe he will do the same thing here?"

"He may try; he will not succeed," promised Russell.

"But this does not offer proof," said Mayor Fletcher with a critical lift to his bushy brows.

"Only because Exeter was not around to stand trial. I understand that the circuit judge has already received a brief on the man and that he is prepared to examine him when he holds court here in March." Russell looked around the room. "I know the man is your son's friend, Mayor Fletcher, but it doesn't change anything; he is a trickster and a criminal—"

"Come, come," said Olfrant.

"There can be no doubt of that," Purvis said heavily. "If only we had had some warning."

"I did warn you," Russell pointed out. "You chose to ignore what I said. Now you must see that I had good reason for my suspicions. I request your permission to detain Exeter for the circuit judge. There are already warrants outstanding for his arrest and there is no reason to refuse me."

Mayor Fletcher took a deep, unhappy breath. "All right, Sheriff; you must do your duty since you took an oath."

"Which you administered," Russell said kindly. "And which your Town Council witnessed."

"I realize that," Mayor Fletcher said. "Very well, arrest that unfortunate young man. I only hope it will not prove to be as . . . as dreadful as I am afraid it might."

"Your son?" Russell guessed.

"Frederick has been . . . friendly with Exeter."

Russell hesitated; he had anticipated this moment with worry and now that it had arrived, he found it difficult to speak. He chose his words with care, trying not to be too blunt. "According to the information I have received, the man's name is Fiske. I'm afraid that he has used a number of aliases in the last few years. And he has bilked others—individuals and communities as well—of a great deal of money."

"Yes, yes. You warned me of the possibility and I knew how it might be. I must take responsibility for not acting until now," said Mayor Fletcher impatiently. "Of course you are correct in enforcing the law. You will have to make allowances for my position, not as Mayor but as a father." He looked at the other two members of the Town Council. "I do not know what to tell you, gentlemen. I wish I had some words of consolation to offer."

"Because we were rooked right and proper," said Purvis after an awkward silence. "And we were. The Sheriff has been very restrained, because he warned us at first."

"I also permitted myself to be distracted by other concerns," Russell said. "You are not alone in . . . laxness."

"Distractions such as the possibility of epidemic disease," Mayor Fletcher agreed. "A more serious problem than one trickster, which is very much to the point." He met Russell's gaze directly. "What do you require of me, Sheriff? Must I sign anything or . . ."

"I have copies of warrants from other towns, and a formal request for detention from the Army. It isn't necessary, but it would be easier if you would give me some form of authorization to act on these warrants. That way there can be no question of authority." Russell looked at the other two Councilmembers. "If you want to act in concert, I'm sure it would be possible." He had intended to soften the blow to the Mayor by this suggestion, but Barton Purvis bristled.

"You are persecuting that young man."

"No," Russell said with alacrity. "I simply hoped to spare any one of you the painful task of—"

"Quite right," said Olfrant. "It is proper that the Council empower the Sheriff." He straightened up. "I think that we will have what you want by this evening, Sheriff, if you wish to put it to use then."

"Thank you," said Russell with misgivings.

Frederick Fletcher faced Russell with an expression between defiance and conciliation on his face. "I didn't break the law."

"You did, you know," Russell said, leaning back in his chair and regarding Frederick in a manner that appeared disinterested. "Technically you can be viewed as one aiding a criminal to profit from his criminality and to escape the legal consequences of his acts. Knowingly giving aid to those breaking the law is considered shared responsibility and culpability. Would you care to tell me why you decided to warn Fiske?"

"Who's Fiske?" Frederick asked, a bit too innocently.

"Your friend Exeter, as you undoubtedly are aware since you have obviously read the documents your father had in his possession." Russell folded his hands and braced them on the table. "What *are* we going to do with you, Frederick."

"What do you mean?" Frederick demanded as his face darkened.

"I mean—as you have surmised—that your antics have gone beyond the irritating and have become actionable. You have assumed that your position as the Mayor's son has conferred immunity on you. That, certainly, would be understandable if you were a child or if this town were still as small as it was three years ago, but you are no longer so young that you can be excused your irresponsibility, nor is Charity the fief of the Fletchers. It never was. Frederick, you have embarrassed your father by your actions: do you understand that?"

"My father is easily embarrassed," Frederick said, sulking.

"That is because he is Mayor here and his bank is the only major institution in this town that has regular dealings with cities and institutions outside of Charity. That imposes a heavy obligation as well as a degree of earned privilege. What happens within his family must reflect on him, either to his credit or detriment, and this escapade of yours is no exception." He stood up and looked stonily at Frederick. "I have your father's permission to detain you, which I would do with or without it."

"Detain?" repeated Frederick, his face paling.

"Yes; I am about to put you in a cell and keep you there for a few days while I decide how best to handle this lamentable situation." Russell's right hand closed around his baton in its holster.

"You can't do that. My father won't allow it." There was more bluster than passion in Frederick's objection.

"He will, you know," Russell said. "And he will not rescue you, no matter what you think."

"I'm his son," Frederick insisted, his voice rising to a childish treble.

"All the more reason for you to be ashamed of what you have done. You have convinced yourself—haven't you?—that you were being a loyal friend, but all you were doing when you warned Fiske was defying your father and me. You want to show that you are above us."

"Don't be ridiculous!" Frederick intended this to be the confident statement of a gentleman and instead he sounded like a petulant boy.

"Come, Frederick." He took the young man by the arm.

"Let go of me!" Frederick yelled and attempted to pull away from Russell's grasp.

His hand tightened; Russell moved quickly and efficiently. "If it is necessary, I will use this," he said, holding his baton up. "I would rather not."

"You wouldn't dare," Frederick said, shocked at the change that enveloped him.

"There is no question of daring," said Russell as he pulled Frederick around. "If you insist on violence, you will have it." He had opened the door to the cells, and one of the barred doors stood open. "This cell is nearest the stove. You will be as warm as it is possible to be in this jail."

"You won't lock me up," Frederick yelled.

Russell shoved the young man into the cell and closed the door. "It's done, Frederick," he said as he turned the key. "I have already told your father that I would do this."

"He won't permit it." Frederick's countenance had turned from flushed to pale. He grabbed the bars with such force that his knuckles were taut and white.

"He already has," said Russell. "And he will rely on my judgment where you are concerned, since he is aware that he does not always maintain the perspective he ought where you are involved. You see, he is not as mesmerized by you as you think he is, and he is not as completely blind to your faults as you believe he ought to be."

"My mother will—" Frederick began.

"Your mother has no role in this, unless she wishes to provide you with supper. Sun Fan-Li prepares food for the jail, but if you prefer other arrangements . . ." He had his baton back in its holster and he was moving toward the door. "If we are lucky, my deputy will discover which way your friend Fiske has gone and perhaps that will aid us in capturing him."

Frederick tried to laugh, but his bravado failed and his voice cracked.

Lorinda Dooley looked miserably at Padre Antonio, then faced Russell across the tiny Lady Chapel at Sagrada Caridad. "They told me I was not to say anything," she began.

"Lorinda," Padre Antonio admonished her.

"I don't mean that the way it sounds," she went on to Russell, all the while glancing uneasily at the priest. "I didn't want to help them, really I didn't, but . . ."

"This is not something you can excuse," Padre Antonio said, his tone growing more stern. "You have endangered your body and your soul by what you have done."

"Father . . ." Lorinda Dooley said, looking as if she were about to cry.

"I'm sure you can tell me without exposing yourself," Russell said quickly, for he sensed that Lorinda was about to panic. He continued in a deliberately low and soothing voice, as if he were speaking to a frightened horse. "I don't want to see you harmed in any way for what you offer me."

Padre Antonio glowered at Russell. "She has an obligation to her faith and her soul," he said, his eyes dark and inflexible.

"She also has a right to defend herself, and nothing will change that. You have your responsibilities in this, Father, but I have mine as well." Russell stared hard at Padre Antonio. "You must do as your office dictates; I don't deny that. But I have my tasks to attend to as well, and I will do as I must."

"So must we all," said the priest as he crossed himself. "I do not want to see anyone harmed," he went on, more to Lorinda than to Russell. "But harm can be done in many ways. You have told me, my daughter, that you have heard things that can bring great danger not only to you and the . . . the women who work at your house, but to the rest of the community."

"I . . . I did not mean to . . . to . . ." Lorinda broke off as she began to cry. "I was terrified, Sheriff. I didn't know what to do. They said they'd kill me and all the girls at the house if I said anything. They told me they'd find out. If I hadn't confessed to Padre Antonio, I wouldn't have . . . He told me that I had to speak or there could be no forgiveness of my sin, because I was responsible for the consequences of my silence." Tears welled in her eyes and ran down her face, leaving tracks of kohl on her cheeks. "I didn't want to speak. You have to understand that. I wanted to remain silent, and if anyone asks, then I will tell them that if it weren't for my priest, I would not have spoken."

"What happened?" Russell asked, too puzzled to be angry at the distraught woman.

"Three men came to my house last week. They stayed for two days, and they . . . amused themselves." As she said the last she glanced once at Padre Antonio. "They said they had not had women for months."

"They were demanding?" Russell said.

"That was part of it." She rolled up the sleeve of her dark serge dress that she wore to church. There were bruises, slate and purple and green, marking her flesh. "I have others," she said candidly. "Padre Antonio has said that Doctor Clayton ought to examine them."

"I insist that he do so," Padre Antonio interjected.

Russell nodded. "I'm sorry to have to put you through this, Miss Dooley, but it would be best if I knew the full extent of what was done. You may tell the Doctor, and he will file a report with me. I don't want to cause you any more discomfort."

"Two of my girls did worse than I. One of them is in bed. I wanted to have the Doctor come see her; I'm afraid she has broken ribs. But she refused. What could I do?"

"If she were Catholic, I would speak to her, admonish her to come forth," said Padre Antonio.

"Miss Dooley," said Russell, doing his best to ignore the determined speech of the priest, "if one of your girls is hurt, you have only to tell me. I know that there are those who do not believe that women who work as you do deserve anything more than what is given out to you, but . . . that is not my opinion. If a woman is to be an outcast because she has carnal knowledge of a man not her husband, then my mother would be among the outcasts. I will not punish you if I have any choice in the matter."

Padre Antonio gave a shocked sigh. "La madre."

"You're kind to say that to me, Sheriff," Lorinda told him; she plainly did not believe what he had said about his mother, but something in his manner had reassured her. "I will ask her to see Doctor Clayton. I've done it before, but I'll try again."

"Good," said Russell. "Now, who were the men who used you so cruelly?"

"Men who ride with Coffin Mayhew," she said, her attitude now resigned. "They came in late and while they were at the house no one was permitted to leave. There was one other . . . caller, and he was ordered out by the men as soon as they crossed the threshold. Then they put money on the table—fifty dollars, and I can't afford to turn that down—and said that the whole house was theirs for the next three days."

"I see," said Russell, saddened that he did.

"I didn't know they were going to hurt anyone," Lorinda went on. "I thought they'd just . . . do what men do to women, and then leave."

"But it was worse than that?" Russell suggested.

Lorinda nodded.

"She confessed to many things. I cannot break the seal of Confession, but if it were permitted, what I would say would shock you," Padre Antonio exclaimed. "I have heard many things, as priests do, but—"

"I'm not asking you to break the seal of Confession," said Russell gently, for he knew that what the priest was saying distressed Lorinda Dooley. "If Miss Dooley or any of her . . . associates wish to speak out, I will hear their complaints. If they do not, there is nothing I can do—or would want to do—to compel them to be specific in their accusations."

"I wish I could tell you more," Lorinda said. "But they promised to do worse to us. I know they would. They would use any excuse to come back and . . . hurt us again." She clasped her hands together, more in distress than supplication. "If it were just me, I wouldn't care. What's the point of it? But there are others, and . . . I owe them something, don't I?"

Russell did not touch her, but his eyes softened. "You are a very brave woman, Miss Dooley. I want you to know that I admire you for that. And I will do everything I can to see you are protected from the men who hurt you."

"They were Mayhew's men. You know what they're like," said Lorinda, her manner more resigned than before. When she lifted her hand, it trembled, and this shamed her. She tossed her head in a show of defiance. "Mayhew won't stop them doing anything they want to do. Mayhew'd like it."

"You will have to resist them if they come back, for your own sakes if for nothing else. You cannot let them simply . . . *use* you. You're worth more than that," said Russell. "Send one of the girls for me. Day or night, it makes no difference, I will come and stop them."

"You can't," Lorinda sighed. "They won't be stopped."

"Oh yes they will," said Russell. "I might be over forty, Miss Dooley, and it may be that you have rarely seen me carry a pistol or rifle, but don't be misled: if I must deal with violent men, I am more than able to handle them. And myself," he added softly. He felt concern for her, and a curious sympathy for her assumption that she could expect nothing from the town.

"Sheriff, I—" She did not go on. "What's the use of it? Why would you bother?"

"Because I am sworn to protect this town and everyone who lives in it —everyone, Miss Dooley, not just those who have money and position." Russell made a quick sign to the priest and was relieved that Padre Antonio stepped back, though he clearly did not approve, giving them a bit more privacy. "If you or your girls are in danger, then I will do as much to protect you as I would do for the Fletchers."

Her laughter was brief and sad. "Thanks for saying that, Sheriff."

"I'm perfectly sincere," Russell said, and saw the disbelief in her eyes, in the angle of her head. "Send for me. Please."

"I hope I won't have to," she said, making a concession to his request. Her words were soft, almost wistful, as if she could not accept his aid no matter how genuine his insistence.

"I share your hope," said Russell quickly. "But it is wise to be prepared, isn't it?"

"If you say so, then I suppose it is," she said to him, her attitude changing swiftly, pragmatically. "I have to get back. I told the girls I was going to church and they will wonder where I am. That wouldn't be good right now." She rose and looked around for Padre Antonio. "Thank you, Father. Pray for me."

"I pray for all sinners, my child," said Padre Antonio, and escorted Lorinda Dooley to the door.

Russell watched them go with a chill that had nothing to do with the winter wind.

14

Donna Elvira was dressed in black and her skin seemed more pale by comparison. "I am going to the Rancho," she announced to Russell as she stood in the office of the jail, her traveling cloak wrapped around her so that she seemed almost twice the size she was. "I intend to continue to run it."

"Fine," said Russell, uncertain of her reasons for telling him this.

"No matter what comes of the war the United States is waging with Mexico. It means nothing to me, that war. I do not care about the outcome. The land was my father's and now it is mine." She lifted her chin. "I will not give it up."

"I don't think anyone wants you to, no matter what happens," said Russell. "If nothing else you have a legitimate claim to homestead, and I, for one, will be glad to have you continue at the Rancho." He nodded toward Luis Guerra, who was doing his best to remain invisible. "My deputy and I will give you the same protection we offer anyone living within ten miles of Charity. If you do not object, of course."

"I will not object," Donna Elvira announced in a tone that suggested that she would accept help only if all other possibilities failed and she had run out of hope and money as well as power. She leaned forward, her fur muff resting on the edge of the desk. "I am going to speak to Mayor Fletcher. I will transfer the money my father left me to the bank here and that should please him." She touched the veil that covered her face as if to remind herself and the two men that she was still in mourning. "He and my father did not get along, but . . ."

"You are not your father," Russell finished for her. He studied her briefly. "I think that you might want to know that I have been going to the Rancho every ten days when the weather has allowed it to see that it was not falling into neglect. A few of the hands have left, and one of the household staff went to San Esteban, but other than that, the Rancho continues as it was. If you are worried about—"

"I am worried about nothing," Donna Elvira announced.

Russell decided to ignore the condemnation in her attitude. "It might be difficult at first, since you are alone, but if you have any trouble, please do not hesitate to send for me." He had been saying that a great deal in the last month, he realized, and briefly it troubled him. He put his concern out of his mind.

"It will not be necessary, but thank you. I wish you to know that I will maintain the Rancho as before." She turned on her heel and started toward the door.

"Donna Elvira," said Guerra from his place near the stove.

"Yes?" She was haughtier than ever.

"It is good you are back," murmured Guerra, whatever else had been on his mind disgarded in favor of this neutral remark.

"Excellent," she declared, and rushed out the door.

"That is one handful of a woman," Russell observed when the door was slammed shut.

"It is her breeding," Guerra said. "She is an aristocrat."

"My father was an aristocrat and he never behaved that way," said Russell before he picked up the stack of paper in front of him. He glanced over the report on the top of the stack, but his thoughts were still with Donna Elvira. "I wonder if she'll be able to stick it out."

"Certainly; it is in her blood." Guerra stood and stretched. "She will be here longer than you and I."

"Perhaps," said Russell.

"We found him late last night, back of the old barn," said Bess Mattington as she sat slumped in the largest of the lobby chairs. "He was frozen by that time—not that it wasn't a mercy, considering."

Russell took a deep breath. "How long had he been missing, do you know?"

"Well, he wasn't expected back for another two days and he had been gone for more than a week, riding the perimeter." She rubbed her face. "I don't know what I'm going to tell Arthur. He's likely to blame himself."

"You couldn't have known that he'd be . . . hurt," said Russell.

"We knew that Mayhew was around, and from the look of that boy, I'd say it was Mayhew got him." She started to cry in a quiet, heedless way. "Arthur's in Santa Fe. There's cattle for sale right now, and . . ."

Russell patted her shoulder. "I'll talk to your husband for you, if you like." He hated breaking such tragic news, but he sensed the pain it would cause Bess Mattington was far greater than his own. He could take the first denial and rage without sharing them, and for the Mattingtons this would be a kindness.

"He was with us from the first. We'd had two others, but one got the bending sickness and the other was crushed in a rock slide, more'n ten years ago. Ralston was all that was left for us from the start. Our daughters are married and they live away from here. Hiram was the one who . . ." She held her hands up as if to push away the knowledge of Ralston's death; her deep-set eyes were haunted.

"It wasn't your fault, Bess," said Russell. "You didn't send him out to die."

"I didn't stop him, either," she said indistinctly. "I could've sent one of the other hands, or sent two of them, but he wouldn't stand special treatment, said that he had to work like all the others." The lines in her face had deepened and she moved as if her body ached. Russell had seen this before, and, as always, he felt incapable of lessening the pain Bess Mattington endured.

"When Doctor Clayton finishes his examination, I'll make a full report," he said, knowing that this was an inadequate promise. "I'll make sure that other towns have the information, so that we can do something toward stopping Mayhew once and for all." He went on more gently. "I know that won't bring your friend back, Bess, but it might make you feel less like he was . . . wasted."

"He wasn't wasted, he was killed. He was butchered," she responded with sudden heat. "Those animals took him and tore him to bits. They peeled the skin off his hands and feet!"

"I know," Russell said as gently as he could.

"They didn't let him die easy, or clean. They made sure they ruined him first." She pounded the arms of the chair in futile protest. "They wouldn't even let him die quick. They had to drag it out. They had to make him sick with it, to harden his soul. You can tell that from how thin he was, and the way his face looked. He shouldn't have had to look like that when he died."

Russell had nothing he could offer in consolation. "I'll do everything I can to stop them."

"You better," Bess Mattington said in a low, fierce voice. "You make them suffer for what they did to him."

"I'll bring them to justice if I can," Russell told her.

"Justice!" She rounded on him, grief now made bitter with anger. "Justice isn't for the likes of them. They're mad beasts, and you shoot them. That's the only justice that will stop them, that they'll understand. Nothing else."

There were no soothing words that Russell could say. He put his hand on her shoulder once more and shook his head. As he got up, he signaled to Dorabelle Schmidt to come to Bess Mattington's aid. He hated the tremendous helplessness that engulfed him, the futility of comfort.

"You leave her to me, Sheriff," said Frau Schmidt. "You do not know what to tell her now, and she does not want to hear what you have to say."

Russell left the hotel and walked down Charity Street toward Henry Clayton's house. His hands were sunk deep in his pockets and his collar was turned up against the cold. As he went, he tried to kindle a sense of purpose in his heart. All that he found was impotent fury. It was useless to be so distressed; rage of this sort caused mistakes and poor judgment. If he intended to stop Mayhew, to bring him before the bench, he would have to restore clarity to his thoughts. He could not afford the terrible frustration that ate at him, for it was a greater danger than Mayhew would ever be.

"You look dreadful," said Henry Clayton as he opened the door to Russell's insistent knock.

"I feel worse than that," Russell admitted with chagrin.

"Because of the Mattington hand?" Clayton ushered Russell into his parlor.

"Yes," Russell admitted.

Clayton said nothing at first. He reached out his hand as if to pat Russell on the shoulder, but held back. "I wish I knew what to say."

"That poor family, to lose their friend that way," Russell said softly. "I don't know—"

"A terrible thing to happen," Clayton agreed. "I don't want to mention this to the Mattingtons, since it would distress them to no purpose, but I think it took at least three days for Ralston to die, and that's a horrible thing to have on your mind."

"It is," said Russell.

"I've gone over the body pretty carefully. The same kinds of wounds that we found on the Vreeland man were on Ralston. The man finally bled to death, but not at first, no, hardly then, but some time later, and not until most of what they did to him had been done. He was alive through most of it, poor devil." Clayton spoke calmly enough, but there was a glazed shine to his eyes, almost as if he had been smoking opium again. "I don't want to say anything more than I have to, Jason. I'll put all my finding in my report, but unless I have to give evidence in court, I don't want anyone to know what he went through." He put his hands together, as if he wanted to pray but had forgotten how.

Russell nodded.

"He's been dead about two days, near as I can figure. He's frozen, so it could be longer, but it certainly isn't apt to be less. Given the state of his fingers and toes, I'd say the most it could be is four days." He sat down abruptly, as if the weight of what he was saying was suddenly too great a burden.

"Two to four days," Russell repeated.

"Probably. It might be more, but . . ."

"But the fingers and toes make you think it was that long." Russell said this without feeling, as if he were talking about a load of wood. It was the only way he could bring himself to speak at all.

"It's torture, Jason, like something out of the Middle Ages. I've never seen anything like it, and I've autopsied a few atrocities in the past, but nothing so . . . methodical. It's as if Mayhew wants to find out how much punishment a body can take." He put his hand to his forehead and rubbed with determination.

"I see," Russell told the air. "I wonder if there are any others?" He did not want to know the answer to his question although it possessed him like a nightmare.

"How do you mean?" Clayton looked up sharply, his features still with distress.

"I mean, I wonder if Mayhew has found any other fellow out by himself, without anyone expecting him? I wonder if he has tried the same thing and worse on victims we haven't yet found." He walked the length of the room. "It isn't impossible, is it?"

"I suppose not," Clayton answered cautiously.

"It sickens me," Russell said.

Clayton was not able to answer at first, and when he did, his voice was strained, as if he had been ill for a long time. "I pray you're wrong, Jason. God, I wish you hadn't spoken of it at all."

"I understand that," Russell said steadily. "But I must consider it. If I don't, I might overlook . . ."

"Don't," said Clayton.

"Where is the body?" Russell had come back down the parlor and was standing a few feet from the Doctor's chair.

"In the back, in my surgery. It's cool in there, not that it matters." He got up awkwardly. "I suppose you ought to have a look at him."

"Yes," said Russell, and followed Clayton down the hall.

"I've warned you what to expect," Clayton said as he stood aside to admit Russell to the surgery. "It isn't easy to look at."

"I didn't think it would be," said Russell, moving toward the examining table where a figure lay draped in an old sheet.

"It's worse than the other one," Clayton pointed out as he drew back the cloth.

"Christ," muttered Russell as he looked at the devastation made of Terrance Ralston. "And he was alive while this was done? Are you certain?"

"I think he was dead when they cut off the . . . the genitals. I hope he was."

"How can anyone do this to another person," Russell whispered as he examined the gaping cuts that crisscrossed the boy's chest.

"I don't know. I don't want to know," Clayton said. "Have you seen enough?"

"More than enough," said Russell as he pulled the sheet over the face once more. "How much did Bess Mattington see of this, do you know?"

"He was partially clothed when they brought him in. She saw the face and arms and chest; possibly the back as well, though it's not as bad as the chest." He had to stop to swallow hard. "I doubt if she saw the rest."

"Good; that's something." Russell leaned back, his shoulders braced against the wall. He breathed deeply, fighting dizziness and nausea. "Make sure he's clothed when you bury him, or if you have to show him to anyone. I don't want the whole thing seen if there's any choice. Put it in your report and leave it at that."

"Yes." Clayton opened the door into the hall. "Let me get you a brandy."

"Please," said Russell as he left the surgery. Little as he wanted to admit it, he was badly shaken. He had seen enough of cruelty over the years to view it stoically. But the ferocity of the wounds on Ralston's body appalled him, and he had to force himself to assess what he had seen in a rational manner.

"Here," said Clayton, offering the Sheriff a glass of brandy. "Medicinal, believe me."

"I do," said Russell, and consumed half the glass in one draught. "I thank you for it."

"I'm . . . I'm in need of some of it myself," said Clayton as he poured a second glass. "I found myself, looking at that man, wishing I had opium. I wanted to lose myself in a dream and be lost to the world. I didn't want to have to look at the things that were done to Ralston. I treated him just last year for an infected tooth."

"You'll only distress yourself, remembering that," Russell said. Now that he had got away from the body, he was able to control his feelings with his usual discipline. "I can't watch you do this to yourself again."

"How do you mean?" Clayton asked, his voice careful and measured, as if he were preparing a medication.

"I have seen you in that dream, you will recall. You are my friend and I don't want to have to witness that . . . that state in you again. It's bad enough to have to see that man, but if I must watch you—"

Clayton put his glass aside. "Drink might do the same to me, one day. It gives a similar consolation." He gave a guilty hitch to his shoulders. "Not that this changes anything for Terrance Ralston, or anyone else that dies hard."

"No," Russell said slowly. "Nothing changes that."

By the middle of December, Charity was wrapped in a mantle of snow as impenetrable as glass, for all the travelers who came through the town. Families stayed indoors as much as possible and those who had to go out were garbed in heavy clothing that made movement difficult. January was no better—snowfall increased and there was a biting wind that drove the temperatures down lower than they had been before even as it whistled derisively at the houses huddled against the rise of the mountains.

"There's another body." Lorinda Dooley was pale as the snow and her eyes stared out of her face with an intensity that was so consuming that Russell worried for the state of her mind. She had taken the one visitor's chair in the Sheriff's office, her coat pulled tightly around her although the stove had warmed the room so that it was almost comfortable.

"Where?" He had risen from the chair behind his desk and was already coming toward her to offer her what little support he could provide.

"It was left in the woodshed. One of the Mayhew gang came back. He was armed, and he made two of the girls please him in . . . in terrible ways."

"I'm sorry," Russell said with abiding sincerity. He looked down at her. "You?"

"No; I was locked in the kitchen. We found the body when he left." She was shaking now, as if caught in the grip of fever. "I know he left it there to . . . warn us. He wanted us to know what he could do if he wanted to. If he came with Mayhew, it was what they *would* do." There was a cold certainty in her voice that could not be disputed.

"Did he threaten you with that?" Russell asked, his hand coming to rest on her arm.

"No. He did not threaten us at all. He said nothing. He did nothing other than . . . what you might expect him to do. He was determined to see us . . ." She sighed. "I don't know why I came here, but I was so worried about the body, and I couldn't think what else to do. I was going to tell Padre Antonio, but if the man wasn't Catholic, he might not want to . . . help."

"He is a priest. He is expected to help everyone," said Russell as reasonably as he could.

"But the man . . ." She stopped once more. "I ought to tell you where to find the body." Her voice was edged with panic and she fiddled with the huge buttons on her coat as automatically as she would have run Rosary beads through her fingers.

"You said in the woodshed," Russell reminded her.

"That's right," she said, seizing on the mundane words with gratitude that struck Russell as pitiful. "He was an old man, a man with a beard that was all matted with blood. There were deep cuts all over him."

"That would be Mayhew's doing," said Russell grimly. "Judging from the other two, it must be the same man doing the same thing."

"I suppose so," she said in a vague way. "It was the most horrible thing I've ever seen. I never knew that it would happen that way."

"How did you discover him?" Russell asked, trying to get Lorinda to move away from her fright. "What were you doing that you looked in the woodshed?"

After a moment she responded. "We needed wood. The house was getting cold, and we needed to heat it. There was no wood left inside," she said reasonably.

"But did you get the wood? Doesn't your cook usually get the wood? Why not this time? Or if—"

"She was afraid. Everyone was afraid. All the girls, my daughter, everyone." She shook her head. "I had to go. Someone had to, and it's my house. I didn't know that the body had been left, or I might not have gone myself." She laughed once, the sound so desolate that Russell felt his eyes sting.

"If you'll take me there, I'll claim it. I'll make sure that Doctor Clayton has it. He'll . . . he'll make a report, so that there will be a record of what was done."

"Oh, God," she whispered, and crossed herself.

"We must have that. For the court," said Russell. "I have reports of the first two already, and if this one is . . . similar, that will help build the case." He cleared his throat, finding the words hard to say. "I don't want to distress you. I don't want you to be afraid. We have to . . . evaluate what we find."

"You're the Sheriff. You're supposed to *do* something," she said, turning on him. "There's a *body* in my woodshed, a dead man. There must be some reason. You have to do something about it." Her eyes filled with tears. "You have to do something."

"I will," he promised her, although at that moment he was not sure what it would be. All the various plans that had suggested themselves to him had been stopped by the weather and the demands of the townspeople, who were all feeling the stress of remaining inside too long.

"They say that you've been a law enforcer for years. Why can't you stop Mayhew?" She met his eyes fearlessly. "What has to happen before you can stop Mayhew."

Russell lowered his head. "I have to find him. If I can find him, Miss Dooley, I can stop him. Because he will have to kill me to stop me."

Lorinda laughed again, this time wildly. "What makes you think that he won't? What makes you think that someone won't find you in a woodshed with the flesh cut off your chest and your arms, and the blood frozen in ropes along your ribs?"

It was a short moment before Russell could answer. "All right; perhaps that will happen to me. But I don't think it will. Because I have been enforcing the law for almost thirty years, and because I intend to stop this man. I am a very determined fellow, Miss Dooley, and I have one small advantage: he does not know about me. If he thinks about me at all, he probably assumes that I am yet another retired sergeant or a man with a gun paid to be tame. I was in Bow Street before I was twenty, and I have worked at my profession every year since then. I have learned a few things in that time, some of them that Mayhew won't be expecting. I will rely on that—on his tendency to underestimate me."

"You don't understand," Lorinda said. "It doesn't matter what you have done before, or where you have done it, or what you think you can handle. You aren't attempting to catch a thief or a run-away soldier, you will be trying to stop Mayhew." She shook her head several times.

Very deliberately he interrupted her. "Show me the body in the wood-shed. I have to start there." He met her gaze with his own, and he saw how close she was to collapsing. "Come. Just show me. I'll do the rest."

She shook her head. "I can't look at it again."

"You don't have to," said Russell as he helped her to rise. "I will tend to it." He wished that Guerra were with him instead of at the Howe Dairy, for he knew that he would want assistance in moving the body. It was possible to ask Henry Clayton, but the physician would have more than his share of work to do once the corpse was brought to his surgery. "Come. I'll walk with you and I'll make the necessary arrangements."

"I don't want to know anything about it. I want the body gone. I don't want to know anything more." Her voice had risen and she tugged at her coat as if it were armor.

"You won't have to. It's my work now." He indicated the door and took her elbow under his hand as he walked beside her.

15

"You'll regret this, Russell," snarled Harry Fiske—otherwise known as Eugene R. Exeter—through the bars at the Sheriff of Charity.

"How?" Russell asked in his most reasonable manner. "What are you proposing to me? I won't permit you to cheat me and you are not a violent man."

"I might change. You never can tell." He made this last as vicious as he could. His young weasel-like face was more pinched than usual and his eyes had narrowed, removing every trace of candor from his expression and leaving only the calculation behind.

"For your own sake, I hope you won't try," said Russell. "You may not believe this, Fiske—"

"Exeter," corrected Fiske.

"Perhaps you'd like a hyphenation?" suggested Russell in his most po-lite manner. "Exeter-Fiske, perhaps spelling Fiske with two small *f*s instead of the usual way. It would look so much more distinguished. Do consider it." He leaned against the bars, his attitude so patient that both men knew he was being insulting. "If you want to trade on being British, it's all one to me, but let me recommend you find something less exalted in tone. I'm not the only person who is going to become suspicious of so grand a name as Eugene Rupert—is it Rupert?—Exeter."

"If I wanted advice from a copper, I'd have asked for it. You can lock me up, but I don't have to listen to you preach." Exeter-Fiske retreated to the far side of the cell. "Leave me alone."

"All right," said Russell, moving away from the cell door. "I don't mean you harm."

"Of course not," Exeter snapped. "You're saving me from myself, copper. Isn't that right."

"For what it's worth, I am not and never was a copper. We Runners didn't wear uniforms with or without copper buttons, and there were no constables among us." He closed the door between the office and the cells. Little as he liked to admit it, he felt he had failed. It was a fortunate chance that he had been able to bring in Fiske so easily and he knew that such an opportunity was not likely to come again. A criminal like Fiske was no real danger, not the way that Mayhew was; the worst that Fiske would do was take money and cause embarrassment. He did prey on those without money and he never set out to harm his victims. There were others who were much more dangerous, and they were the ones who gave Russell restless nights and uneasy days.

About thirty minutes later, Luis Guerra stormed into the jail, his hat crusted with snow. He said nothing to Russell, but slammed over to the stove and pulled off his coat. He refused to look at Russell and his jaw was so set that the muscles stood out on his face, turning his features to a mask.

"Would you like to tell me what's troubling you?" asked Russell when Guerra had tossed his coat aside.

"Why should you care?" demanded Guerra. He pulled a mug off the narrow shelf by the stove and reached for the coffee pot.

"You'll burn your hand that way," Russell pointed out, saying nothing at the protesting oath from Guerra as his fingers touched the hot metal. "Sit down, Luis," he said. "Tell me what the matter is. I'm willing to listen to anything you wish to say to me."

"It's nothing. Nothing I can do anything about. Not that I would." He sat down abruptly.

"Get a cloth and pour us both some coffee. It's worth drinking, for a change." Russell rubbed his eyes. "If you're only going to sulk—"

"I'm not sulking," Guerra informed him grandly.

"All right, what are you doing?" Russell asked.

Guerra did not answer; he got up and poured the coffee as requested and handed the larger mug to Russell. "It doesn't matter anyway," he admitted.

"What doesn't matter?" Russell inquired with asperity. "You're talking in riddles, Luis."

"I guess I am," said Guerra, retreating to the stove once more. "You'll think I'm a fool."

"I doubt it," said Russell.

"You will. *I* think I'm a fool. Worse than a fool." He stared down into the coffee. "It's Donna Elvira."

"What has that infernal woman done now?" Russell sighed.

"It's not what she's done," Guerra said quickly.

"What is it then?" Russell prodded.

"It's Frederick Fletcher," Guerra blurted out.

"What does *he* have to do with any of this?" Russell said. "Luis, forgive me, but I've missed something."

"He's courting her," Guerra said baldly.

"You're joking," Russell said, and at once realized he had made a mistake; he strove to correct it at once. "How could that happen? Mayor Fletcher would not tolerate . . ."

"What does he have to say about it?" Guerra scoffed. "Mayor Fletcher doesn't see beyond the doors of his bank."

Russell took a long sip of coffee and for once did not relish the taste. "Frederick Fletcher is paying court to Donna Elvira Arreba y Corre." He listened to the words as if hearing the sound of them would lend them some sense.

"Frederick Fletcher wants her land. He sees the miles and miles she controls and he imagines himself profiting from it." Guerra spat, deliberately missing the spittoon.

"Luis," Russell began, then shook his head. "Do you think that Donna Elvira would allow herself to be taken in by someone like Frederick Fletcher?"

"I think she sees the end of the Spanish land grants and wants to hang onto the Rancho, no matter what it requires to do that. If she must marry someone like Frederick Fletcher to achieve her ends, she will." He cleared his throat. "She's right to worry. The United States is winning the war against Mexico. We all know that. It's just a matter of agreeing on a price for the land between here and the Pacific Ocean. That won't take long now that everyone knows that it's almost over. They've had the Texas Territories to practice with; you know it won't take long. She's desperate,

Jason." He rarely used the Sheriff's given name and when he did, it was an excellent indication of the extremity of his moods.

"Desperate enough to consider Frederick Fletcher? Come, Luis. You can't believe that."

"Why not?" Luis countered hotly. "She is a beautiful and wealthy young woman with lands of her own and . . . and Frederick is precisely the sort of man who would protect her interests as his own." This last was a statement of such cynicism that there was almost nothing Russell could think of to say in response.

"What about the question of religion?" he asked at last.

"Why should either of them care about that?" Luis jeered.

"If they do not, you may be certain that their families will, and their priests and ministers. Donna Elvira is a Roman Catholic and the Fletchers are Protestants. That's no minor difference, Luis." Russell took a deep breath, knowing that he was risking giving serious offence. "You will have to allow that Protestants do not marry Roman Catholics."

"Frederick Fletcher would marry a squaw if she had as much land as Donna Elvira does," Luis stated.

"Not if his family had anything to say about it. If you think that George Fletcher is about to permit—"

"He wants to see the town consolidated," Luis said. "If permitting his younger son to marry a Roman Catholic will bolster his position in the town, you may be certain he will do it." He drank the rest of his coffee and poured a second cup without asking permission to do so.

"And why does it matter so much to you?" Russell asked, coming to the heart of the problem as deliberately as he could.

Luis shook his head. "It shouldn't."

"But it does." Russell drank the rest of his coffee so that the silence between them would not be too obvious.

"All right. I have no right to want anything else other than . . . whatever I have now." He turned and met Russell's eyes. "She would never consider a man like me. Eventually she will marry someone and that will settle everything. But I never thought it would be someone like Frederick Fletcher." He said the Mayor's son's name as if he were mentioning underwear.

"Do you have some reason—other than your dislike and your personal concerns—to believe that there would be difficulties with the match?" Russell spoke crisply, as if he were conducting an investigation, which in a sense he was.

"I think that he is determined to get as much money and power with as little work as he can. I think that he likes the notion of taking a good Spanish girl and turning her into someone respectably American—for he is one of those who does not think of Mexicans as Americans." Luis shook his head. "There is no law against any of that, is there? In fact, some might think him generous to do so much for a woman who might lose all her land if Congress does not uphold the land grants." He stared down at his boots. "I don't know what to say."

"Do you want her for yourself?" Russell asked in his most neutral tones.

"In my dreams, sometimes. But she would not have me. Her father was hidalgo enough to . . ." He shifted his subject. "Hidalgo comes from the words hijo de algo meaning the son of something. Don Maximillian told me that years ago, so I would understand how different he was from the rest of us. As hidalgo he was the heir of the great ones—the grandes of Spain. For him that was so important that nothing else was . . ."

Russell set his mug aside. "I will have a word with the Mayor, in private. I can't assume that it will make a difference, and I will not tell him what you have said. If he approves, then there is nothing more I can do, or will do. If he does not approve, Frederick may have to make other plans."

Guerra looked genuinely startled. "You would do that?"

"Of course."

He was so startled that he was not able to speak at all. He wrung Russell's hand and smiled for the first time that day. "Oh." He smacked his forehead with his open hand. "I ought to have said this first time. The body you found in the woodshed a week ago?"

Russell was still. "Yes?"

"He's been identified." At once he was contrite. "I'm sorry, Jason. I ought to have said it first thing, but the other was on my mind, and since it . . . it didn't mean anything . . . I didn't . . ."

"Everything and everyone addressed to this office means something, no matter how trivial you or I might think it or him." Russell tapped the desk. "Well? Who is the . . . victim?"

"I have the name written down," Guerra offered, holding out the little notebook Russell had given him. "I did it just as you told me. I asked to have the name spelled. I copied exactly what I heard."

"Cole Ritchards came into town and Doctor Clayton asked him to look at the body. He identified it as Charles Holt, a carter out of Denver." He kept his eyes on his notebook.

"Ritchards is certain?" Russell demanded.

"He said the man bought logs from him occasionally. He said he'd warned Holt about the danger of trying to haul in winter. He said—" He looked away from the notebook and the Sheriff.

"What did he say?" Russell asked.

"He said that . . . that if Holt was stupid enough to try to get a load of wood down the mountain in winter, what else could he expect to happen to him?" He closed his eyes. "I don't know what else he might have said."

Russell nodded once. "I can guess. Cole Ritchards doesn't have a very high opinion of his fellow-man, does he?"

"No," Guerra admitted gratefully. "He told me I ought to write it down."

"You did the right thing. You're not responsible for what other people say, but you have a duty to report it." He let his breath out slowly. "A carter from Denver. Another man alone."

"According to Ritchards, he was married, or had a woman at least, and they had children, but he couldn't remember how many of them, or how old they might be." Guerra crossed himself furtively.

"God help them," Russell agreed. "I suppose I'll have to make inquiries about them. They have to be notified."

"Do you have to do that?" Guerra asked.

"Yes. I hate it." He slumped. "I'll talk to Smilin' Jack. He'll probably know how to reach the man's family." He stared up at the ceiling. "By the way, Harry Fiske is back in the cells. Make sure he gets his supper if I'm out."

"Fiske?" Guerra said.

"Or Exeter, whichever suits you." He felt immeasurably tired.

"You caught him." Guerra was very pleased with the news.

Russell shook his head. "Child's play."

"But you caught him."

"Bess Mattington could have caught him," Russell said. "One of the Howe children could have caught him."

"But he was armed," insisted Guerra.

"He had a gun, if that's what you mean," Russell corrected him. "He was more frightened of it than he was of me. The gun's in the cabinet, by the way." He jerked his thumb in the general direction of the locked cabinet on the walls.

Guerra nodded several times, as if the repetition would add emphasis to his determination. "I will see that he is guarded at all times."

Russell wished he could put off paying another visit to Henry Clayton's house but knew that it had to be done at once now that he had a name for the most recent victim of Mayhew's ferocious cruelty. "I might come back in a couple hours," he said as he pulled on his fur cap.

"I'll make sure that Fiske stays put," Guerra vowed.

"Fine. That's fine, Luis," Russell said in a remote tone as he pulled on his coat. He would have to clean and oil his guns tonight, he decided. The volley-gun would need to have its action checked—it had nearly jammed the last time he had fired all fourteen rounds—and his No. 5 Paterson Colt needed its case repaired. Russell was almost to the door when Guerra stopped him with two words.

"Jason; thanks."

Russell nodded and left.

"I am almost convinced you're serious about this," Mayor Fletcher said as he stared at Russell over the top of his holiday cup.

"I am serious," Russell said in his most polite manner. He had not wanted to attend the Mayor's annual Christmas function but knew that his refusal would be interpreted as a deliberate insult by George and Agatha Fletcher. "In England we call this Boxing Day, when gifts are presented to the poor of the parish and to those servants and others employed by the estate."

"You're changing the subject, Russell," Fletcher said, his expression more dogged than usual.

"I most certainly am," Russell said in his best and most affable way.

"I'm not going to be maneuvered into consenting to a plan that I regard as irresponsible and dangerous." Mayor Fletcher wagged his finger at Russell.

"I'm not a schoolboy, Mayor," said Russell with just enough humor to make it appear that he was not offended by the attitude displayed by Fletcher. "I have an obligation that is part of my office and if you expect me to live up to that obligation, you will have to understand that from time to time I must act in ways you do not find . . . acceptable." He indicated the forty-three guests in the room. "Ask them, if you are not convinced by me. All of them want to be rid of Mayhew. He will not come to us. It follows that I must go to him. Doesn't it?"

"And what then?" Fletcher threw out his chest. "I believe that I have something to say about what you can and cannot do."

"Yes, you do," Russell said. "But I am constrained by the law, Mayor. We are all constrained by the law." He caught sight of Henry Clayton and raised his cup toward the physician.

"And I am warning you, Russell," Fletcher went on with great determination, "that you are to do nothing without the specific authorization of the Town Council."

Russell smiled. "Fine." He inclined his head the way he could remember seeing his father do a quarter of a century ago. "Call a special meeting."

There were many things Fletcher disliked and having his hand forced was very near the top of the list. He glared at Russell. "How can you make such an unreasonable demand, and at this time!"

"I can because I must," Russell said as he raised his cup again. "Let me congratulate your wife on her refreshments. She has outdone herself." He took one of the hard, dark finger-sized cakes that were set out on a tray. "How did she manage it? Charity is so remote, I'm astonished you could offer so much to your guests."

"My wife is a very careful housewife," said Fletcher, torn between gratification for the compliment and irritation for being got off the track once again. "Certainly this is a very special occasion for all of us. It *is* Christmas."

"Boxing Day," Russell corrected sweetly. "Perhaps before New Year we can attend to the matter? I would hate to have to take matters into my own hands simply because you were occupied with other problems." He stepped back. "I have demanded too much of your time; your other guests . . ."

"Russell . . ." Fletcher was saying even while Russell strolled away toward Henry Clayton.

Liam Cauliffe and Henry Clayton joined the hastily convened meeting of the Town Council, which was held in the parlor of the Fletcher house. It was already dark out and snowing lightly and all the men grumbled about the circumstances.

"My wife has had to delay supper as well, gentlemen," said Mayor Fletcher. "However, I agree with Sheriff Russell that we must quickly agree on how best to proceed."

Barton Purvis, whose house was the closest to Fletcher's, glared at the others. "I can't see why it was necessary to speak tonight. Tomorrow morning would do as well and would be much more convenient."

"Shall I tell the townspeople that your convenience is more important to you than public safety?" Cauliffe asked in his most bland tone. "I'm sure that will interest them, particularly when the time comes for your reelection."

"And there will be elections in two years won't there," Cauliffe ventured. "Eighteen hundred fifty, as I mark it, is an election year." He was enjoying himself tremendously, though his expression was dour as ever. Only the glint in his eyes revealed his high pleasure.

"Yes, it is an election year and of course we will hold elections. That is the correct way." Olfrant waved his hand as if to brush away bothersome insects. "You demanded this meeting. I fail to see why it is required." This last challenge was directed at Russell. "The Mayor has said that you have decided that we must take action against Mayhew."

Russell nodded. "Not quite; what I believe is that *I* must take action against Mayhew, which is a very different thing."

"You speak as if you expect to sashay out into the mountains, lasso the fellow and bring him back at the horse's tail," said Purvis, deliberately exaggerating his tone and manner to what he assumed was like the trappers and ranchers who lived around the town.

"If it were so simple a matter, I would have done that months ago, when I first discovered the Vreeland body." Russell spoke softly, with deceptive casualness. "I don't wish to underestimate the man, and that is why I realize that steps must be taken or every traveler approaching this town will be in mortal danger."

"You've got a knack for the dramatic," Mayor Fletcher said.

"Stop your nonsense right now, George Fletcher." Cauliffe spoke so suddenly and with such emphasis that the room was loud with silence.

"What do you mean, nonsense?" Fletcher demanded after he had recovered himself enough to feel insulted.

"Precisely what I have said. Here you have the Sheriff saying the first sensible thing I have heard in regard to Mayhew and you all behave as if he was a recalcitrant youth seeking glory. That's not the case. You are dealing with an experienced and seasoned man who has just informed you that he is prepared to risk his life for the safety of this town, and for that you should be willing to hear him out with respect." He swung around to face Russell. "And you will do me the courtesy of accepting what I say without caviling. Is that understood, Jason?"

"Yes, it's understood," Russell said in an undertone.

"Good." Cauliffe turned back to the Town Council, and took deliberate advantage of their sheepish attitudes. "For the sake of Our Lord, do not insist on belittling what the Sheriff is doing. I truly believe that none of you has the least appreciation for what Jason Russell has done for you. It is a strange compliment for him: it indicates that he has done his work so well and so competently that you have not been aware that he was doing it. You hired him to keep the peace, and that is precisely what he has done. Because he has succeeded, you assume that there was nothing to it. Don't you?" This last rhetorical question was delivered as if Liam Cauliffe stood in a pulpit rather than before the Town Council.

"You recommended the man. Of course you defend him," Hosea Olfrant began.

"Egad! listen to the carking fool!" Cauliffe thundered. "I recommended him because he was far and away the best man for the job I knew or knew of. That he was willing to accept the work was surprising to me, since he does not need the salary he requires you to pay him." He paused, his eyes raking over his tiny congregation. "Instead of realizing your good fortune, you have made up your minds to regard what is being done for you as nothing more than the most minor of custodial tasks. What must I do to persuade you to reassess your—"

"Liam, please," Russell said, now acutely uncomfortable. "Let me handle this, won't you?"

"Why? So you can undo everything I am trying to establish here? No, Jason. You must hear me out, too." Cauliffe joined his big, knotted hands. "Are any of you prepared to go out looking for Mayhew and his gang? No? Are you willing to bring in the bodies of his victims and make a report from Doctor Clayton's findings? No? Are any of you willing to ride to the outlying farms and ranches, no matter what the weather, every ten days, to be certain that everyone is safe? No? Are you willing to—" He broke off. "Of course you're not. Jason Russell is. If you cannot see the value of that, you're past praying for." He rounded on Henry Clayton. "I've had my say. Perhaps you can make them understand."

Clayton shook his head. "I haven't your fervor, Preacher Cauliffe," he said as he rose to address the Town Council. "As Liam Cauliffe told you, I have examined the victims of Mayhew, and my findings are on record at the jail, both for the judge when he arrives and for any legal inquiry that might be made later. I've seen only three bodies of Mayhew's victims, but I must tell you that each one is worse than the one before. Whatever possesses this man, it is growing stronger and his capacity for inflicting damage increases with every . . . opportunity. Based on what I have seen, it is my opinion that the assaults and injuries will increase in severity and that the number of victims will probably rise as time goes by." He stopped to put his hand to his brow.

"Are we to understand," said Purvis with a mixture of timorousness and arrogance, "that you think Mayhew will grow bolder and more—"

"Destructive?" suggested Clayton. "Yes, I do. I've spoken with the Sheriff, and little as I like the notion—I'd be lying if I said otherwise, Jason—I am convinced that it is the only reasonable way to deal with the threat that this creature poses to Charity." He sighed. "I've seen the bodies, gentlemen. I've examined them carefully, and I tell you now that the man who can do that to another man is one of the damned."

"You make it sound like there are devils in the woods, the way the Indians claim." Olfrant was attempting to scoff but he could not look at either Clayton or Russell; he tried addressing Cauliffe. "It's almost mythic, isn't it, Reverend Cauliffe?"

"Indian devils may be mythic," said the minister caustically, "but if you are trying to confuse Indian legends with Coffin Mayhew, you're more of a cozener than I thought." His Scots burr had grown very strong now and he regarded Olfrant with irritation. "And I will thank you not to blaspheme."

Mayor Fletcher slapped his hands onto the table. "In the meantime, Sheriff Russell, what do you propose to do about this lamentable situation? You say your plan will work; you will have to prove this to me."

Russell shook his head slowly. "I wish I could explain it to you gentlemen. When I was a Runner, one of the things we were taught to do was to track a criminal, to follow him before he knew he was being hunted. We were encouraged to act quickly, in order to have surprise on our side. If we wait until Spring, Mayhew will be ready for us, and he will have taken measures to keep us from reaching him. That much is certain. The man may be mad as a Bedlamite but he is not stupid. Therefore the only chance we have to stop him without endangering half the men of this town is to pursue him now, in winter, and quickly." He noticed that he finally had Purvis' attention. "I think that with care I can bring the man in with minimal bloodshed and with less risk than a full-fledged manhunt must entail."

"When you say full-fledged manhunt, Sheriff, what do you mean?" Purvis asked as he held his pencil over his notebook.

"A manhunt would have to involve most of the able-bodied men in and around Charity. Half would have to ride into the mountains, probably in three separate parties in order to cover the most ground. It would not be a secret expedition and there is no way it could surprise Mayhew. The other men and some of the women would have to guard the town, by which I mean that there would have to be armed barricades established on all the roads leading into town. Otherwise Mayhew or his men would be sure to shift their activities to Charity, as a warning that no one was to come after him again. The manhunt would take time, possibly as much as a month. It would be very costly, gentlemen, both in hours and commerce lost and in potential harm to all the people in and around this town. There is an excellent chance that many people would be maimed or killed if Mayhew decided to wage a campaign against us." He leaned forward, willing the Town Council to accept his proposal. "I will inform my deputy of where I intend to go, and we will establish signals that he will be able to follow. Consider: I am proposing to risk two men—one of them myself—instead of half a town. Even if the two of us fail, you will have lost less than if—"

Liam Cauliffe interrupted. "Be perfectly aware, gentlemen, that when Jason Everard Nicholas Russell says *fail*, he means *die.*"

16

Between the delays of the Town Council, a drunken brawl at Lorinda Dooley's that put three men in jail and one in Henry Clayton's surgery, and a four-day blizzard, January was more than half over by the time Russell set out on his hunt for Coffin Mayhew.

"I'll ride to the second line cabin on the Mattington ranch tomorrow," said Guerra as he watched Russell adjust the girths of his Hussar's saddle on Rajah.

"Fine."

"Make that two of us, Sheriff," said William Red Pony, who was putting Daniel Calvin's farrier's tools in order.

"¿Como?" Guerra burst out, rounding on the Indian. "You, you are not his deputy—"

Russell pulled down the stirrup iron and said, "That's very generous of you, Red Pony, but it isn't necessary."

"I know these mountains," Red Pony said reasonably. "And no one pays any attention to an Indian. There are some who know that Guerra is your deputy, and that could increase risk for everyone." He set aside three heavy rasps. "I have an obligation to you, Sheriff."

"Don't be silly," said Russell as he adjusted the browband on the bridle and then buckled the throatlatch. "I think your argument makes sense, and I would appreciate your help. So would Guerra if he gave it a moment's thought." He clucked to Rajah to back him out of the stall.

"I can do this without help," Guerra announced ominously.

"I don't doubt that," said Russell. "But why should you? Red Pony has offered you valuable assistance and the most sensible thing would be to accept it. For my sake, if not for yours." He checked the sheaths holding his volley-gun and baton, then tugged once on the thongs holding his bedroll to the cantle.

Guerra flushed. "I am ashamed," he muttered, then looked at William Red Pony. "You are most welcome."

"Thank God for that," said Russell as he swung into the saddle. "Someone open the door for me, will you?"

*   *   *

Drifting snow obscured most of the road; Russell picked his way through the trees, hoping that the footing would support Rajah. Above him the sky was filmed over, glarey and bright but without direct sun, shining like gunmetal. He had another three or four miles to reach his first stop: Cole Ritchards' largest cabin. For the last hour he had occupied himself by questioning his motives for taking on the hunt for Mayhew. While he knew it made some sense, now that he was in the barren chill of the mountainside, he was not as certain as he had been at first that it would be possible to track and find Mayhew in January. In the comfort of his office with the fire in the stove, the hunt did not appear to be overwhelming. Now that he was out in the snow-muffled silence, his eyes rimmed with ice and his ears burning with cold, he feared he had been rash.

"Hold on there, fellow," he said to Rajah as the horse shied at a sudden rush in the undergrowth. "Whatever it is, you're bigger."

Ahead, a small fox broke cover and ran, belly-down, over the snow.

"My half-brother would give him the chase," said Russell to his horse. "On one of your half-brothers, most likely. Not that the Hunt would cover ground like this." He patted Rajah's neck. "I know it's hard going, old son. Just do the best you can."

Rajah blew out through his nostrils and continued to wade through the snow.

When at last the cabin came in sight, most of the mountain was deep in evening shadow. A tang of smoke in the air told Russell that the misanthropic Ritchards was waiting in his cabin as he had indicated he might be, if he decided that it was worth his while to help the Sheriff. Apparently he had reached his decision. It gave Russell scant comfort.

The Sheriff dismounted a few yards from the cabin and called out a greeting.

"You can come in, Russell," called back Ritchards. "But don't look for nothing from me. I got no food to spare, no ammunition and no time to go after anyone."

"Wouldn't dream of it," said Russell, leading Rajah around to the back of the cabin and making the best of the slight protection of an open shed.

By the time he had watered and fed his horse, it was dark enough that Russell had difficulty making out the cabin among the mass of trees. He floundered over the snow and onto the uneven steps to the door.

"I wouldn't've done this except for Holt," said Ritchards when he had poured out a dark liquid he called coffee for the both of them.

"I appreciate that," said Russell. His gloves, cap, and coat were draped over a sawhorse near the stove, steaming in the warmth.

"Holt was as much a dolt"—he sniggered at his version of humor—"as the rest of the world, but he didn't deserve to die like that. I never seen anything like him, and I seen lots, including some of the heathenish things the Indians can do." He scratched his beard.

"Red Indians?" Russell asked, knowing full well it was what Ritchards meant.

"Sure—what other kind'f Indians are there?" He took a pouch of chewing tobacco from his pocket and bit off some.

"The ones in India," Russell said.

"That's a daft thing," Ritchards stated in a satisfied way, as if it confirmed his low opinion of mankind.

"The people of India had the name first," Russell said, and tasted the silt-like coffee.

"It's still daft," Ritchards said, contented to think the worst. For the better part of two minutes he stared reflectively and sardonically at the stove, as if his gaze would control the heat of the fire. Then he said, "You got any idea where to look for Mayhew yet?"

"Not precisely, no." Russell disliked admitting this and he spoke grudgingly. "Have you?"

"I might and I might not." He paused to spit in the direction of the stove. The tobacco smell was sharp on the air.

"Does that mean you do, or that you have a good guess?" Russell inquired after a moment.

"It means that I think I know where they were three days ago, for what good that could be to you. They could be a long way from that place by now, o'course, and it might not have been Mayhew at all." He leaned back in his rickety chair.

"Well?" Russell asked when Ritchards did not go on.

"I'm not saying that this'll be any use to you," Ritchards warned.

"Yes, I understand that," was Russell's weary answer.

Apparently it was satisfactory. "Y'see," Ritchards said, refusing to be rushed. "I was out toward the east, cutting up half a dozen trees on the edge of an avalanche. A big one like that brings down rocks and trees in its path. Most of the trees stay buried until spring, but the ones at the edge are easy to get. It saves me having to cut them, not that you get much lumber out of it—firewood's the best you can salvage. Most of the trunks are cracked lengthwise." He spat again.

Russell resigned himself to waiting for the whole tale. "This was two days ago?"

"When I saw the men, yeah." He stared across the room with distant eyes. "It was early afternoon, and I was stacking cut branches, when I heard horses coming, half a dozen of 'em or so." He drank his coffee, and there was a subtle alteration in his expression, as if speaking of real danger somehow lessened the contempt he showed for all of life. "I was under cover of the brush, and the logs I was clearing away pretty well hid everything. If that was Mayhew, I guess I was lucky."

"And what makes you think it was Mayhew?" Russell asked.

"Some of the men were talking, and one of them joked about the way the man they had just killed died. One of them was laughing. Lordy, Lordy, I don't want to hear a laugh like that again this side of Hell." He drank more of the coffee, his wad of tobacco making a lump in his cheek.

"The man they had just killed," Russell echoed. Somewhere out in the cold there was another body, possibly more disfigured than the previous three. He swallowed hard and did his best to keep his voice steady. "Did they—"

"They didn't say who or where, if that was what you're getting at," Ritchards said, sounding more subdued than Russell had ever heard. He hesitated. "I guess you better have it all. One of the men called another one Coffin, and I can't think who else that might be."

Russell nodded, sorting his thoughts. "Was there any indication of where they were going?"

"One of them said something about an old roadhouse on Cowley Pass Road," Ritchards said after a short pause. "At least, I think that was what they were talking about. I wasn't going to stop and ask."

"There isn't a roadhouse on Cowley Pass Road," Russell stated.

"No, not now. But six, seven years ago there was one. A family from Kansas started it, thinking that they'd get a jump on the new settlers. Just a bit too much of a jump; there wasn't much business. I don't know how they made it through the first winter. Finally they got one of the hauling companies to use it as a remount station for a year or two." He chewed with more determination. "Wasn't much of a place. Just four rooms, a stable, and a couple of outhouses. They charged fifty cents for supper."

"And what did that buy?" Russell inquired, knowing the price was high.

"Something hot to eat. Where else was there to go for it?" He spat once more. "They cleared out four years back. The place has stood empty ever since."

"Why hasn't anyone mentioned this to me before now?" Russell wanted to know.

"Most of 'em probably don't know about it. The folks in Charity—well, most of 'em—arrived after the roadhouse was gone. It's a good twelve miles from town, and since no one's there . . ."

"No one except possibly Mayhew and his gang," Russell corrected with irritation. It had not occurred to him to ask about abandoned buildings, which he would have done in India or back in London. But here, in the

Texas Territories, he had assumed that with the land so newly opened, there could not be deserted buildings. It was an inexcusable oversight, he chided himself. It was the sort of error he would not tolerate in a green recruit.

"Troubled, Sheriff?" Ritchards mocked, some of his habitual sardonic attitude returning.

"Yes." He put the mug aside. "Tell me about this abandoned road-house. Where is it and how do you get there?"

Ritchards shook his head. "Off the Cowley Pass Road, near the turnoff for the Colorado River, maybe a quarter mile from the La Reina Virgin spring." He smiled with half his mouth. "But you don't know those places, do you, Sheriff?"

"Tell me how to find them." His sense of determination was growing stronger, renewing his flagging spirits. "Anything you can tell me—"

"You've got most of it already. I'll draw you the best map I can. That might make it a little easier." He rounded on the Sheriff. "I'll say this, Russell: you got more guts than most of 'em but that just means you're a bigger fool than they are. You think you can go out there and get rid of something like Mayhew. Unless you shoot him down like a mad dog, he'll take care of you the same way he took care of the others. And they're too dumb and too scared to find another lawman like you, back in Charity. They'll end up toadies to Mayhew or to some bastard just like him who'll pin on a badge."

"They already have a bastard with a badge," Russell said with irony tinging his voice.

Ritchards shrugged. "You're saying it, not me." He got up and went to the stove, pulling the door open with his boot-toe as he reached for one of the sections of log in the box near it. "I don't want to discourage you— don't think I could even if I wanted to—but Mayhew has at least six men in his gang. There's only the one of you. Guns or no guns, that's pretty bad odds." He shoved the log into the stove and kicked the door shut.

"I'm aware of that," said Russell flatly.

"Just so you're not kidding yourself. I expect Fletcher to be an idiot, but you've got a glimmering of sense. It'd be a shame to see you get wrecked for someone like Fletcher." He came back to his chair and sat once again.

"Fletcher didn't want me to try to find Mayhew. He was worried about the money as much as anything." Russell smiled faintly. "Bankers."

"Loobies, all of 'em, if you ask me." Ritchards was quiet again. "Tell you what, Sheriff. You want me to meet up with that Mexican deputy of yours, I'll do it if there isn't anything else taking up my time."

For Ritchards this was a generous offer and Russell responded to it in that light. "I would appreciate it more than I can tell you, Ritchards. Thank you."

"Pleasure, I'm sure," said Ritchards, executing a travesty of a bow from his chair.

Russell was not put off by this reaction. "About the roadhouse . . ."

"I knew you'd get back to that one time or another," said Ritchards. He gave a long, put-upon sigh and closed his eyes. "I suppose I might as well do it. If I don't, someone else might, and who knows what could happen. Knowing you, you'd ask one of Mayhew's men and never know it." With his best long-suffering expression, Ritchards got up and went to the sack where he put the ashes from the stove. He prodded around there until he found a good-sized lump of charcoal. This he took out and blew on to get rid of most of the ash clinging to it, and then he scuffed a clear space on the floor. Bending over from the waist he began to draw. "Come over and have a look, Sheriff."

Russell obeyed, drawing up his chair and leaning forward, his notebook open on his knee.

"Y'see, we're here," said Ritchards, making an *X* near his left toe. "Now this"—he sketched in a jagged line—"is the ridge to the north of us. On the west end, there's a steep drop, and a couple of creeks feed down to the river." He indicated all these features with quick, clumsy lines which Russell copied into his notebook. "You keep that ridge on your right and you follow the old trail that goes this way"—once again the charcoal left a track over the floor—"until you come to a hollow with two fallen pine trees. They make a kind of cross. You'll know them when you see them."

"Will they be above the snow?" Russell asked as he continued to copy the information Ritchards was giving him. His pencil needed sharpening and one projecting bit of wood scratched the paper of the notebook, almost tearing it.

"Probably. They were yesterday. Anyway, there you go to the right. It's not a sharp turn, and it takes you up the slope past an old trappers' camp. You can see the skin sheds still, though they're falling down." He spat one last time. "From there, you follow the hill around to the left and that will bring you out about a mile east of the roadhouse. The trail's partly snowed in, but you won't have any trouble making it out." He straightened up. "I'll stick around here for the next three days for your deputy to come."

"I'd appreciate it. Guerra and William Red Pony should be a day or two behind me. We agreed upon that, but they will go to the Mattington line cabin first. You're second on their list, first on mine. We decided that we'd cover more territory that way."

"I don't hold with Indians. Never did. Still, if he's with your deputy, I'll tell 'em what I told you." He gave a sarcastic grimace that might have been a smile. "Think that's enough?"

"More than enough. I'm grateful." Russell made a few more notes and then put his pencil back in his pocket.

"Tell me that in a week, if you're still alive and have all your skin on you," Ritchards said, and reached for more chewing tobacco.

Despite his misgivings, Russell found that Ritchards's instructions were easier to follow than he had hoped they would be. What had appeared incongruous drawn in charcoal on a rough plank floor proved to be a fairly accurate rendering of the landscape features Ritchards had indicated. The snow was deep and Rajah went slowly through the drifts, occasionally whinnying with distress when he sank to his withers.

"Hold on, fellow," Russell said after one especially bad incident. "Keep going. You're doing fine." He patted the horse's neck with his gloved hands and wondered if he would need the second pair of reins he had tucked into supplies. He had learned that precaution years ago in India and knew that he was still alive because of it. Carrying a second set of reins was as much superstition as prudence for Russell, and he knew it.

By midday he had reached the two fallen pines, and he paused to give Rajah a nosebag of grain and to chew two incredibly tough sticks of jerky himself. When he tightened the girths and got back into the saddle, he had a brief, intense desire to turn around and ride back to Charity. "Craven," he said aloud to himself, and set Rajah moving on the trail.

By sunset he was near the place where the roadhouse ought to be. Russell drew in and checked his volley-gun and his No. 5, frowning as he felt how stiff the freezing cold made the action of the gun. It had almost blown up in his hands once; it might happen again. He adjusted the saddle so that the guns could be warmed by Rajah's body.

Little though he wanted to do it, Russell found a dense copse that provided cover from the weather and any prying eyes that might be about. He cut down branches and made a shelter of them that was large enough to hold both Rajah and himself, if not in comfort, at least with a degree of protection that he valued more than other advantages under the circumstances.

After giving Rajah more grain and some water from melted snow, Russell ate more of his jerky and some of the heavy, cold pudding that Frau Schmidt had insisted he take with him. At the time he had thought she was being too solicitous but now he was glad to have the heavy, sweet concoction. He took the remnants of the meal and buried them in the snow some distance from the shelter so that any animals that found the food would not find him as well, and then returned to his horse, curling up beside the big creature to get what sleep he could.

By morning, Russell was stiff and aching with cold. He woke at first light and cursed as he tried to move. His hands were awkward as paws and when he got to his feet, he walked with difficulty. He made sure Rajah was fed, then went away from the shelter to relieve himself. The two-day growth of beard on his face was scratchy and his clothes were beginning to smell. He itched on his shoulders and back, and had to ignore the urge to scratch. When he returned to the shelter, he informed Rajah that "I'm chilled in all the wrong places."

It was useless to try to obliterate all traces of where he had been. Russell could think of no way to smooth the snow so that there was no sign of his presence. He took the time to break a few low-growing limbs off the trees, hoping that some of the disruption of the copse might be attributed to the breakage, at least to the casual eye. When he had Rajah saddled and ready, Russell took him to the far side of the copse and mounted.

He rode parallel to the Cowley Pass Road, keeping in the shadow of the trees whenever he could. Good sense told him that it was not practical to approach the roadhouse directly, although this prudence would not bolster his position if he were discovered. When he reached the turnoff Ritchards had described, Russell deliberately went past it by almost a quarter of a mile so that if the road was being watched, his presence would not arouse suspicion. Only when he knew he could not be seen from the turnoff did he pull Rajah around and start toward the roadhouse.

There were horses in the corral behind the roadhouse and a thread of smoke coming from the chimney that stuck up from the roof like a diseased thumb. Russell rode as near to the buildings as he could without leaving the cover of the trees. He dismounted and gripped Rajah's nostrils to keep him from whinnying a greeting to the others of his kind.

"Steady, old son," he whispered as Rajah tried to break free of his hold. "Don't give us away." He pulled his horse back into deeper shadow, braced his back and one foot against a tree and settled into waiting.

For over an hour nothing happened. The most difficult thing Russell did was shift his weight to keep his feet from falling asleep. He took five minutes to make notes about the roadhouse and everything he could observe from his vantage point, and then he resigned himself to the boredom of surveilance. The hardest part of watching was to keep from becoming drowsy, or permitting his attention to wander. Long ago he had been taught various methods for directing his attention at something uninteresting for long periods of time, and he used them now: he kept his eyes moving constantly, changing the pattern of his search regularly. He looked at the corral, then at the low sheds that adjoined it, then at the back porch of the roadhouse, then at the road leading up to it, then at the three visible windows. The next time he began with the back porch, then the road, then the corral. By varying the order of his inspection, Russell was able to keep from becoming too familiar with what he watched.

After an hour, he saw a figure in one of the windows. He leaned forward and concentrated, trying to discern as much as possible about the person standing in the roadhouse window.

"Not very tall," he muttered, using the sound of his own voice to sharpen his attention. "Light hair. Leather coat." He narrowed his eyes as the person turned. "A woman," he said, in some surprise. No one had ever mentioned a woman with the Mayhew gang. "But why not?" he whispered to the air.

He felt rather than saw Rajah bring his head up sharply, ears forward. And then something slammed into his shoulder. As he fell forward, a glancing blow struck his head; he was unconscious by the time his face hit the snow.

17

"He's coming out of it," said a voice that seemed to be at the far end of an echoing tunnel.

Russell tried to open his eyes and was rewarded with a surge of dizziness. Any movement made his headache worse.

"Throw some water on him," said an amused voice, a voice with a strong accent Russell had heard in England, from natives of Yorkshire.

"Gordon, not yet," a woman's voice protested. "He'll come around. Give him time."

"What for? We'll get down to business as soon as he's ready." The tone was condescending now. "What's the matter, Solange?"

"Don't do it anymore, Gordon. For me?" There was no pity and no whine in the request. "You promised the last one would be the last one. You gave me your word."

"I lied," Mayhew—for Russell was certain the Yorkshireman was Mayhew—chuckled.

Two other men joined in, one more tentative than the other.

"This is a lawman, Solange. He came hunting me. I didn't ask him to do that. Do you want him to take me back so I can hang?" Under the taunting there was menace now.

"Someone had to come after you, Gordon. You said that yourself," Solange said, but now her words had the sound of an old, ritualized argument. "Can't you leave him alone?"

"He'd just come after me again," Mayhew told her. "If you don't want to watch, don't stay here. I didn't make you stick around for the others, did I?" There was the sound of approaching footsteps and Russell felt a large hand grab his jaw and force his head upward. "Well, lawman?"

His head rang like a smithy but Russell made himself open his eyes and look at the Yorkshireman who had captured him and would very likely be his murderer. "What?" The word was little more than a croak, but it was enough to satisfy Mayhew.

"You'd come after me again if I let you get out of here." He had rotten teeth and his cheeks, where the beard did not grow, were deeply pockmarked. His pale-green eyes were deep-set under a large, narrow brow. Thinning, oily brown hair framed his face. Looking at Mayhew, Russell knew that the man was young enough to be his son.

"Yes," Russell grated. "I'd come after you."

Mayhew sank his hand in Russell's hair and dragged his head back, cracking it against the central post to which he was tied. "I can't let you do that." He relaxed his hand enough to give him slack enough to slam Russell's head back a second time. "Does it hurt, lawman?"

Russell strove to clear his vision, doing his best to keep the two intersecting beams overhead from multiplying like wooden daisy petals. He had seen Mayhew's type before and knew that denial and stoic resistance would only goad him to more violent acts. "Yes."

"Good." Mayhew let go of Russell and stepped back. "Think about it; get ready for what I'm going to do to you later." He laughed and all but the woman laughed obediently with him.

For a long, hideous moment Russell feared he would vomit. His whole throat felt as if it were being tickled with twigs. He swallowed hard twice, three times, and the sickness passed as he struggled to banish the images of Mayhew's victims from his thoughts. He let his eyes move, the apparent aimlessness of his gaze concealing his first close observation of the roadhouse—the main room—and he supposed that this was the main room of the four Ritchards had mentioned—was littered with broken tables and benches as well as other oddments including two large copper tubs for heating water. Some of the legs of the tables were stacked near the fireplace, ready to feed the blaze that had been kindled there. In four of the windows were torn curtains; the rest were barren, dusty, flyspecked.

Russell strained against the ropes that held him more to find out how stout the fibers were and how strong the knots than with any hope of breaking free.

"What makes an old man like you pin on a badge?" Mayhew asked, circling his captive. "You're not young enough for the game. You're no match for me. Why'd you try?" When Russell was silent, he was struck across the face. "I asked you a question, old man. I asked you two questions."

Russell took longer to recover than he actually needed, sensing that Mayhew would do less now if he thought Russell was more damaged than he actually was. "It's my job. It's been my job for close on thirty years," Russell said at last through bruised lips. He wanted to build on Mayhew's belief that he was decrepit, for such an assumption was to Russell's advantage.

Again laughter, this time more derisive than at first. "Your job. Like making shoes." He indicated the others with him. "Well, you're trying to stop us doing our job, old man. I won't have it."

"Don't hit him again, Gordon," said the woman.

"Why not? You going soft on him? You got any reason to help an old man after what Da did to you?" The fury in his voice was raw as an open sore.

"Just don't hit him again, not while I'm here. You said you wouldn't do any of that when I was around." She came to his side and put her square, chapped hand on his shoulder. "Because of what your Da did."

He pushed her hand away. "So you don't want to watch?" He was abruptly uninterested. "Come on. Wells is waiting for us, anyway. This old man will keep until we get back." He spun around and his fists bludgeoned into Russell's body. With a curse he pulled back, his knuckle in his mouth. "His bloody belt!" He held up his hand, showing the cut, as irate as if Russell had attacked him deliberately. "Bugger all!"

It was agonizing to move; ropes cut into his arms and shoulders, breathing made him retch. Russell wished he could faint even as he struggled to hold on to his consciousness. He had to listen to what was said, he knew that, he clung to that determination through his buzzing head and spotted vision.

"How long you going to be gone, Gordon?" Solange asked, a slight tremor in her voice.

"A day, maybe two at the most. Those two women have some good stock and unless I miss my guess, they'll have stores we can take when we're through with the . . . rest of it. We'll need time to pack it up, and who knows how long they'll last. Some women are tough, Solange. Some of them fight back. One of those two is going to be a fighter. She'll take time." He brought his heel down on the uneven flooring with the impact of falling rocks. "I'll get back when I get back. You got enough here to keep you through another month. If I get delayed, you wait here, like always. Understand me?"

"I understand you," she whispered.

Mayhew came over to her and tweaked the lobe of her ear. "You bet you do," he said, his manner threatening and teasing at once.

"Just be careful," she said unsteadily, taking a step back from him.

"I'm always careful. Tarnation, woman, I got a good plan this time. Those two ladies won't know what's what until I'm on the porch. They'll see the lawman's horse and they won't know who's on him until they can see my face. It'll be too late then." He made a signal and the men fell into step behind him. "If you get worried in three days, you can send word to Morris: he'll know if anything's happened to us." He pulled the door open and the frigid wind rushed in. "Make sure the old man's alive enough for some fun when we get back. We'll need us some amusement." He was still chuckling when the door closed again.

Russell listened, hearing the preparation outside, the sounds of horses being caught and saddled, the muffled thud of hooves as Mayhew and his men rode away from the abandoned roadhouse. He thought of Cloris Bell and Maude Rossiter, and he hoped fervently that Guerra had reached them already, for then they would know of their danger, horse or no horse. He had to keep from cursing when he thought of Rajah being used so dishonorably. In spite of his determination, he moaned.

"Mister?" Solange said, approaching Russell, but not coming close enough to touch him.

"Mayhew . . ." It was all Russell could say. There was a hard, hot pain at the base of his ribs. Oh, God, he prayed without hope. God, something's broken. He tasted blood at the back of his mouth. He took a deep, uneven breath. No, nothing broken after all, but a deep bruise, one that would require time to heal. He might even bleed inside—that worried him, because it would weaken him in subtle and dangerous ways before it took its full toll of him.

"Lawman?" Solange asked, a little nearer. "You hurt bad?"

He tried to deny it, but the pain roared through him and he thrashed in his bonds, crying out before he fainted.

Somehow she had managed to free him and to drag him onto a make-shift pallet near the hearth. There were three vile-smelling blankets wrapped around him, and his head, he realized, was pillowed on his saddle. The room was darker than before except for the small pool of yellow light from the lantern hanging from the main ceiling beam, and the spill of brightness from the open hearth.

"How long?" Russell asked when he saw her come toward him. His voice was no more than a thread, the words bumps on his breath.

"A couple, three hours, more or less." She carried a cup of something steaming in her hand. "I got some tea for you, the kind the Indians take for sickness."

The idea of swallowing anything was repugnant. "Not yet," he said.

"You'll dry up without it," she said sensibly, and knelt beside him. "Don't mind Gordon. He . . ." She could not finish. A hard vertical line between her brows deepened as her words trailed off.

"Don't mind him." Russell started to shake his head in disbelief, but the movement disoriented him.

"He's not always . . . what you think he is. He can be a good man, sometimes. He hasn't always done . . . the things he does now." She brushed her hand over his brow. "I think you got a fever."

"Small wonder," he growled. Speaking required more of an effort than he wanted to provide.

"Come on, drink just a little of this. If a sip won't stay down, then you don't have to take anymore just yet." She put the rim of the cup to his lips.

The liquid smelled of roots and herbs, thick and earthy but not unpleasant. Russell let a little of it run into his mouth, astonished at how parched his tongue and throat felt. "Thanks," he said when he trusted himself to speak.

"A little more." She pressed the cup insistently against his lower lip. "Lawman."

"Jason Russell," he corrected her, and somewhere in a remote part of his mind crazed mirth romped and hooted at the absurdity of his predicament, and the magnified importance good manners had assumed in it.

"I'm—"

"Solange," Russell said.

"Solange Waters," she said, and tipped more of the tea into his mouth, ignoring his sputter of protest. "You drink that down, Jason. You'll feel better if you do."

Since he felt no burning and no sudden spasm shook him, Russell did not resist her order. Though it was difficult to swallow without coughing, he managed, and was oddly satisfied that he was able to do this. As he lowered his head back against the curve of his saddle, he hoped that the tree was not ruined by this handling. A Hussar's saddle was not designed to be a pillow; he did not want this one broken, for it would be almost impossible to get another, and he disliked the charro saddles of the Texas

Territories. It would take the better part of a year to get another sent from England, and he was certain that the saddlers in the Texas Territories could not be trusted to make one. Resolutely he forced his mind back to the current danger. He fumbled his hand free of the blankets and ran his palm over the seat, noticing that the volley-gun was missing. Then, unexpectedly, his knuckles brushed against the end of his baton, still in its scabbard. He withdrew his hand at once, hoping his expression had not betrayed him.

"Something wrong?"

"My gun," said Russell, trusting she would accept his explanation. He did not want her to know that he had one weapon left to him.

"They took it with them. Where'd you find a shotgun like that?" She had risen and was walking toward the hearth.

"In Australia," he said.

She paused in her gathering of wood to build up the fire. "Where's that?"

"South and east of India, below China," said Russell, knowing that she was more and not less confused by his additions. "It's a very long way from here. It's been a penal colony, a place where men like your Gordon might be sent, instead of to prison."

"It's got to be a strange place, with guns like that." She paid no notice to the last as she tossed three chair legs onto the fire and brushed her hands off one against the other.

"It *is* a strange place," he agreed, thinking that she would think any description he gave her of the animals there had to be tall tales. "But you can find guns like this in England."

"Oh, England," she said with a slight smile, as if that explained everything. "Gordon's Da"—her face darkened—"he came from England. So did my Da. My Mamma came from Calais. That's in France."

"I've been there," said Russell. The worst of the tension was fading out of him. He resisted the urge to sleep.

"Have you?" She threw another two pieces of wood on the fire before she straightened up and stepped back. "What's it like?"

"It's a seaport. Lots of ships there, most of them making the Channel crossing. There's some fishing out of Calais." Like most Britons, he put the emphasis on the first syllable of the word rather than the second. "What did your mother's family do?"

"She said they were poor. I don't know more than that. They came here when she was twelve or thirteen, something like that. She didn't go back." Her face was reserved and distant, as if she were almost as far away from him as the French port was. "Get some rest. I'll wake you up for supper."

If Russell had had any strength left, he would not have gone along with her instruction, but already his eyelids were treacherously heavy and his concentration fading. He made a brief, futile effort to life his head again, but without success. After a short resistance, he slept, awakening only when he felt her hand on his forehead again.

"You don't feel as hot as before." Her attitude was efficient now, and pragmatic. "I ought to tie you up."

"I'm not going anywhere," Russell said ruefully. "Even if I could walk —which I doubt—you said that Mayhew took my horse, didn't you? How would I get out of here? Walk out in the night through the snow?"

"All right. I won't tie you up yet." She went to the hearth and poured out more of the herbal tea. "You got to drink more of this. Otherwise you'll get worse, and I don't have any other medicines here." As she administered the dose, she seemed more jittery to Russell than she had been before. Impulsively he caught her wrist in his hand as she started to pull the cup away.

"Solange. What's wrong?"

She looked away from him. "What makes you think something's wrong?"

"You're nervous, you look unhappy and your eyes are sad," he said, choosing the most obvious, outward signs of her distress.

"It's nothing. I'm alone here with you. I don't know you and we're all alone together." She got up quickly and moved across the room from him. "I'm going to make supper soon. You want to try to eat something? We don't have much, just a little stew and some hard bread."

"I'll try. I don't know if I can eat anything," he said, watching her. "Why is being alone with me so difficult? I'm hardly in any condition to harm you." He saw her touch the fire tongs in a furtive way. "Even if I could, I wouldn't. My fight is with Mayhew, not with you."

She gave one short bark of laughter. "Gordon's Da said that, too." The light from the fire put her face into sharp relief, showing one side in flattering amber brilliance, the other into stark shadow.

"What about Gordon's Da?" The last came out breathlessly as he tried to brace himself on his elbow without success.

"Nothing." She started toward the adjoining room, which Russell knew had to be the kitchen. "I'll soak the bread in the gravy from the stew. You can start with that."

Russell lay back, feeling defeated. "All right. That would be wonderful." He said the last automatically, as if he were still a child and being cared for by his mother.

A series of clatters came from the kitchen, none of them sudden or

uncontrolled. "You traveled a lot," Solange said as there came the sound
of sizzling fat.

"A fair amount, I guess." Russell had never given much significance to
his wandering.

"You like to travel?" Another bang accompanied this, one that sounded
like a slammed door.

"Not particularly," said Russell, surprised at his candor.

"Why'd you do it?" The noise from the kitchen abated as Solange
settled in to cook.

Russell took a deep breath, feeling tightened muscles and battered flesh.
"It seemed the sensible thing to do, under the circumstances."

"Like traveling with Gordon," said Solange in a low voice.

It was a moment before Russell trusted himself to answer without demands. "Possibly."

"Gordon's my stepbrother," she said. "We're family."

"Oh."

"I'm three years older'n him." She paused to do something that scraped
metal on metal. "I'm thirty-one."

Russell thought that his impression was correct: Mayhew was young
enough to be his son. For some reason he could not define, knowing this
filled him with despair. "How long have you been traveling with Mayhew?"

"Eleven years," Solange replied, sounds of stirring accompanying her
words. "A little more. We left . . . home in the fall." She volunteered
nothing else, and after a little pause, Russell tried again.

"Your parents were married, is that it?"

Solange waited before she answered. "Yeah. A couple years after my Da
died, Gordon's Da showed up, Gordon and his little brother with him.
Said that he and Da were cousins or something, and that he wanted to
take over the family. Mama was almost out of money, and with three
children, she didn't know what she was going to do. She did fine sewing
and similar things, but that didn't bring in enough money. So she married
Gordon's Da, and he moved in with his boys."

"What happened? Did you run out of money? Did he take advantage of
your mother?" Russell had seen such things happen many times before,
and his sympathy was both muted and genuine.

"No; nothing like that." A pan slammed on the stove and Solange
changed the subject. "This is almost ready. You want me to bring you
some hot water to wash your hands and face?"

"That would be very nice," said Russell, capitulating for the time being,
though his curiosity was piqued. Little as he wanted to admit it, he was

tired and he welcomed a brief rest before attempting to eat. He leaned back and closed his eyes, waiting for Solange.

"Here; let me do your face. There's some blood in your beard. I want to get it out." She had come back and knelt down beside him.

"I appreciate that," Russell said, mumbling a bit as he shook off the first encroachment of sleep. "Let me take care of my hands, though, will you?"

"Sure." She frowned as she went over his face, and when she was done, she rocked back on her heels. "Here. You can do your hands."

He took the wet cloth and obediently cleaned up. "How bad is the cut?"

"You got one on your cheek and one over your eye. The one over your eye bled more, but your cheek is swollen." She reported this without emotion. "I'll put a salve on them after supper."

He handed her the washcloth. "Thank you."

"It's nothing." She did not get up at once. "Why'd you come after Gordon?"

"I've told you—it's my job." He could see she was not satisfied with this answer. "Do you know what your step-brother has been doing?"

"He's . . . been strange, the last couple years. He wasn't like that before." It was not an answer, but it was all she was willing to say. Carefully she rose and went toward the kitchen.

"What was he like, before he changed?" Russell called after her.

"He was strong. He took care of me." This time the sounds were of preparation, and shortly Solange emerged from the kitchen carrying two large white bowls, both with steam rising from them. She carried large spoons as well. "The one with the bread is yours," she said as she knelt beside him and set the two bowls side by side on the floor.

This time Russell was better able to push onto his elbow, though it hurt. "Thank you," he said as he took one of the spoons. Now that he could smell the gravy-soaked bread, he discovered he was hungry.

"Go ahead. I don't pray anymore." She had taken her spoon and was dipping into her bowl. "Gordon's Da was a preacher, part of the time. He said that the Lord moved in him." There was so much anguish and venom in the last statement that Russell set his spoon aside and gave Solange a long, troubled look.

"If you want to tell me, I'll listen," he said, knowing how well this offer had worked with the men he had known in London and India and Australia. "I won't repeat what I hear; you have my word of honor."

She sighed. "I . . . Gordon doesn't like me to talk about it. I don't much, either."

"You don't have to say anything if you don't want to," Russell assured her, and started to eat, chewing gingerly.

Solange took a few more bites, and then, staring into the fire, she started to speak.

18

"At first, we were all real happy about Gordon's Da coming. Mama stopped fretting, and it was real nice to have a father in the house again, even if it wasn't Da. He was a good man, Mama said he was, and his boys were well-behaved. Their Da made sure of that, using a belt when they did wrong, and praying with them afterward." She drew up her knees and locked her arms around them. "It went along well enough for a while. Then Mama took sick, and things changed around the house. You don't know what it can be like when that happens."

"No, I don't," Russell said, recalling his mother fondly.

"No," said Solange, shaking her head at her memories. "It wasn't too bad at first. My sister and brother worked hard, and Gordon and his brother tried to be as much help as they could. But Mama got worse . . . as she got worse, Gordon's Da took to saying long prayers over her and to telling God to heal her or he would have to do something about it. He was like someone in a fight. Sometimes he would shout at her, too, telling her to accept God and healing. I . . . I used to stand in the room and want to put my hands over my ears because of the way he would shout." She stopped for a short time, her eyes and her thoughts so distant that Russell was fairly certain she was no longer aware of him. "When Mama died, three years after she took sick, Gordon's Da was in a state about it. God had failed him and he decided that he would . . . prove something about that. At first all he did was pray more, and make the rest of us pray along with him, sometimes for hours and hours. Then he changed . . . He started messing with me whenever I was alone. I got so that I didn't want to be in the house, but if I stayed out, then Gordon's Da would beat me with his belt, and he'd go a strange color while he did it, breathing all funny."

Russell listened to her with sympathetic detachment. He had heard of instances like this, and unlike many of the lawmen he had known, he rarely attributed the problem to a flirtatious step-daughter or niece. He wanted to tell Solange this, but would not break into her reverie to do so. He fought off his weakness and hurt well enough to sit up.

"I tried to keep away from him, but it got worse and worse. He was always watching me. He would wait for me and catch me alone. He'd . . . put his hand under my skirt. He said I was tempting him, just like my mother had tempted him. He said she had died for tempting him, and that if I didn't do what he wanted, God would kill me, too. He said that it was my duty, as my mother's oldest daughter, to be his wife. He said that it was part of Scripture that I do this. He kept *at* me and *at* me until I was half-crazy with it. I told Parson about it, but he got mad at me for speaking against Gordon's Da." Her words were almost a chant, coming out of her steadily, the intensity of her feeling demonstrated by the slow rocking she began in cadence with her speaking. "I wanted to run away. I wanted to die. I wanted to kill Gordon's Da. He was always putting his hands on me and telling me that I was a servant of the Devil, as Eve was, that it was my nature to lure him. He said that whatever happened to him because of the temptation was my fault, that I was to blame for all of it. I didn't know what to do. I couldn't talk to anyone about it, and there was nowhere I could go to get away from him.

"Then one day, while Gordon's Da was trying to pull my bodice open, Gordon caught us. He was real upset. When his Da told him that it wasn't his business, that I was to be his woman, and that Gordon would have to go along with it, Gordon got all upset, and said that he knew better. He said he'd heard me crying at night and he knew that I didn't want to be messed with anymore. He had a terrible fight with his Da, and at the end of it, Gordon was standing up and his Da was out cold. From that day on, Gordon protected me. He really took care of me. He made sure nothing more happened. He wasn't much more than a kid then, but he made sure his Da stayed away from me. Every time his Da tried something, Gordon would beat him up. I was . . . I was so grateful. I think . . . I loved Gordon more than anyone else in the world . . . I wanted to do everything for him. You see, I thought that it was because he was my brother that he did this, so when he asked me to run away with him, I said I'd go. I didn't consider that it might be something more than just brotherly concern that made him ask. I was . . . I was—"

"Innocent," Russell said as gently as he could.

Solange turned and stared at him. "Yes," she said a bit later. "I guess I was at that."

Russell was shaking with pain and exhaustion from the effort to remain sitting, but he willed himself to overcome both. He reached out and put his hand on her arm. "I'm sorry, Solange. I'm sorry I can't undo it. I would if I could."

She nodded, hardly moving her head. "That's kind of you," she said, unable to look at him again. Compulsively she resumed her story. "We ran away together, and I thought . . . I don't remember what I thought, but I didn't know what Gordon expected. When I found out, I . . . I wanted to . . . I was so ashamed. I never knew how bad it would be. But I was so grateful still. Don't you see? He'd kept his Da from doing what he ended up doing to me." Now she was crying. Impatiently she wiped the tears from her face. "After a while I figured that so long as it was going to happen anyway, it might as well be with someone who would keep the others away. I reckoned that Gordon was better than many another might be." Her breath was ragged and her face was mottled. "It *is* better, isn't it?"

It took most of Russell's remaining strength to drag himself close enough to Solange to put his arm around her, but he managed it. He drew her head down to his shoulder and held her as she wept, saying nothing while she tried to purge herself of the abuse that had festered in her for so long.

Morning was overcast and dank, the cold permeating everywhere. In the aftermath of the previous evening, both Russell and Solange were wary and fatigued. Over an otherwise silent breakfast, Solange broached the matter.

"I don't want you to think that I was trying to influence you last night," she said, her attention on heating more of the herbal tea for him. "It wasn't anything like that. I don't know why I started talking that way."

"I don't think that," Russell said evenly. "I think you needed to say those things to someone and I was handy. I'm a stranger."

"It's easier to talk to a stranger, sometimes." She had brought one of the few intact chairs for him to sit in, and she had helped him to be as comfortable as possible. "I don't mean that I want you do to anything."

"But do you?" Russell asked, and immediately modified his question as he saw her back stiffen. "There isn't a lot I *can* do, but if you think of something, tell me, will you."

She filled a cup with the tea and finally looked at him. "What would be the point? Gordon wants to kill you, the way he killed . . ."

"The way he killed his father?" Russell suggested when she did not go on.

"I didn't tell you that!" There was terror in her eyes now, and she trembled as she watched him. "I didn't."

"No. You didn't have to." He held out his hand and when she reached for the cup to give it to him, he shook his head brusquely. "No. Give me your hand, Solange."

Reluctantly she did as he ordered. "What are you going to do?" She was frightened still, her hand quivering as his fingers closed around it.

"I wish I could comfort you," he said. "That's all."

Immediately she pulled away. "No."

"May I ask why not?" When she would not respond or look at him, he added, "I may be a bastard, but I was taught to be a gentleman. My father couldn't give me the name, but he did try to see I learned the manner. You have no reason to be afraid of me, Solange."

She was staring out the window at the grey vastness of the snow. For a short time Russell was not sure she had heard him, let alone understood what he had said. Then she asked. "A bastard? Really?"

"Really." He tried to reach his cup and nearly overturned his chair in the process.

"You're not well enough for that yet," she said, he good sense coming to her rescue. She reached the cup for him and made certain he had a good hold on it before she moved away from him once again. "What kind of man was your father, do you know?"

"Oh, yes," said Russell as he drank the tea. "He was old nobility, an Earl. My mother had been hired to tutor his younger brothers and sisters. They fell in love. He was only twenty when I was born, and my mother twenty-two." He saw he had her interest, and that these revelations made her more comfortable about what she had said to him the night before. "He did the right thing by her, since there was no way they could marry. He established her in a place of her own and he saw that she and I were cared for. Eventually she opened a school for girls, in the country, but that was after I was in school myself. My father saw that I was educated and that I had a decent occupation—I was a Bow Street Runner. He even provided for me in his Will." He paused. "I have a half-brother who is the Earl now, and who is afraid that I will make some claim on him or the estate beyond what my father left. I've never been able to convince him otherwise. Part of the trouble is that he's six years younger than I am. He believes that there might be some way I could deprive him of the title— not that I want it, because I emphatically do not—and so he fears me."

"Why does he think that?" Solange asked, her shoulders less rigid.

"Because I suspect that is what he would do if he were in my place. He is a man filled with the longing to possess things and people and all the rest of it. He measures himself by everything he has." Russell was shocked to hear the sorrow in his voice, and the undercurrent of bitterness. He had always supposed that he had put such feelings behind him.

"But you want something of him," said Solange, now standing beside him, looking down into his face. "What is it?"

"I guess I have always hoped he would accept me, that he would take me at my word and know that he had no reason to be concerned about me. His oldest son writes to me, when his father permits it." He met her eyes. "They are the only family I have."

Solange put her hand on his shoulder fleetingly. "That's too bad."

Russell nodded, confused by the turmoil he felt in the wake of his admission. He had intended only to provide a balance to the revelations Solange had made the previous night, but somehow he had become caught up in what he was saying, and old scars that he rarely felt anymore had become tender again. He decided it had to be the result of the beating he had taken, and his chagrin at being caught that brought on the conflict that welled in him. "Do you have anymore of that tea?"

"I'll get it," said Solange with ill-concealed relief.

"You're worried," said Russell. It was now almost four days since Mayhew had left. For the last day and a half a storm had howled over the mountains, piling up snow in massive drifts so that the land outside—what little they could see of it—was foreign to them, most of the recognizable features being swathed in frigid disguises.

"I'm getting worried," she corrected sharply as she paused in the act of breaking up two more benches for firewood.

"Mayhew will have found shelter somewhere. He won't try to ride here in this weather unless he's totally mad." Russell was recovered enough that he was able to walk with only mild discomfort, though he was still stiff and he tired more quickly than he liked. "Let me help you with that," he offered.

"I can do it," she said, going on with the work.

Russell sighed. "I'd like to help. You've done so much for me that it would please me to do something for you." He went and took a few of the sections of wood from her hands and carried them to the hearth. "There? You see? No relapse."

"I'll take care of it," said Solange in a remote tone of voice.

Russell stood back and let her tend to the chore. When the fire had been built up again and there was a good stack of wood in the bin, Russell tried again. "We're snowed in, but there ought to be something I can help with."

"There's nothing," she said, going to the kitchen without looking at him.

He followed her. "What's the matter, Solange?" he asked as he watched her examine their dwindling supplies.

"Gordon'll be back soon," she said, slamming down a wedge of hard cheese and taking a knife to it.

"Yes." The word hung in the silence between them, fatal as a bullet. "I don't . . ."

"You know he plans to kill me, don't you?" Russell said softly. "You know that he's killed others, and now he's going to kill me."

She began to force the blade through the hard cheese, rocking it through the unyielding stuff. She refused to look at him. "He saved me."

"Yes, he did. But that was years ago. And he exacted a price, didn't he?" Russell was being more blunt than he had intended to be at first, but he was becoming desperate, not only for himself, but for Solange Waters.

"He saved me," she repeated vehemently.

"He wanted to," said Russell.

She glared at him. "Don't speak against him. If he hadn't done what . . . he did, worse would have happened to me." She had cut up most of the cheese and was looking for a pot to melt it in.

"All right, I won't speak against him," said Russell in a resigned tone. "But Solange, I have to keep in mind that when he returns, I am a dead man." He said it harshly and deliberately, and he would not be swayed by the militant light in her eyes as she faced him.

"He won't do that." Her declaration was a bit too high to be completely convincing.

"Why?" Russell asked, handing her a pot from the rack over the stove.

"Because he won't. For me." This last was muffled. Her head was down as she put the cheese into the pot and added some flour and pepper to it.

"For you?" Russell laughed in a soft, sad way. "Oh, Solange, if you ask it, it would only make it worse for me. Keep still, and maybe I can taunt him into doing it quickly. Otherwise it will . . ." He thought of the bodies he had seen and shuddered at the memory.

"He'll do what I ask," she insisted defensively as she slammed the pot onto the stove.

"Will he." Russell stepped back. "Don't put that to the test, will you." He turned away from her, feeling suddenly desolate and fearful.

"I have to put it to the test," she said. "I have to do it." She was speaking more to herself than to him. "Gordon's always said that he'd give me what I wanted, what I asked for. He'll have to . . . He won't kill you, Jason. I won't let him."

Russell stared toward the cold-frosted windows. "Have you seen what he does to his victims? Do you know what he does?"

"He kills them." She admitted this with difficulty.

"Oh, that's the least of it." He looked back at her, and his demeanor was grim. "I've seen what he does. It sickens me. Your Gordon ties his victims down so that there is no chance for them to fight him or to escape. That's the first of it. Then he cuts them with a heavy knife; not deep enough to kill them, but so that they are completely helpless. He cuts muscles and tendons so that there is nothing the victim can do. By the time your Gordon is through with them, even if they were not held by ropes, they could do nothing, for they have been totally crippled. If any of his victims survived, they would have to remain bedridden or in an invalid's chair, which someone else would have to push. They could not lift an arm to feed themselves, or hold a pencil to write. They could not stand or walk or get from a chair to a bed without help. There are other things your Gordon does as well, atrocious things that—"

"*Stop it!*" She flung herself at him, outraged and consumed with anger. The force of her blow knocked him backward against the door frame and almost threw him off his feet.

They struggled together in the doorway, he striving to keep his balance as well as to hold her at bay, she attempting to scratch his face and bite his hands.

"Solange," he said, and was rewarded with a shriek.

"Don't talk like that! Don't say those things! You're wrong! *You're wrong!*"

"I've seen the men he's killed," he told her, teeth clenched and breath coming explosively as he cursed his weakness. "I know what was done to them. I have reports in my office. I'll show them to you. You can talk to Doctor Clayton." He was panting now, and he trembled with the effort of resisting her wrath. "Solange. Please."

"Gordon doesn't *do* that!" She shoved him, striking his shoulders with both her hands. "Take it back!"

"No." He staggered but stayed on his feet. "Solange, I am not trying to defame him. I am telling you what I have seen." He moved away from her, out into the main room of the roadhouse, standing near the hearth.

"Someone else did it. One of his men must have." She came after him, determination in her expression, her movements almost predatory.

"Do you really believe that? It's his gang. His men do what he tells them to do. You've said as much yourself. Do you honestly think that if he had a man in the gang who killed that way without his consent that your Gordon would permit that man to live? He couldn't take the risk, Solange, everything else aside." He set his stance, preparing to endure another onslaught.

"He wouldn't!" It was a scream, begging for agreement, beseeching Russell to deny what he had said.

"He would. He has. And he will do it to me when he returns." Russell said it with calm certainty, though his body tightened with revulsion as he spoke.

Solange drooped suddenly, her head going down, her shoulders sagging. "I . . . I won't let him."

"You won't have any say in the matter," Russell said, oddly moved that she would be concerned for him. "And if you try, as I've already warned you, it will only make it worse. Keep quiet."

"He said he'd never do anything . . . like that . . . where I could see it." She sounded less convinced now.

"What choice is there? The way the snow has piled up, he won't be able to take me to another of his hideouts, and this roadhouse isn't big enough for you to hide from what he will do. You might go out into one of the sheds, but . . ." He decided to take a chance on her change of mood and came toward her. "He *will* kill me, if he gets the opportunity. He will cut my body until it is useless."

Her wail was abject. She leaned her head against his shoulder and cried, a high, keening sound like a lost dog might make late at night. "He won't," she said, misery possessing her.

Russell hesitated, then put his arms around her. "It's all right, it's all right," he murmured, though they both knew this was a lie.

"I'll stop him," she said a little later. "I'll make him promise to live up to his word." She was no longer weeping, though her eyes and nose were red, and her lips were more chapped than before.

"Be sensible, woman," Russell admonished her. "Promises mean nothing to your Gordon anymore. They might have once, but that time has long passed."

She began a half-spoken protest, then shook her head. "I suppose not."

"No." He kept his arm around her shoulder as he led her nearer the fire. "Accept that, Solange. The step-brother who saved you is different now. Now he likes killing." From here he could smell that the cheese was starting to burn in the pot, and he left her to tend to it.

While he was in the kitchen, Solange called after him. "We could run away?"

"Where?" he asked as he set the pot on the coolest part of the stove, his hand protected with a dirty rag.

"Away," she said vaguely.

"You tried that once and . . ." He stopped, not wanting to add to her pain. "Besides, once the weather breaks we'd be easy to track. We can't get far and all they'd have to do is—"

It took a moment for her to make another suggestion. "Could we get word back to town, to get help?"

"Possibly, but there's a similar problem, to say nothing of the risk of encountering your Gordon on the way. He would not be very pleased if he discovered either one of us out of this roadhouse." He was equally certain that Mayhew would treat such betrayal with greater ferocity than he had shown so far. "Besides, we're on foot, and they are mounted."

"Does that make much difference in this much snow?" she asked with forlorn hope.

"Yes it does." He put the rag aside and came back to the hearth, sitting beside Solange, putting his arm around her once more.

"Suppose we leave now, while it's still snowing. We wouldn't leave any tracks, would we?"

"For a while. The storm won't cover them up at once, and if your Gordon . . ." He shook his head. "We'd probably get lost, and end up freezing. Not that that mightn't be more pleasant than what Mayhew has in mind." Finally he asked a question that had burned in him since Mayhew had left them alone. "Solange, if you could leave him, would you?"

"Where is there to go?" She ran her fingers over the frayed hem of her skirt. "Where could I go?"

"Away from him." Russell knew the answer already.

"If there was a place I could go, I might," she said after considering Russell's question. "I don't have much education, I don't have very good manners. I don't want to be a whore, and I haven't the knowledge to be anything else." She closed her eyes.

"If there was a place to go, would you go there?" Russell persisted.

"Jason—"

"Would you?"

She stared blankly at the door. "I . . . I don't know. I hope I . . ."

He had to stop himself from trying to shake the answer out of her. "What do you hope?"

"I hope that I would still know a place like that if I found it. After all this time, I can't be sure I would." She leaned against him, her gaze still fixed on the hem of her skirt.

Russell thought back to England and India and Australia and wondered if he was still capable of recognizing a haven when it appeared. His doubts warred with his memories while the fire burned down and Solange sheltered in the bend of his arm.

19

Two more days had passed by the time Mayhew returned with only three horses and four men accompanying him. They arrived not long before midday, the two riding double ten minutes behind the rest. As soon as they had unsaddled their mounts, they came hurtling into the roadhouse, all with shouts of relief that was underscored with a frenetic bravado which might easily turn to weeping or violence without warning. Mayhew himself was the last through the door, and when he saw Russell standing free and on his feet, he bellowed for Solange and snapped out orders to tie the Sheriff up at once.

"Gordon," Solange said with wary delight as she came into the main room. Belatedly she remembered to smile at him. Her apron had a sprinkling of flour on it, and she was wiping her hands self-consciously. "I was afraid something might have happened."

"You were? Well, isn't that strange. Something did happen," he announced, coming to her and grabbing her by the upper arm. "Why'd you let him loose?"

"I talked her into it," Russell said, seeking to forestall any argument or confrontation that might erupt at the slightest provocation.

"He was hurt. He's still not in good shape, and since it was snowing . . ." She faltered and was silent.

"It's not snowing now. Sky's blue as cornflowers. In case you hadn't noticed. And he doesn't look that hurt to me." He shook her. "What is the matter with you? You turning on me? I told you to keep him tied up."

"He was hurt," she said again, this time with more force. "He ran a fever and he couldn't do anything. He was out of his head, Gordon, and real sick with pain. I took care of him, like you told me to do."

"I didn't want you letting him run tame around the place," said Mayhew, then he released her and stepped back. "All right. Make sure he can't get loose." He spun around to face Solange again. "What is there to eat?"

"Not very much. I was making some biscuits . . . There's some pickled beef left, and a couple potatoes that haven't sprouted yet. Didn't you bring anything back with you?" She asked the last in alarm.

"No, I didn't bring anything with me," he said with heavy sarcasm. "I didn't have the chance." He swung back toward Russell, who was now secured to the central pillar once more. "You're a clever one, Russell. I'll say that much for you. God, but I was sure that I'd get in like that." He snapped his fingers next to Russell's face. "Those women weren't fooled when I came up on your horse. The pretty one held a gun on us; she said that your deputy had told her you'd be gone for a week. Took a shot at me, too. She got Saul, just blasted a hole in his chest, cool as you please."

Russell was relieved, even grateful that the Cousins had not been deceived on his account. He could not rid himself of a sense of responsibility for their welfare.

"Saul's dead?" Solange asked.

"And Ben. We had to leave Lucas behind. They got our horses, too." He regarded Russell with defiance. "Your horse went down, Sheriff. Real early in the game. He had his legs shot out from under him and he almost took me down with him."

"Poor Rajah," Russell muttered, hoping that the horse had not been left to bleed to death in the snow, but knowing that he probably had.

"So we had to get out of there quick." Mayhew looked at the remainder of his gang. "The others are expecting us to join up with them in a week or so. They're on the road to Denver. Old Morris'll take care of them until we arrive."

Out of habit, Russell made a mental note to recall what Mayhew said, although he was reasonably certain that he would not have the opportunity to put his information to use. "What about the Cousins. Are they all right?"

"The women, you mean?" Mayhew said. "I shot one of 'em, but the other wasn't hurt that I could see. Make you feel better, Sheriff? Don't be too happy about that. I'll take it out of your hide." His laughter was not quite under control and Russell flinched at the sound of it.

"Gordon," Solange said, so eagerly that it was obvious that her response was contrived, "why don't you or a couple of the men go out and bring in a deer? I can do a good roast with venison, and it'll last a while, so if it starts to snow again, we'll still have something to eat and it won't matter that we're so—"

Mayhew struck her a backhanded blow. "Quiet!"

"Mayhew!" Russell barked. "If you're going to lift your hand to someone, lift it to me."

"No, Jason," Solange protested, crouching near the hearth.

"No *Jason?*" Mayhew scoffed. "Jason, is it? Jason. What started this?

You're calling the Sheriff by his Christian name. How'd that come about? When did it start?" He took two steps toward Solange, then reached down and dragged her to her feet. "Was that before or after you let him get his hands under your skirt."

"Gordon!" Her face brightened with indignation. "I told you he was sick. I told you I took care of him. You know that I wouldn't allow anything else to happen." She tried to pull out of his grasp without success.

"I know that you can't keep a determined man off you," Mayhew said, gloating over her shock and dismay. "You couldn't keep my Da off you, you couldn't keep me off you. You couldn't keep him off you, could you?" He struck her again, this time with his fist.

As Solange cried out, Russell strained against the bonds that held him. "Mayhew, stop it."

"Why? You want to come to her rescue now that you've had a taste of her." He strolled over to Russell and stared at him with hard, flat eyes. "Doing the right thing by her, are you, Sheriff?"

"Not as you mean it. I haven't done anything to Miss Waters that compromised her. She gave me excellent care, and I am grateful to her for it. It means nothing that she uses my given name, not in the way you interpret it." He wanted to hit Mayhew, to force him to apologize, to give him back the humiliation he dished out so casually, to batter the man into unconsciousness. The force of his emotion alarmed him, for he rarely succumbed to so powerful an impulse and had come to believe that such compulsions were dangerous, and foreign to his nature.

"How noble of you. Gracious, what my Da would call a right gentleman. How'd that come about, Sheriff?" He leaned forward and spat in Russell's face.

Russell could not wipe the saliva away; the feel of it on his skin was as galling as acid. He brought his anger under control and deliberately taunted Mayhew. "It's easy to do while I'm tied up, isn't it? Goodness, what a brave fellow you are when there isn't a chance of an even fight. What's the matter? Are you afraid that the others will find out how incompetent you are?"

He was rewarded with a punch to his face and his solar plexus. "I don't want to hear anything more out of you."

"Of course not. The truth isn't pleasant, is it?" Russell's breath came in gasps, but he went on relentlessly. "You can't defeat two women, for the Lord's sake."

Mayhew hit him again, a deep, driving punch that caught Russell at the base of the ribs and took his breath away. "No more!"

It took all his will for Russell to make himself speak. "Why? Because you'll hit me again? That won't prove a damned thing." He made an effort to focus his eyes. "You're a coward, Mayhew. That's all there is to it."

"I'll kill you!" Mayhew vowed.

"While I'm tied up, naturally," Russell said, breathing through his mouth to keep from revealing how little air he had left.

"*No!*" Mayhew reached over and grabbed the front of Russell's heavy jacket. "No, not you. You're going to find out just what kind of fighter I am."

This was what Russell had been hoping for, but now that it was a reality, he had to ignore the rush of fear that went through him. "What do you mean?" he mocked. "You'll fight me? I don't believe it."

"You'll believe it soon enough," Mayhew said grimly, and signaled one of his men to cut Russell's bonds. "I'm going to like killing you, Sheriff. I'm going to cheer every time you bleed."

Covertly Russell glanced around for his saddle, and saw it in the shadows on the far side of the room. He was gambling his life on being able to reach his baton before Mayhew could sever any of his tendons or cut a major blood vessel. "That's assuming you can hurt me at all," he said evenly, pleased that his voice neither rose nor shook as he spoke.

"It'll be me and you, right now. And once you're disabled, I'll take my time carving you up, so that you'll last longer. I don't want to have to miss any part of it." Mayhew looked insolently at Solange. "This time, stepsister, you can watch. You better watch. And you better be on the right side, or you'll pay the same price he does."

Solange shrieked, turning away from Mayhew. "Gordon!"

Mayhew laughed. "Keep that in mind," he said to Russell. "You can make this hard on her, too."

"Leave her out of this," Russell said.

"Why? So she can stab me in the back some night? You'd like that, wouldn't you?" He stood back while Russell pulled himself free of the ropes that had held him to the pillar. "You ready, Sheriff?"

One of Mayhew's men reached to hold Russell back and was abruptly reprimanded by his leader. "But Coffin . . ." the man protested.

"You let him be. I'm going to show him who's the better man, is all." His Yorkshire accent was stronger now, the power of his emotion carrying him back to his youth. "All right, Sheriff." He pulled a long, lethal skinning knife from the sheath at his belt. "You think you can take me—come and try."

Russell did not move. "You have the knife. You come to me." He was able to imbue his words with icy contempt which hid the sinking sensation that engulfed him. He stepped away from the pillar and slid back toward the corner where his saddle rested.

"Afraid, Sheriff?"

"I'm unarmed. I'd be foolish not to . . . respect that." He tested his body, hating the aches and hurt he found as he moved. He had covered half the distance to his saddle when Mayhew rushed at him, the knife held in front of him. Russell jumped back as the blade swung toward him.

"Coffin!" the oldest of his men shouted. "Let me give him a knife, to make it even."

"I'll take mine to you when I'm through with him," Mayhew said through clenched teeth. He followed after Russell as the Sheriff continued to retreat. "What's the matter? Not so brave now that you have to fight?"

Russell feinted to the side as the knife moved again, and this time he felt it nick his jacket. "Bloody sod."

Mayhew laughed at the insult. "Your names won't hurt me."

"Poltroon." Russell's heel touched the flap of his saddle. He dropped swiftly to one knee and reached back, fumbling for his baton.

"Planning to throw the saddle at me?" Mayhew scoffed. "What would it do?"

"Not the saddle," Russell muttered to himself as his fingers closed around the head of the baton. As he pulled it from its sheath, he knew that he would not have the strength for a long fight. Already he was breathing too fast and he felt sweat on his forehead start to run into his eyes. This he dashed away with the back of his hand as he brought the baton up to guard his neck and torso.

"A *stick?*" Mayhew screamed. "You're going to beat me with a stick?"

"Yes," said Russell quietly, taking hold of his weapon with both hands. Now that he had the familiar baton in his grasp, he settled automatically into the light crouch he had been taught so many years ago. His legs were not as springy as he would have liked—I'm getting old, he thought as he moved forward—and he was too sore to bob and weave properly, but he used the one advantage he knew he had: he had often fought knives before, but Mayhew had never fought a baton.

"What's the matter, Sheriff? You think I'm a bad boy? You want to cane me?"

"I want to bash your skull in," Russell said casually, and flipped the lower end of the baton quite suddenly, rapping Mayhew's right arm.

Mayhew shouted at the sharp pain that radiated from the blow, and switched knife-hands.

Russell had anticipated the move and the upper end of the baton was already descending toward Mayhew's shoulder as his fingers closed on the handle of the knife.

"Bastard!" bellowed Mayhew.

Russell smiled, parrying the thrust that Mayhew aimed at his neck. He moved another step nearer his antagonist. He said nothing, not wanting to waste what little air and strength he had remaining to him. He slid on the balls of his feet, the soles of his boots never leaving the floor.

"I'm going to cut you up in pieces," Mayhew yelled, his voice high. "I'll leave you in the snow for the wolves." The last word was cut off as Russell's baton slapped into his knee. He staggered, his face going white, and when he steadied himself there was a look about him that made the other men in the room go silent.

Though it was risky, Russell kept up his counterattack. He twirled the baton, moving it from one hand to the other in rapid shifts that made a barrier as impenetrable as a shield before him. Twice Mayhew attempted to break through the defense, but both times he drew back, once with his knife-blade ringing from the impact of Russell's baton.

"Getty! Move around behind him!" Mayhew shouted to the youngest of his men.

The youth hurried to obey, but shrieked as Russell spun and caught him with his baton full-force between the legs. "Don't," Russell advised him as he shied away from Mayhew's charge.

"You're dead, Sheriff," Mayhew hissed. "Dead."

"But not yet," Russell made himself answer, aghast at how weak his voice was.

"I want time to get even," Mayhew shouted as he sliced toward Russell's neck.

The knife caught on the baton and slid down the shaft. Russell moved back, spinning his baton once more.

"Tricks!" Mayhew jeered.

Russell ignored the jibe, his attention wholly on deflecting the blade.

Mayhew reached for one of the metal plates on the fireplace mantle and threw it at Russell. It clanged into the baton, then flew crazily across the room. Mayhew had already seized the next plate and flung in Russell's direction.

"Use your gun, Coffin," his oldest man advised.

"Not yet," Mayhew declared, with one plate to go.

This one glanced off Russell's brow and left him with a gash over his right eye. Blood ran down his face, but he could not take the chance of stopping to wipe it away.

"Gordon, please!" Solange cried out. "Let him alone."

Russell wanted to tell her to be silent, that her begging, rather than placating Mayhew, only drove him into a greater frenzy. He dodged the bench that Mayhew swung at him, and almost fell against the central pillar where he had been tied.

"Coffin, that's not right," said the tallest of his men, and in the next instant crashed to the floor as the bench slammed into his chest.

Mayhew was insane with his battle, and now he pressed toward Russell, his knife moving as swiftly as the tongue of a snake. He bent low and swiped at Russell's legs, giving a bark of satisfaction as he saw red well in the cut cloth. He moved faster, and grinned as the Sheriff retreated before him.

Russell's vision was clouded, speckled with dark motes that obscured the room and Mayhew. He could not get enough air into his lungs and he felt as if he were about to break in half. He knew that he was not moving the baton as quickly as he should, and his grip was no longer as reliable as it had been moments before. He wanted the fight to end.

"I'll gut you, Sheriff," Mayhew crowed, sensing victory within his reach. "I'll spill your innards all over the floor and make you tie 'em in knots for me."

Just then Russell missed his footing and he skidded perilously close to the pillar. His grip on his baton weakened, and it swung erratically in his hands. He lifted his arm to protect his head, and felt his baton shiver as Mayhew's knife struck it again. He waited for the cold invasion of steel, hoping he could trick Mayhew into cutting something vital so that he would die swiftly.

Mayhew raised his knife and brought it down so furiously that it took him a second or two to realize that he had not succeeded. Only then could he see that the blade was broken, and that half of it was embedded in Russell's baton. He started to take one step back, but the metal bit into his thigh, and he fell forward, knocking Russell to the floor beneath him.

Two of Mayhew's men started to rush forward when one of the windows shattered and the muzzle of a carbine thrust in with the icy wind.

"Hold everything," said Luis Guerra.

As two of Mayhew's men reached for their guns, a second window on the opposite side of the room was broken and a second gun barrel intruded. The men held their positions, only their eyes shifting from one window to the other.

On the floor, Russell shifted Mayhew off him and sat up, his expression dazed.

"Sorry we took so long, Sheriff," said Guerra. "It was tough going."

Russell nodded, not entirely convinced that the situation had altered so abruptly or so advantageously. He got slowly to his feet, pulling his baton out from under Mayhew, who had grasped his leg with both hands in a futile attempt to contain the steadily pumping blood. With an impatient gesture, he signaled one of the men to help his fallen leader. "Get a tourniquet on him."

The tallest of the outlaws hastened to obey, moving furtively, almost apologetically, as if he feared that Russell would change his mind and let Mayhew bleed to death.

By the hearth Solange gave way to soft, hysterical tears.

"The door's not locked," said Russell, bending to pick up Mayhew's revolver. He held it negligently in one hand. "Guerra, you come in first. Is that William with you?"

From his vantage point outside the window, Red Pony answered, "I said I'd help out."

"So you did." It was difficult for Russell to speak, and he strove to slow his breathing, taking in great, long breaths that made his chest hurt. He glanced toward Getty, who was huddled on the floor, then motioned to the other outlaws. "Over there. Against the pillar. Backs to it. Hold hands."

One of the men started to protest and was immediately silenced by the other.

Mayhew had begun a slow, mindless crooning as the tourniquet was tightened around his thigh.

The door opened and Luis Guerra came into the roadhouse, his carbine angled at Mayhew. "There's a lot of snow out there." It was his version of an excuse.

"True. It slowed them down." Russell wanted to lie down and close his eyes. He was exhausted and his body was so sore that it hurt to move at all. He pointed toward the two men at the pillar. "Tie them up."

"Right away, Sheriff," said Guerra, acting so promptly that it appeared he wanted to make up for his earlier delay.

"Red Pony; come in." Russell indicated the door and took a better position to guard the room while Guerra was occupied.

Getty started to reach for his pistol and thought better of it as William Red Pony came through the door with his carbine at the ready.

"How many horses did you bring?" Russell asked.

"Our two and Gryphon," said Red Pony, looking down at Mayhew. "So that's Coffin himself."

"Yes," Russell said. "We're going to be one horse short."

Red Pony shrugged, then said kindly, "It's too bad about Rajah."

"Yes, it is," said Russell, wondering what horses his half-brother had shipped to him and when they would arrive. "Is Gryphon all right?"

"Fine. A little stiff from the cold, but fine." He caught sight of Russell's Hussar's saddle. "We've got a charro saddle on him."

"Better leave it. The saddle-tree is broken on mine." He hated to admit it, but did his best not to show it. "Are we going to have decent weather for a day or two? I don't think we can make it back to Charity before nightfall."

"Should have," said Red Pony, watching as Guerra tied up Getty, paying no attention to the young man's protests.

Russell nodded twice. His pain was subdued enough that he trusted himself to walk over to Solange Waters and put his hand on her shoulder. "It's over," he said gently to her when she turned her tear-streaked face up to him.

"What's going to happen?" The words came out in gulps as she did her best to stop crying.

"We're going to take Mayhew and his men back to Charity. The rest is up to the circuit judge. He'll probably hang, Solange." He had not meant to say it so bluntly, but there was no gentle or graceful way to convey such information. "I'm sorry, for your sake. Not for his."

She gave way to sobs, but nodded, her face set as she absorbed his blow in a long series of blows. "All right."

Russell moved away from her and went to see how Mayhew was getting on now that the blood flow had slowed.

"I'm cold," he said, looking up sideways at Russell. "If you did for me, I'll kill you."

"You've tried that already," said Russell. "Lie still. You'll live to stand trial if I have anything to say about it."

"Do you want me to take over, Sheriff?" Guerra asked, holding out a length of braided thongs. "I can tie that man up and take over the tourniquet, if you like."

"Whatever you prefer," said Russell. "There are some other gang members with someone called Morris. We'll have to bring them in later. For the time being . . ." He studied the room, and then, as an afterthought, bent to try to pull the shattered knife-blade from his baton.

20

By the middle of February all of Mayhew's gang was locked in the Charity jail. Russell appointed Martin Corley and Liam Cauliffe as temporary guards, so that at no time was the building untended. For once neither Mayor Fletcher nor the Town Council objected to the additional expense.

"You're healing up well enough," said Henry Clayton to Russell as he finished his third examination of the Sheriff in as many weeks. "But you're going to have to be careful for a while longer. I'm not sure, but I think you've had enough internal bleeding from the beating you had to bring about some permanent damage."

"I doubt it," said Russell as he buttoned his shirt. "Why don't you have a stove back here, Henry? This place is as bad as a snowdrift."

"Perhaps you're right," mused Clayton. "You feel well enough to complain, and that generally counts for something. And if I had thought about it, I would have a stove back here. But, sadly, I had the house built in the spring, when such things weren't so important."

Russell shrugged. "What do you recommend for the stiffness in my shoulder?"

"Being a decade younger," said Clayton. "And easy, regular exercise. You might have a word with that pagan Red Pony. He might have one of those brews of his that can help. Don't let him know I suggested it."

"I'll admit I'm surprised you did," said Russell as he got to his feet. "But I'll take your suggestion. While I was in India, I learned not to despise what the natives offer, though I once got into a serious quarrel with a Cherrypicker over it."

"Regiments can be narrowminded." Clayton looked away. "I've had the Cousins in. They're both doing well. I don't think you need to worry about them now, Jason."

"Perhaps I don't need to, but I probably will," he said. "I keep thinking that they came to grief because—"

"They would have come to more grief if you hadn't made the preparations you did, and if you hadn't sent Guerra around to all the outlying ranches so that everyone knew you were gone and were prepared, in case something happened."

"I still think they should not have been left alone," said Russell with a self-deprecating half-smile.

"That's probably why you're Sheriff here," said Clayton with a cool glance, then added awkwardly, "Smilin' Jack brought me some opium. I told him not to bring any more, but then I . . . well, I . . ."

"Then you changed your mind?" Russell said.

"I'm afraid so. I got to thinking of what the dreams can be like, and how sweet they are, and . . . I said . . . I can't give it up, not entirely." He looked desperately at Russell, beseeching Russell with his eyes for understanding.

"You know what I think, but . . ." Russell clapped his friend on the arm. "Just let me know when you decide to use it, so that I'll be prepared."

Clayton nodded silently. He made his way to the door, then turned back. "I meant it about your asking Red Pony. Those Red Indians have some very useful preparations."

"Thank you," said Russell, recognizing the repeated suggestion as the peace offering it was intended to be.

"I want you to know that I think you've been very fortunate. When I think about Mayhew and the corpses we've seen . . ."

"I think I'm luckier than I have any right to be," said Russell, following Clayton to the door.

"Have you heard about Cauliffe?" Clayton asked as the two men went down the hall.

"He said he's planning to settle down here, if that's what you mean. He's talked to Fletcher about the best site for his house, and he told me last night that he was considering getting married." Russell shook his head.

"Did he mention who?" asked Clayton as they neared the front door. "It's none of my business, of course, but I am curious."

"No, but if you care to make a little wager, I'd put my money on the Widow Schmidt."

"You're joking," said Clayton, but without any real shock.

"No," said Russell. He put his hand on the door latch. "Is raising horses all right? It won't make my shoulder worse or lead to other troubles, will it?"

"Oh, I shouldn't think so," said Clayton. "Are you really going through with it?"

"I've staked out a hundred-forty acres on the east side of town. I'd better be serious. I've given Fletcher two hundred dollars and he's authorized to send another two hundred to Denver once the road is open and safe." He smiled at Clayton. "I'm assuming that my half-brother will have sent the horses guaranteed to me in our father's Will."

"Is there any reason to suppose he won't?" asked Clayton with some curiosity.

"Not really. He isn't the sort of man to abrogate the provisions of a Will." Russell stepped out into the brisk March air.

"I'll see you again in a week, here, and we'll find out how much damage you still have." Clayton stepped back. "Let me close the door, or what heat I have will be gone."

Russell waved and went down into the street.

George Fletcher's face was mottled plum and white, and he was so furious that he gobbled when he tried to speak. He pounded his desk with his fists and poked a finger at Russell. "I expect you to do something about this dastardly state of affairs!" he finally got out. "You're Sheriff."

"What state of affairs, Mayor Fletcher," asked Russell in a deliberately calm manner. "What's happened?"

"That *woman!*" he announced. "That despicable woman!"

"Which despicable woman?" Russell inquired, taking out his notebook and already writing Lorinda Dooley's name.

"That Spanish woman, that Donna Elvira!" thundered the Mayor, all but choking. "I expect you to—"

"What, precisely, has she done?" Russell wanted to know, since he had not anticipated any difficulties with Donna Elvira.

"She's married my son!" Mayor Fletcher declaimed as if he were a tragic actor in a Greek drama. "She has made him her husband."

"I see," said Russell, who did not. "When did this happen, and where?"

"She took him to San Esteban. That priest, that Roman spy, that Papist, married them! No decent Protestant clergyman would take such flagrant advantage of a youth like Frederick."

"Are you saying that Frederick was compelled to marry Donna Elvira?" Russell asked, his pencil still poised although he was no longer making notes.

"No, of course not. But there are limits, and I do not want a Roman Catholic in the family. I told Frederick that, after you gave me that timely warning. I was sure he understood. In fact, I am certain that he understood. But this morning, when he finally returned from her Rancho, he said that his emotions ran away with him and he decided that he must marry her." This turbulent explanation was almost more than the Mayor could bear. He hit the top of his desk with his fists and glowered at the Sheriff. "What can be done?"

"I honestly don't know," said Russell. "I'd speak with Padre Antonio, if I were you. He probably won't be any happier than you are about this." He saw the disbelieving expression in George Fletcher's eyes and went on, "Roman Catholics are as committed to their religion as you are to yours, Mayor. So far as I am aware, neither your son nor Donna Elvira have broken any laws. Both are of the age of consent—she is over fourteen and he is over sixteen—and both are of sound mind."

"I doubt that," grumbled Fletcher.

"You may doubt it all you like. There isn't a judge in any part of the country who could undo this union. I'm not sure, but I think that the only way a priest would annul the marriage would be if Frederick were impotent, or if either had been married before to someone still alive. At least, that was what the Irish priest told me in India." He shook his head. "It's one way for Donna Elvira to protect her inheritance. And your son might care for her as much as he claims." He cocked his head and looked at Mayor Fletcher for a long moment. "I'd make the best of it if I were you, sir. I would put as good a face on it as I could. If nothing else, you'll gain access to a great deal of property."

"Spanish land grant!" Mayor Fletcher said with contempt. "What sort of claim is that?"

"It might be a very good one, depending on what Congress decides. Now that the United States owns all the land from the Atlantic to the Pacific, the Congress will have to decide about the land grants. There are too many of them to ignore them." He waited. "If Congress strikes down the land grants, then your son may continue to hold the land by right of marriage acquisition. If Congress upholds the land grants, then he holds title to it through his wife. Either way Frederick gains the largest single holding for thirty miles in any direction." Russell put his notebook away. "If there's nothing else, Mayor?"

"It's all very well for you to be so cavalier," sulked George Fletcher. "It isn't your son who's marrying a Spanish Catholic woman with a temper like hot peppers."

"True, but it isn't as if Frederick were your only child. You have others, and most of them will probably find partners more to your liking. To have one who displeases you is not the worst possible development." Russell was silent for a moment. "I don't believe that there's much more to be said."

"I'll remember this, Sheriff," said Fletcher.

"Fine. And remember also that I will ask Padre Antonio to call upon you in case there is anything the two of you might be able to work out between you. I'm not trying to discourage you, Mayor Fletcher, I am only trying to uphold the law, as you hired me to do."

Fletcher struck his desk again, this time abruptly, and he turned away, making a show of picking up a stack of papers and reading through them as if the Sheriff had left the office already.

"Will you be going to Denver for the trial, Sheriff?" asked Dorabelle Schmidt when word had finally come that the road was passable. There were five new faces in the hotel dining room, and Sun Fan-Li was caught up in producing meals from new shipments of food which had arrived at last.

"I must, I'm sorry to say. I've arranged for Luis Guerra to be temporarily appointed acting sheriff so that there will be someone here who can act officially. I won't be gone one day longer than necessary." He poked at the remnants of his pork roast soaked in apple juice, realizing how much he was going to miss Charity.

"What about the building? Will that go on while you're away?" She had braced her elbows on the table and was watching him in a manner Russell thought of as protective, as if she were his older sister and he no more than eight.

"It had better; I've authorized payment and I expect to see some progress when I return." He reached out and patted the table near her hand. "My only misgiving is that I will not be here. I'll miss your hotel."

She waved the compliment away impatiently. "What about your horses? When do they arrive?"

"I wish I knew. I hope before high summer. I'd like to have some mares in foal by September and that won't be possible if the string doesn't arrive for another four months. Incidentally," he went on in another voice, "Bess Mattington will be bringing in three mares for me. I've been out to inspect and ride them, and they are excellent for my purposes. Calvin's will take them while I'm gone. If there's any difficulty, refer them to the Mayor, for he has records of the transactions at the bank."

"If you wish," said Frau Schmidt, then flushed as she looked up and saw Liam Cauliffe coming toward the table. "You have company, I think."

"*You* have the company, you mean," said Russell, faintly amused by the shy courtship these two were carrying on.

"Ach, nein, not me." She started to rise, suddenly flustered, but Russell indicated her chair, and she remained where she was.

"I've been looking for you, Jason," said Cauliffe as he took the seat across from the Widow Schmidt. "I understand you're the one I have to thank for tying up all the labor in town."

"Possibly. But wait a month or two and you will have more able-bodied workers than you know what to do with. Now that the United States has established its borders, there will be a flood of men and families coming." He saw doubt in the faces of the others. "Well, you have both said that each year brings more travelers and newcomers than the last. Why should that cease when there is so much new opportunity?" He looked up as Sun came from the kitchen with a fresh pot of coffee. "Yes, please, Sun."

"Your favorite," said the cook as he poured out the dark liquid. "Your current supply ought to last you two months unless you decide to drink more of it."

"Thank you," said Russell. "I'll get more while I'm in Denver."

"I wish you Godspeed on that journey," said Cauliffe very seriously. "Men like Mayhew and his ilk cannot be tolerated if we're to prosper here."

"No," Russell agreed darkly. "They can't."

"How many men is the Army sending for escort, do you know?" Cauliffe went on.

"I've been told there will be ten men. I hope that's so, because otherwise it will be difficult standing guard over them, and I would not like to have to fight them again." His eyes were distant as he said that, and filled with horror.

"Are you afraid of Mayhew?" Cauliffe asked before he could stop himself.

"Yes, but not for the reason you might think: I am afraid of him because he almost made me what he is, and that . . . that is more than I could bear." He took the handle of his coffee cup between his thumb and fingers, but did not lift it.

"What do you mean?" Cauliffe said, feeling a strange sympathy for the Sheriff.

"I wanted to kill him. For a few seconds while we fought, I would have enjoyed killing him." Russell's voice was as distant as his eyes and quiet with grief.

"But Jason—" Cauliffe began only to be cut off.

"Mayhew likes killing. I never want to like it. I've seen what that lust does to men, and I thank God that I've been able to keep clear of it. But now if I say that, I tell a lie."

"Hardly a lie," countered Cauliffe. "It was the heat of battle."

"I've been in battles before and never felt that," said Russell somberly while his coffee cooled. "I never want to feel it again. It's a sickness rotting the soul."

Frau Schmidt and Reverend Cauliffe exchanged glances, both of them worried. "You're too severe with yourself, Jason," said Cauliffe at last.

"Am I? But what if I'm not? What will I become then? One of the damned," he said answering his own question without apology.

"Goodness, Sheriff," said Frau Schmidt, not quite able to conceal her shock at his language.

"I've killed men before. Four of them, to be precise," said Russell as if he were reciting a geometric theorem. "Each time it left me . . . loathing myself. I did not want to kill, I did not enjoy the killing. With Mayhew it was different, as if he had a contagious disease, like the worst smallpox." He drank all his coffee at once.

"Jason, you must learn to forgive yourself," said Cauliffe in the same tone he would use to a guilt-stricken parishoner.

"I almost resigned my post." Russell stared at his cup as if he had never seen it before, was not certain what it was. "But who would take my place? Someone who wanted killing? Someone who was not sickened?"

"And so you are still Sheriff," said Frau Schmidt with obvious relief. "Gott sei dank."

Cauliffe touched Russell on the arm. "And testifying—will this trouble you?"

"Very much," Russell admitted. "Which is why I must do it. I never want to forget, not for an instant, what I might have done." He stared around the room, then called for Sun. "More coffee."

Russell's stable was half finished when he returned from Denver, six weeks after he had left. His house was little more than a frame and a bit of roof, but he went to inspect it with all the satisfaction—he told himself— of his half-brother inspecting one of his estates.

"It will be very fine," Luis Guerra told him as Russell tried to describe, unsuccessfully, all his plans for his horse farm. "You have seven mares now, don't you? A very good start, I am told."

"Yes; Donna Elvira sold me two of her Spanish mares for ruinous prices," Russell said, secretly pleased at being able to afford what Frederick Fletcher's wife demanded.

"What of your English horses?" Guerra asked, uncomfortable at the question but still wrung with curiosity.

"They're coming," said Russell with a confidence he hoped was not misplaced.

Guerra walked around the large oval arena that stood at the front of the house. He paced it off. "Why do you need this? You will have the whole mountainside for pasture."

"This is for training," Russell reminded him. "And I will have some small paddocks as well. I don't want to turn out those range-broke ponies you see everywhere. I want to raise fine horses, properly trained and bred.

This country is made for them and I intend to—" He broke off as he saw
Cloris Bell riding up the road toward his incomplete house. "Good afternoon," he called out to her.

"Afternoon to you, Sheriff," she called back. "You got time for a word
or two with me?"

"Certainly," said Russell, strolling toward her. "What can I do for
you?"

Cloris swung out of the saddle. "I've been up at the Mattington ranch.
Miss Waters went with me. She said she wanted to start going out in the
world a little." She paused awkwardly. "Since Mayhew was hanged,
she . . ."

"I know," Russell said kindly.

"Well, the long and the short of it is that Bess Mattington wants to
take her on as a help at the ranch. Solange is staying there a few days, to
try it out. She wanted you to know what she was doing." She twisted a
length of rein in her hands. "She's looking for a man, she told me, one
who liked her."

"The Mattington farrier is a good man," said Russell. "About her age,
too."

"Does that . . . bother you?" It was a much blunter question than
good manners permitted her to ask, and she looked away, seeing Guerra
attempting to be invisible.

"Not really, but thank you for your concern." He smiled at Cloris Bell,
one of the first open smiles he had offered since he started his hunt for
Mayhew. "I wish her well, and . . . aside from the years—of which there
are too many—there is the question of Mayhew. If she tried to remain
with me, even as a friend, neither she nor I would ever be rid of him." He
looked up at the blue of the bright spring sky. "This way, we'll both heal."

"I see," said Cloris, showing some sign of comprehension. "She's very
fond of you, Sheriff."

"And I of her. Which is why I wish her every joy in life, and that
includes being free of Mayhew. And me." He thrust his hands into his
pockets and meet Cloris' eyes directly, with a trace of amusement deepen-
ing the lines around them. "Dear me; were you thinking about making a
match?"

"It had occurred to me," Cloris admitted. "I . . . I said something
about it to Bess Mattington and she all but laughed me out of the room."

"I have admired her good sense since I first met her," approved Russell.

Cloris did not speak at once, and when she did, it was on another
subject altogether. "One of her hands just came back from Santa Fe," she
told him.

"Trouble?" Russell asked.

"No." Suddenly she smiled. "He said that there were five men with forty-three horses there asking directions to Charity. He reckoned that with so many horses and on unfamiliar roads, they would probably arrive in five days."

This time Russell beamed at her. "Thank you. Thank you very much for telling me." He indicated the half-finished stable. "So long as you're here, would you like to be shown around, or would you simply like a leg up?"

Cloris shook her head. "I'd like to see your stock when they arrive. But there are chores to do, and—"

He smiled as they shook hands. "A leg up, then."